Gentle

Gentle Footprints

an anthology

Bridge House

British Library Cataloguing in Publication Data

A Record of this Publication is available from the British
Library

ISBN 978-1-907335-04-4

This edition published 2010 by Bridge House Publishing
Manchester, England

All Bridge House Books are published on paper derived
from sustainable resources..

Acknowledgements

A huge number of people have been involved in putting this book together and it is impossible to mention them all by name. But I do want to thank Born Free for their tremendous help in collating all the facts and approving all the stories and organisations we have approached, particularly Lauren Smith for putting up with my continual bombardment of emails. And of course to Virginia McKenna for the foreword and for being so supportive of our efforts.

Thanks must also go to the cover artist, Colin Wyatt and to all the artists that contributed the line drawings, Colin Wyatt, Justin Wyatt and Ashley James. They make this book extra special.

Thanks to Gill James, founder of Bridge House Publishing, author in her own right and assistant editor on Gentle Footprints, as well as everything else she does. A special thanks must also go to Martin James, our designer who turned this into the book you're holding and of course the one who not only keeps us all on track but is also responsible for sending out all the books, Nicola Rouch.

And finally the biggest thanks must go to all the authors, including Richard Adams, for supporting and contributing to this book – without them there would be no book! I appreciate their passion for animals, their drive to raise awareness not just about the book but the featured animals – and all their work on our Blog. None of this would have been possible without them.

Visit our Blog:
http://gentlefootprintsanimalanthology.blogspot.com

Born Free is a dynamic international wildlife charity, devoted to compassionate conservation and animal welfare. Born Free believes wildlife belongs in the wild and works to phase out zoos and stop animal exploitation. Born Free rescues individuals and gives them lifetime care. With local communities Born Free protects lions, elephants, tigers, gorillas, wolves, bears, dolphins, turtles and many more species in their natural habitat.

Find out more at www.bornfree.org.uk

Charity no: 1070906

Contents

Introduction

If you are holding this copy of Gentle Footprints in your hand but you haven't bought it yet, I urge you to do so. Money from the sale of every copy will be donated to The Born Free Foundation for their valuable work. And it's not just about donating because in return you will own a wonderful collection of beautifully crafted stories about wild animals, ranging from the octopus to the elephant. Each story was carefully selected to remain true to the wildness of the animal and the Born Free edict that animals should be born free and should live free.

The idea for this book came from my story *The Red Queen* published in Bridge House's *In the Shadow of the Red Queen* (2009) which deals with a scientist's last ditch efforts to save the Ocelot wildcat from extinction. I decided to donate my royalties to a pertinent charity. I chose Born Free. And that's when it happened – a w*hat if* moment followed by a *wouldn't it be good to...* and the concept of an annual charity book and Gentle Footprints was born.

I am delighted with the response and support we've received but we couldn't do it without you choosing to buy this book. So if you've read this far I hope it is now part of your collection...

I will let Virginia McKenna OBE, Patron of The Born Free Foundation begin by telling you about her life with animals and her work for this great charity. And then I will talk about our guest writer, known for his animal stories, Richard Adams.

Debz Hobbs-Wyatt

Foreword by Virginia McKenna OBE

As someone who, for over 45 years, has been fascinated by animals, animal issues and their relationship with humans, I have been intrigued by this diverse and yet symbiotic collection of stories.

Each writer has, of course, his or her own style, personal passions and individual focus on their chosen subject but, without exception, one is drawn into the narrative and enters, briefly, the particular world or moment being revealed.

Although, as a child, I had always shared my life with 'pets' (a word I am not quite comfortable with, although I recognise its intent!), it was not until 1964 – when my late husband Bill Travers and I went to Kenya to work in the film *Born Free* that I really began to try and understand animals. Their individuality, the way their minds worked. For us, at that time, the animals were lions. Not 'pets'! But, strangely, I discovered little difference in the way one began to relate to them.

The book *Born Free* by Joy Adamson was, of course, the catalyst. The relationship between Joy and her husband George with Elsa the lioness, illuminated a hitherto unimaginable friendship between humans and a wild predator. Incredibly Elsa remained, until her early death from a tick-borne disease, loyal to her human friends. She always remembered them, returning to visit them in camp, bringing her cubs to show them and, finally, dying outside George's tent.

George was our 'lion man' on the film, and through him we learned never-to-be-forgotten lessons about animals and how to 'be' with them.

The way we treat, manipulate and exploit other species still remains a huge and tragic issue in the 21st

9

Century. This is something that our charity, The Born Free Foundation, has been grappling with for over 25 years. There are many wonderful, courageous people out there trying to instil compassion towards wild animals, to educate both children and adults to understand that suffering, pleasure, fear, protectiveness, jealousy are not emotions exclusively human.

We strive to lead lives that can, in some way, fulfil us and allow us to be ourselves. Animals deserve that same opportunity. They do not deserve to be trapped, sport-hunted, killed for their ivory, held captive, trained to perform.

And that is what is special about these stories. Many are told from the animals' point of view. A point of view too rarely heard and now, at last, here for us all to read about and relate to.

The 'Spirit of Elsa' is still with us.

Virginia McKenna

A Few Words about Richard Adams

The name Richard Adams has, for a long time, been associated with one particular furry animal, the rabbit – and not just one rabbit but a whole family of rabbits that many of us have come to know and love. Of course I'm referring to his first and perhaps most well known novel, *Watership Down*. But since *Watership Down* was first published in 1972, he has published over twenty titles that include both collections of short stories and novels that have established him as foremost well-known English writer, with international acclaim.

But Richard Adams hasn't written only about rabbits. His characters include the great bear in *Shardik*, his second novel, and one he says he is most proud of (published 1974), escaped laboratory dogs in *The Plague Dogs* (1977) a particular favourite of mine and General R.E. Lee's horse, *Traveller* (1988).

His work is not exclusively about animals (for example, he told me the character with whom he became most preoccupied while writing, was Käthe, the female protagonist of *The Girl in a Swing* (1980)). Yet animals do feature prominently in Richard Adams's work. So it seemed only right that I should invite Mr Adams to contribute to this special collection. When I told him we were trying to raise awareness and funds for The Born

Free Foundation, he said he would be delighted to support our efforts. And when I asked him if he could write us an introduction, he looked across the table at me and said, "But aren't you going to ask me to write you a story?"

You can imagine my delight – and I am most pleased that Gentle Footprints includes his new and original story *Leopard Aware.*

When I met Mr Adams recently, what I really wanted to know was what it is that inspires him to write about animals. Is it simply his lifelong love of animals or does it go deeper? He told me he has always been an animal lover – his library stands wall to wall with books – many of which are fictional and non-fictional books about animals. Then we talked at some length about his work with animals, and it immediately became clear he is more than just an animal lover – he cares strongly about the way they are treated.

In 1984 Richard Adams was President of the RSPCA. Since then he has been actively involved in advancing rights for animals. I, myself, first met Mr Adams when I was sixteen and involved with campaigning against the killing of seals for fur and the trade of furs in the EU. I remember the first time I heard him speak out against these atrocities. His eloquent words were so emotive and powerful I remember being grateful the animals had someone like him on their side.

Richard Adams still follows and supports campaigns for animal rights, and when I interviewed him recently he spoke of the recent ban on dancing bears in India, a great victory he spoke about with deep satisfaction. He also told me that recently the EU has banned the import of animal fur from outside the EU. It has been a long fight and it

12

took me back to when I was sixteen, watching him speak for the first time about the seals.

As Richard Adams has such a great love for animals, it is unsurprising that they feature prominently in his work. I have no doubt his works have inspired many other writers, including those that have contributed to *Gentle Footprints*. But what I really wanted to know was what writers inspired him.

I was interested in how many great writers have written about animals. We all know that animals feature notably in children's fiction but it seems less so in adult fiction. So I put this to Mr Adams. I asked him about *Watership Down*, a story he originally made up for his own children. We often hear terms like *cross-over* fiction to refer to books that can be appreciated by children and adults. *Watership Down*, amongst many other accolades, won the *Guardian Children's Fiction Prize* in 1972. It is popular with children and adults alike. When I mentioned this, he leaned back in his chair, looked at right at me and said, "There are no such things as children's books, just books that children like to read." And he told me he once received a fan letter from a six year old about *Watership Down*.

We then talked about the themes in *The Plague Dogs* and *Shardik*. I told him I remembered reading Henry Williamson's *Tarka the Otter* (first published in 1927) and how those sad last lines in the novel still resonate with me. He told me about Williamson's *Salar the Salmon* (1936), which follows the journey of a five year old salmon retuning to the place of his birth.

"Which animal story do you like the most?" I asked.

"Walter de la Mare's *The Three Mulla-Mulgars* (1910) aka *The Three Royal Monkeys*," he answered without hesitation. He went on with animation to recall the

13

story of the three monkeys, their perilous journey to the valleys of Tishnar and their adventures on the way. He described this as the best fantasy animal story he'd read and how he fondly remembers reading it as a boy. He emphasised how much he admired the invention and the imagination in Walter de la Mare's writing.

I only hope that the stories in *Gentle Footprints* might one day resonate in some of you.

Is there anything Mr Adams still wants to write? He told me that although there is nothing specific, he thinks there is still another novel in him.

Finally, I asked Mr Adams to tell me about the story he wrote for *Gentle Footprints* and why he chose the leopard as his animal. It presented a challenge, he said; he not only wanted to write something special for this book but also something original. "There is a limit," he said, his hands pressed firmly against the table, "to what an animal feels and experiences. I don't think", he said, "that animals think in any sort of language, as we do. They don't reason in sequence in their minds. Rather, they are visited with sudden emotions and impulses upon which they act. That's not rational, but of course it works for them."

I will leave you now to enjoy Mr Adams' story *Leopard Aware*, but before I do, I want you to think about how important each and every story is in raising aware-ness and an appreciation of the true wildness of the animals as you read about them.

Richard Adams' feeling for animals extends beyond just writing about them, and this is what I want the take home message of *Gentle Footprints* to be. So if after you've read the stories you decide you want to be involved, please look at the information provided by Born Free to find out what you can do. If everyone does one thing, we are another step closer to a better world for the animals.

Richard Adams has written about animals, spoken about animals and fought for animals for many years and I am so grateful that we have been able to work together on another animal project, since that's where it all started.

So all that's left to say is, enjoy!

Debz Hobbs-Wyatt, 2010

Leopard Aware

By Richard Adams

Heat. Slow, enveloping heat. Not strong heat. "From above" heat. Even heat all round body. Even heat on ground. Ground all round. On ground off ground on ground all ground. The air all round. From "long way off" air. Air speaking. All kinds of speaking but first of all, "no danger" speaking. Pad pad pad pad going along pad. Draw in air cool breathe out old air. Going along pad. Draw in air cool breathe out old air warm warm air cool air warm air cool air. What? What? Air talking. What? Don't know, but safe pad pad pad pad feel safe.

So all goes together now. In breathe out breathe air talking pad pad pad pad. Rough ground stumble stumble now smooth again under body. STOP STOP What? Conscious. New. All together smooth heat all round four pads up and down regular up and down. Breathe in air speaking all sorts of speaking. Confusion confusion but Ahhhh! Old air speak again of what? New smells too many. Stop. Sniff take them apart one by one. But this is new, dribbling into the mouth, dribble dribble drool. Spit spit it out, but what now? All together now. heat breathe sniff sniff and pad pad under pad stones pad ground soft ground speaking pad air coming in, out in out all sorts of messages from air and TEETH and CLAWS this is

16

POWER this is POWER no longer apart but all together ears hear blasted flies get away. Flies damn flies. Swift sniff nose smells nose talks nose chatter babbles mouth dribbles. Pad pad pad pad faster slower *I* say whether faster slower *I* say. Mouth bites AND TEETH snap snap. All together whatever I say. This is ME – ME – . No more one thing and another but THIS ME. I am all ONE. I AM AN ANIMAL. My teeth, my claws, my fur my nose my tail swish swish swish.

Ah now I feel. Feel from belly. Belly speaks HUNGER. Get belly food. So – sniff on the air AHHH that was quick yes air talking smell good this is the way, yes. Pads run I say pads run.

Long time goes by as I run and run and run towards smell. YES I RUN but now no smell so says run slower. The THING mustn't be frightened but this THING always frightened. Whole life frightened listen and smell. So I must go this way go away air go away smell of me pad pad STOP BELLY. CROUCH. Lie flat HEAD DOWN LOW.

Time passes slowly I creep creep but now THING now THING stop, alarmed, and sniff sniff I all drooling expectation now. Mustn't make least noise O BLAST CRACKLE STICKS CRACKLE O BLAST STICKS UNDER ME STOP THING WARNED THING gets message THING turns turns now run. All long legs long legs all clutter of legs but for me all dash out dash out towards THING dash DASH now nothing nothing but THING all running leaping away and I running empty belly says FASTER but THING FASTER TOO I leap nothing but faster faster and THING faster but faster faster faster and THING faster but now I closer can smell THING but can smell its smell, hear its breath I am nothing but hurtling leaping claws out leap not far enough. Soft soil under claws THING AH THING SLOWER now again I'm LEAPING AH CLAWS INTO SOFT FUR THING'S fur on flank and claws cling cling smell of BLOOD THING'S BLOOD THING struggles but slower slower now THING STUMBLING falls on side and I panting growling onto it all noise nothing but noise nothing but biting bloody biting. BLOOD WARM TASTE BLOOD SHLOOP DRIBBLE ALL PLEASURE GNAW TEAR GULP.

THING dying slower slower and I drooling drooling all over fur on its flank. Then rip it apart ANIMAL ALL CLAWS ALL TEETH ALL TEARING.

Now eating eating gulp swallow belly nothing but eating tearing biting. AT LAST BELLY FULL.

LYING not eating now lying across bloody fur belly had enough ah satisfaction. I Nothing but all satisfaction licking bloody claws NOW other animal come small teeth small claws coming all round me. Small animals snivelling snatching GET OFF MY PREY MY PREY BUT Come BLOODY FLIES BUZZ BUZZ snatch ahhh snap I'll give you snap snap. Air cooler, close eyes rest FULL BELLY.

Drowsy. TIME PASSES

Small animals come WARY WARY snatch up run away come back snatch up run away thieves. Pads tired jaws tired snap yawn snap Flies oh let them have it. Drowsy. don't want more now belly full now all right all right you can have it. Get up slowly now wandering away. Cool air light less cooler evening wash tongue lick lick clean clean blood mouth dribble blood cool air gentle but what does air say NO DANGER near drowsy sleep SLEEP.

TIME PASSES

Days nights cool on fur find water drink gulp drink. Sniff nose air speaking speaking all time now I make use of

18

wind air no danger no hunger. Thirst need drink to satisfy. Listless, here tree, climb tree. Drowse lying along thick branch. Dusk dim dusk. Hear owls hunting. New day sun smell on wind hear herd passing. Hooves. Come closer herd zebra. No interest hooves gone smell big water glitter water creep closer herd of flamingos all wings wings splat splat leap clutch blatter blatter kill only one eat.

TIME PASSES

Day air very warm. Lying easy under trees then air from up wind brings NEW SMELL. I listen to smell. Smell not go away. Smell pulls me slowly up wind.

Richard Adams

~~~~~~~~~

Leopard Facts

Species: Leopard (*Panthera pardus*)

Location: Leopards have the widest range of any species of cat in Africa and Asia.

Habitat: Leopards are superb climbers and their spotted coat ensures they are well-hidden amongst leaves and bushes.

Behaviour: Big cats must defend their home-range or territory from others. Smell is an important form of communication and big cats spray urine and rub their scent on trees and bushes around their territory, as well as leaving scratch marks, to warn others to keep away.

Leopards are solitary creatures, living and hunting alone. When young, their mothers teach them the skills needed to survive on their own.

Conservation Status: Africa's leopard subspecies are not considered in immediate danger of extinction but the IUCN[1] Red List, which lists all threatened species of animals, classes Asia's leopard subspecies as 'Endangered' and 'Critically Endangered'.

Threats: Throughout the world, countless thousands of big cats are kept in appalling conditions in zoos, circuses and private ownership. Even in modern zoos tigers, lions and other big cats repeatedly pace, frustrated because their hunting and territorial instincts are denied.

Action: Born Free Foundation has two sanctuaries in South Africa for leopards rescued from zoos, circuses and other captive facilities. The Born Free Foundation also works to campaign and raise awareness of the problems associated with keeping leopards in captivity.

To find out how you can get involved in leopard projects visit www.bornfree.org.uk/animals/leopards.

---

[1] IUCN – The International Union for the Conservation of Nature

Homecoming

By Abi Burns

At first I was not sure what it was. The light was fading and mist beginning to seep from the ground. Cornwall is a place of extremity and strange light effects, where land, sea and sky meet and are sometimes indistinguishable. Nowhere is this more so than West Penwith where I was born. This is a wild place, the very far tip of the country – jutting out defiantly into the Atlantic, next stop America.

I had spent the afternoon walking a favourite stretch of the coast path, somewhere I always felt close to my father. Since losing him last year I had returned home to Cornwall often and would find myself back at these cliffs. Sometimes I would bring mother and we would sit in the car looking out at the sea and talking about Dad. Now black clouds were gathering. They were edged in white-gold by the low sun and the great expanse of ocean was darkening, yet dancing with light, as if sprinkled with burning sparks of magnesium.

There it was again. Something was definitely moving in amongst the granite outcrop near the cliff edge. My eyes strained to decipher shapes in the gloom. Gradually a human figure emerged from the dark mass of rocks, facing me and, I could just make out, waving and beckoning. I looked around but there was nobody else on the path. I

21

hesitated – it was getting late and I was reluctant to leave the path or linger any longer on the cliffs. Like anyone from these parts, I know not to underestimate how treacherous this coast can be. The car was still a good half-an-hour walk from here. Still, I should go and find out what was going on, perhaps there had been an accident.

I began to pick my way down through the gorse and lichen-splashed boulders. You have to tread carefully here. This ground is riddled with holes, mine shafts and adits, which have caught out many an unsuspecting walker or dog. The legacy of mining is everywhere, derelict engine houses dotting the treeless moors and desolate cliffs amongst the prehistoric burial sites and stone circles. At one time the sea itself ran red with the ore disturbed by tin excavation.

As I neared the edge of the ravine where I had spotted the figure, I could see a rising wind whipping the top of the rollers into spray. I had a twinge of apprehension. Even on the calmest day, a storm can close in from nowhere. The countless wrecks littering the seabed bear testament to the savage fury the elements can display. Then I saw him. A man was crouching on a rock no more than ten feet back from where the granite stacks plunge away to the sea.

"Are you OK?" I shouted.

No response.

He was looking out over the ravine, searching for something. I could see his face in profile – he was perhaps late fifties, dark haired with a moustache.

I called again, "Hello, is something wrong?"

This time he heard and turned to look. He was Cornish, I was sure; older than my first impression with the look of someone who had seen hard times. He indicated for me to come closer and turned back to the sea. I felt a surge of annoyance at the lack of explanation so I shouted: "What's the matter? I don't want to come any nearer the edge."

He turned and studied me, then pointed somewhere down in the gully, his other hand cupped behind his ear.

When he spoke his voice was hoarse, urgent: "Hark, did 'e 'ear 'em?"

I followed his gaze and tried to hear anything over the waves crashing below. Mordros – the Cornish word for the sound of the surf – has no English equivalent. There on the edge of the cliff it seemed to envelop everything; the sea, the spray and the wind, overwhelming the senses.

But then somewhere, over the mordros, I did hear it – a haunting cry drifting above the sea and the spray and the wind.

"*Kee-aw, kee-aw*".

I could scarcely believe it and, even though I had never heard it before, I knew instantly what it was and it was strangely familiar. The man was observing my face intently, waiting for a flicker of recognition. His black eyes, sharp and questioning, met mine. I smiled in astonishment and nodded. And he knew that I understood.

It is curious how some experiences are primordial, transcending any particular time. And so it was that late afternoon standing on the wind-blown cliff, listening to my first chough. That cry, a link to the past, my past, and a link to my father. To the Cornish, the chough is more than just a bird. It is a legend, the symbol of a people. It even perches on top of our coat of arms, supported by a miner and a fisherman, for nothing is more Cornish than a chough.

Since being knee-high I remember my father talking about this great icon; chows he would call them. I would hear fantastical stories of how King Arthur's soul had passed into the body of a chough when he died, his blood staining the beak and feet that incredible crimson colour. When choughs return to Cornwall, my father would promise as he tucked me in, it will signal the rebirth of Tintagel's king. And then of course, and my favourite of all, there were the tales of the last chough.

Forty years ago my father had travelled up the coast to an isolated stretch between Watergate Bay and Mawgan Porth in a pilgrimage to see that tragic creature. The year before, one of that last pair had been found dead so, by 1969, only a single member of the race survived. For the next six years, this chough kept a lonely vigil – for choughs pair for life – before finally disappearing at an age of twenty-six or more.

As a child the image of that last chough had seemed impossibly sad. I would lie in bed and picture that solitary bird patrolling along the storm-swept cliffs and felt sure that there could not be any loneliness greater than being the last of your kind.

There it was again – "*kee-aw, kee-aw*" – and this time nearer, though from which direction I could not tell. Wind gusted up from the ravine and I crawled along the granite outcrop on my hands and knees, favouring the security of the rock over any pretence of elegance.

"Can you see him?" I shouted scanning the cliffs.

"Away jus' beyond yon rocks. 'll be back soon enough." He indicated to an outcrop further along the headland. Now only a few feet away I could just make out the man's pallid complexion, mottled red and etched with scars and lines. Most likely the result of a life mining, until recently the most common form of employment round here.

"Have you seen it already?"

24

He nodded. "Sure 'nuff. B'aint one though. 'Tis a proper chattering – a score mebbe." I stared at the man in disbelief. Since a pair of choughs miraculously appeared back in Cornwall eight years ago, possibly straying over from France, they had delighted everyone by making their homes here and breeding. For my father the return of the chough had heralded hope for a nation and a language waiting to be re-born. There had been occasional reports of a few birds together but I had never heard of anything like twelve. That would indeed constitute a 'chattering'.

But then suddenly I saw them.

They were wheeling round the headland, like black wind-blown leaves against the dying sun. How many were there? I desperately tried to count as they appeared: four together, and then several more, followed by another group, I think, of five. They separated and regrouped as they climbed on the up-draught from the ravine. Then one by one they would turn and drop with their wings closed as if in free-fall, somersaulting and tumbling through the sky until, at the very last moment – just when it seemed they would be snatched by the surging waves – they would swoop up in an air current and begin their miraculous climb again. The whole display gave the impression of being directed by some unseen choreographer. And every now and then one would cry that unforgettable *kee-aw* which pierced even the incessant roar of the sea.

Three came directly overhead, and close enough to see the curved scarlet beaks and the broad fingered wings, as they soared on the air currents. They swept round and settled on the short grass on the other side of my outcrop, calling to the others which followed and alighted effort-lessly despite the gusting wind. Now, as they hopped around the cliff edge, moving quickly as they probed and dug in the short turf, I could clearly count twelve birds.

I am not sure how long they stayed. As they investigated the ground for insects, kee-awing to each other – each cry accompanied by a flick of their tails – I was aware that the experience had an unreal feel to it, as perhaps all those of great significance do. I felt a shared moment with those who had been out on these cliffs in days gone by, watching a chatter of choughs go about their business when they were a common sight. I wondered if they too had marvelled at the aerial acrobatics, the birds' sheer joy at being – for there was no other explanation for their elaborate show – and felt a shiver on hearing that haunting cry.

Then suddenly, as if on some cue, all twelve took off, dipped down into the ravine, skimmed low over the sea and disappeared around the far headland. Just as quickly as they had come, they were gone. As if they had never been there.

"Proper 'andsome birds they be."

I had almost forgotten about my companion and realised, as I nodded agreement, that I was holding my breath.

"'Tis 'ow they should be. Free to go as they want. We belonged 'em in cages when we was children. 'Em as survived would get tame but most never got used to bein' caged. I use to think 'ed died of a broken heart."

Quite possibly I thought. "What made you want to keep them in cages?"

"Weren't too many about even back then. They'd fetch a good penny for gentlemen from up country. 'Tis partly why they disappeared. There were that many caught. A good many traps was set on these cliffs. I remember seein' a chow caught in a gin. It were flapping about an' its leg were broke and t'other kept swooping down to it making a terrible shrieking. I were only a boy but I couldn't bear the noise and I stepped on th'spring and let it go. I'd 'ave bin half killed if the'd seen us. I don't know whether it lived but it flew off with its mate. That were the last pair I ever saw."

"Well, I guess the rarer the choughs got, the more sought after their skins and eggs became. It's a vicious spiral."

"'Es. Times was hard and us could make more for one clutch of eggs than two weeks toil underground. Father'd clamber right down cliffs or into the shafts to get t'eggs. And a good few folk fell trying."

"Did you mine too?" I asked.

"Sure 'nuff, we worked just below these 'ere cliffs. I'd be a mile out 'neath the sea bed and could 'ear the sea clunkin' boulders round a few foot above us when storms came in. Then I was in the arsenic works, scraping it off the walls of the chimney."

Arsenic, that would explain the pale complexion, I thought. What a way to make a living, or try to. It was no wonder that egg collecting was tempting for men struggling to feed their families. I remembered my father talking about what caused the choughs' disappearance, about how times had been so desperate that men were prepared to scale sheer cliff faces to provide rich folks with pets for their gilded cages or eggs for their cabinet collections. Even as a child I was struck by the pointlessness of it all. And now standing there on the cliffs my eyes fixed on the headland where the choughs had vanished I wondered again what it is about human nature that makes people need to possess things at all costs.

The dark clouds were overhead now and a cold rain began to fall; large, insistent drops which stung my face.

"Well, I'd better be going. This rain looks set in." I said, then hesitated and smiled. "Thank you. For calling me over I mean. I can't believe that I have seen twelve choughs – a real chattering. I wouldn't have missed it for the world."

He nodded. "'Es. I thought it'd be worth a shufty."

"Nice to meet you. And thanks again." As I made my way back over the rough ground to the cliff path, I noticed he was still in the same position, facing out into the wind and rain, where the choughs had gone.

The next weekend I was back at the cliffs with my mother. It was a long walk for her but I desperately wanted her to see a chough. She had been sceptical when I had told her I had seen twelve.

"Are you sure they weren't rooks?" she had asked gently.

"No, Mum; they were choughs alright. I could see the red beaks and feet as sure as you are standing there." She had told me that large chatterings of choughs had not been seen in Cornwall since the thirties and then they were restricted to the coast much further east. "They must be doing better than anyone realised if you saw a dozen."

We scanned the ocean hopefully. Slow, round, Atlantic rollers came in, each one catching the sun's orange glow on its swell, before crashing into the rocks hundred of feet below. Today there were only gulls soaring over the ravine, their thin cries piercing the bluster of the wind. I found myself thinking about the man I had met.

"There was a man here, Mum. He pointed out the choughs to me. When he was a boy, they used to have choughs in cages to sell on to collectors. His dad used to climb down mine shafts to get eggs."

My mother looked puzzled. "He couldn't have been from Penwith then. The choughs had all gone from these parts over a hundred years since."

"But he was from round here I'm sure. He was a miner and said he worked beneath these cliffs – a mile under the sea – and he worked in the arsenic mines too."

"Those mines have been shut since the thirties, maybe earlier. He must have been confused, my lovely. Not sure what's true and what's story by the sound of it."

I felt indignant – had the man been lying to me? He had been so believable and yet the dates just didn't add up. Perhaps his mind was fuddled by years breathing fumes and dust but he seemed lucid enough.

My mother spoke as she looked out over the sea: "This is a thin place, you know. There's not the usual barrier separating the past and today. Perhaps your friend slipped between the two. It's a place of spirits, to be sure."

I looked inland to the patchwork of fields six thousand years old and the ancient moor with its cromlechs and tarns. In Penwith the past is everywhere and somehow seems as real as the present.

Somewhere, on the edge of consciousness, I could hear that haunting cry *"kee-aw, kee-aw"*. I shut my eyes and could still picture the choughs, gliding on the updraft then rolling and tumbling down towards the green waves: those magical birds with their blood-red beaks, back again like dark ghosts in the far west sky.

Abi Burns
Abi Burns has a degree and PhD in Zoology and worked as an animal welfare scientist for a number of years. She now works as a nature writer and artist. Animals have always been her first love and she has far too many paws and claws at home. In 2009 she was named BBC Nature Writer of the Year. Her first book will be out next year.

www.abiburns.co.uk

Dedicated to Georgie: Well done on seeing your first chough, my darling. Hopefully the first of many!

~~~~~~~~~~

Chough Facts

Species: Chough (*Pyrrhocorax pyrrhocorax*)

Location: Southern Europe, spreading eastwards to the Middle East and south East Asia into western China. Although their range is large, the chough is highly localised. In the UK the red-billed chough is restricted to the west coast of Wales, Scotland and the Isle of Man. The chough has only recently returned to the Cornish coast.

Habitat: Choughs forage on grassy cliff top farm grazing sites, looking for insects and small invertebrates, and preferring low-intensity farmed areas such as sheep and cattle grazing. They also feed on dung and other soil invertebrates that thrive in these areas.

Behaviour: The chough nests in recesses in cliffs or in suitable buildings. Breeding pairs remain for most of the year roosting close to the nest site. Those not yet mature form flocks and roost communally on cliffs and buildings. Nest building begins in March, and by early April there should be eggs. Five is the average size for a clutch. They are highly social birds and learn important behaviours from the other choughs at the communal roost sites.

Conservation Status: IUCN classify the red-billed chough as 'Least Concern'.

Threats: Intensive farming of grazing areas has degraded the quality of food available for the chough. They have only returned recently after careful management of critical areas.

Action: N/A

To find out more about the choughs in Cornwall contact the **Cornwall Wildlife Trust**. The Cornwall Wildlife Trust is Cornwall's leading local charity working to protect and enhance wildlife and wild places. The Trust is passionate about all aspects of nature conservation. It is a membership organisation that depends on members' support as well as a fantastic team of volunteers.

The Cornwall Wildlife Trust, the RSPB, the National Trust and the Cornwall Bird-Watching Preservation Society work together to protect habitats suitable for the chough. Choughs returned to Cornwall in 2001 and bred successfully in 2002, the first time in 50 years. There are now around 20 choughs in Cornwall, which are regularly spotted in Penwith between Pendeen and Gwennap Head, and on The Lizard between Southerly Point and Kynance. Everyone involved in their conservation is looking forward to seeing their population grow.

To find out more visit www.cornwallwildlifetrust.org.uk.

Meena

By Dulcinea Norton-Smith

Dancing, dancing, ever dancing, feet moving, heart thrashing, breath ragged, hoping for death.

Onwards, ever onwards, Meena dances. Her feet lifting and falling in the prance which has been programmed into her limbs and muscles, into every fibre of her being. Her feet chap and bleed. With every step they sting and throb. Her joints ache, she feels them creaking. She is young but feels as old as time. She feels so old, so tired; all hope lost.

Meena curses her vanity and her greed for more. She should have heeded her mother's word, not strayed from her side. Always hoping and dreaming of adventure and now only wishing to stop. Stop the adventure she never really wanted. Just for one moment, just a moment's peace; a moment to rest, a moment to die.

Dancing, ever dancing, feet moving, heart thrashing, breath ragged, hoping for death.

Meena had strayed from her den, from her siblings' sides as Mother slept and her brothers and sisters tumbled and nipped at each other's ears. They were cubs at play in the dusty heat but she had wanted more than the life of a bear. She had wanted excitement and adventure; then she had seen the men, the men with guns and clubs. Her curiosity pulled her forwards, away from the sweet smell of the den, away from the warm heartbeat of Mother, the big safe paws of Father.

Dancing, dancing, ever dancing, feet moving, heart thrashing, breath ragged, hoping for death.

Meena longed to stop but when she did the rope through her nose was pulled by her master. Blinding, searing pain making her eyes water and her ears ring; the bitter, salty tang of blood hitting her tongue and sliding down her throat. So Meena dances onwards without stopping, without resting.

Dancing, dancing, ever dancing, feet moving, heart thrashing, breath ragged, hoping for death.

Meena thinks of Mother; longs for Mother. She remembers the sweet smell of milk, the earthy smell of the den, the yips and growls of her siblings. Now Meena smells dirt and dust, blood and sweat. She hears jeers and tinny, jangling noises over and over, shouts and curses assault her if she stops. Mother is dead now, shot by the guns of the men. Meena's brothers and sisters followed her to see the men. Meena was the one who had fun, she was the one who had adventures. She was the one worth following, who always thought up great games for her brothers and sisters to join in with.

The cubs went to the men, the men had smiles. The sticks they carried scared the cubs but their smiles drew them in; smiles and offers of food, sweet food. The cubs

33

got closer, led by Meena; Meena the fun, Meena the brave, Meena whose energy found great things for the cubs. Not this time. The cubs had been clubbed. Their ribs had been fractured and their heads had taken the rest of the blows. They crumpled and slumped into unconsciousness. Meena tried to run but her fur was grabbed by a man. She saw Mother running towards her, bellowing. Father bounded after her, stopping to stand on his hind legs to roar a warning. The men panicked and rushed around but they had big black stick; sticks that shoot bears. Father and Mother fell. Meena felt a thud on her head. She fell asleep.

Dancing, dancing, ever dancing, feet moving, heart thrashing, breath ragged, hoping for death.

Meena awoke to dance. She knew not how to dance, merely how to lift her feet as the music played on. Lifting them to keep her raw, sliced pads from staying in the dust for too long. Moving onwards so that the rope wasn't pulled. Not a real dance; a dance of joy or love. A fake dance; a dance for survival, a dance for peace.

Dancing, dancing, ever dancing, feet moving, heart thrashing, breath ragged, hoping for death.

Hungry, so hungry; always hungry and aching for food. There is never enough food. Mounds of it for her master, her captor, but never enough for Meena.

Her master tosses scraps from his table; gristle and bone and not much of that. Meena's teeth are filed too short to eat the bones properly. They don't hurt now but her very bones remember the filing. Rough stone moved backwards and forwards in her mouth, shaking and scraping her teeth, making them rattle. Making her skull buzz. She cringes now at the memory.

Meena's ineffective gnawing sends splinters of bone to stick in the roof of her mouth. Her tongue is swollen and dry, it is difficult to swallow, sometimes difficult to breathe. Her swollen tongue brushes against the splinters of bone, jangling at all of the nerves in her mouth and giving her a headache. Her mouth swells and throbs, the flesh festers, the splinters become a part of her.

Dancing, dancing, ever dancing, feet moving, heart thrashing, breath ragged, hoping for death

Meena is thirsty, always thirsty. Her mouth is coated with the dust of the villages. Her throat is always dry.

They travel through the hot, Indian villages. Each village is the same as the next, each village the same as the last. She is forever moving on, never stopping, always dancing. Wherever they travel strangers throw coins at her feet but they are not for her. For her there are shouts, laughter, stones and sticks thrown and rotten food. The children stare but they do not move. Some laugh, some shake in fear, some cry. Meena feels they are crying for her, that their young eyes see her pain.

Dancing, dancing, ever dancing, feet moving, heart thrashing, breath ragged, hoping for death.

Meena dances. How many months have passed? How many years? It's impossible to tell and impossible to care anymore. It is many years since she last wept and wished for Mother. Now she just wishes and hopes for death; a quick death not this living death. She knows that she will dance to her death. Perhaps it was punishment for wanting more from her life. A punishment for wanting more than the life of a bear. Oh for the life of a bear again! The carefree life of a bear, a free bear, a wild free bear; a bear with a future. Meena's heart weeps for the bear she could have been, for the mate and cubs she could have had.

Dancing, dancing, ever dancing, feet moving, heart thrashing, breath ragged, hoping for death.

Meena still feels the wild in her, such a small, ever fading sliver of the wild but still it is there. She gazes to the wilderness. She wants to forage for food and climb trees with her cubs and mate. Her heart weeps.

She longed now for the life of a bear, a wild free bear, a carefree bear; it was not to be.

The people laugh and jeer as she dances. They throw the coins violently; at her feet, her stomach, her head. Her captor looks on proudly and greedily, snatching for the coins thrown to the ground, pulling hard on the rope if Meena slows her steps.

Her nose throbs, her feet are raw and her mouth swollen. Even sleep barely dulls the pain. The pain of living and the pain of dancing is worse than the pain of dying could ever be.

Dancing, dancing, ever dancing, feet moving, heart thrashing, breath ragged, hoping for death.

Never a day of rest, never a day of peace; the dance goes on and never slows. Night time brings peace and memories. Memories of Mother, of the warmth of her bulk, the silk of her fur, the comforting smell and taste of nourishment as Meena suckles at her breast. Meena sinks into memories if the safe feeling of Mother's warmth as she dreams of adventures not yet started. The security of Mother gives her false confidence and hazes the real danger of the world.

As Meena wakes from her dreams of childhood and freedom the pain returns. The pain in Meena's feet, mouth and nose, the pain in her heart and then numbness; shallow, empty, black, numbness but never empty or numb enough. There always remains a tiny shard of pain in her heart. She wishes that the black emptiness were deeper, deep enough to sink into and find comfort in.

Soon she is dancing again; dancing without thinking, trying not to feel, too tired to fight. The footsteps tick away with the beats of her heart as she dances the dance of her death. Keep on going, keep on going; Meena wishes for death.

Dancing, dancing, ever dancing, feet moving, heart thrashing, breath ragged, hoping for death.

One day Meena awakes, she sees her captor dragged away. His legs kick and he struggles and shouts. Now he is the prisoner being dragged from all he knows by his captors. Meena is confused, excited, hopeful. Her heart leaps but she pushes it back into the safe cage of numbness, knowing that they must just be new men, new captors, a new dance. Maybe a quicker death.

Meena waits for the pain, the abuse, the dance, but it doesn't come. The rope is removed, scraping the raw skin and cracking free of the dried clumps of blood as it comes out. The rope being taken out hurts more than Meena could ever have imagined but soon the rope is gone and the pain eases. Meena's feet are bathed and covered with thick grease. It is slippy but soothing and her feet start to heal. A woman strokes Meena's fur as men hold her mouth open. Splinters of bone are removed from her mouth but it takes a long time and a lot of tugging to remove the shards.

Hours pass, then days; many, many days. Months pass then more months; many, many months. Men and women come to see Meena and her healed nose begins to pick up their scents, each one different, each one unique. They do not hit her, they stroke. They do not snarl, they smile. They are like Mother and Father. They are her family now.

Her new family bring food, soft food and Meena eats and grows fat. Yet they look at her with sadness. She grows healthier in body but she feels her soul slipping. She is tired, so tired, all thoughts of adventure are gone. That cub she once was died a long time ago.

Meena no longer dreams of Mother. Her dreams are of dancing. Memories.

Dancing, dancing, ever dancing, feet moving, heart thrashing, breath ragged, hoping for death.

Waking still brings sadness; a dull, aching, weary sadness. She is safe now and loved but she mourns for the cub she was and the bear she could have been. She mourns for the mate and cubs that she never had. The kind strangers watch on and the men and women have worry in their shining eyes.

Meena wants to stand. Her head tells her to live, to fight for this new, sweet life, but she is tired, so tired and weary and the forever peace of death is calling to her heart. Meena sleeps once more and dreams now of her siblings. She goes to join them as they roll in sweet, fresh grass and drink crystal cool water from a bubbling stream. They are older now but still play like cubs, nipping and barking. Her Father and Mother watch from the den. Her adventure is done and with peace in her heart she stops dancing and joins her family.

The men and women mourn as another dancing bear whispers their last breath and with her last breath Meena smiles at the gift they gave her; the gift of dying in peace, no longer dancing.

Dulcinea Norton-Smith

Dulcinea has had short stories published in several books and magazines including in anthologies with Bridge House LLP, Wyvern Publications and Rebel Books LLP. She is currently writing a YA historical novel called *Blood & Clay* and editing an anthology called *Mertales* which is due for publication in October 2010.

Dulcinea also owns and runs the writer's and artist's online forum Pen & Palette (www.penandpalette.co.uk)

Dulcinea's story *Meena* was inspired by the Hans Christian Anderson story *The Red Shoes*.

~~~~~~~~~

Dancing Bear Facts

Species: Sloth bears have been used as dancing bears in India (*Melursus ursinus*)

Location: Most sloth bears live in Sri Lanka and India, but they are also reported in Bhutan, Nepal and Bangladesh.

Habitat: Sloth bears inhabit thorn forests, wet forests and grassland.

Behaviour: Sloth bears are nocturnal and are noisy, busy bears. They share home ranges 13 sq km (8 sq miles) in size with other sloth bears. This is a much smaller area than other bears, probably because their favoured food – ants and termites – is available year round. This availability of their food means they do not have to hibernate in winter.

Conservation status: With just 8,000 remaining, sloth bears are classified by the World Conservation Union as 'Vulnerable'.

Threats: Sloth bears are at risk from being poached from the wild for use as dancing bears or for their body parts for use in traditional Chinese medicines. In addition, illegal trade continues to pose a threat as sloth bear cubs are illegally captured from the wild and sold.

Action: Born Free Foundation supports the work of International Animal Rescue (IAR) as they rescue the dancing bears and provide them with a safe haven – in December 2009 the last dancing bears in India were rescued by IAR and a coalition of NGOs (Non-Governmental Organizations). Born Free helped IAR to build a vet clinic at their bear sanctuary in Bannerghatta, India to provide specialised treatment for the bears already rescued.

To find out more visit about the work of IAR visit www.iar.org.uk.

To find out more about the Bannerghatta appeal visit www.bornfree.org.uk.

When Darkness Falls...

By Bookey Peek

Honey badgers get into trouble. Naturally. The Guinness Book of Records doesn't write you up as the Most Fearless Animal in the World for staying at home and eating rice crispies. No sir. Badgers are out there, ready to take on all comers regardless of size or ferocity. Which is absolutely appropriate for something with skin like India rubber, an armour-plated skull, four centimetre long claws and a jaw like a gin trap, but not so healthy for the delicately constructed human who just happens to be accompanying the said Badger on his journey back into the wild.

I found him at five o'clock one evening on the banks of the Mathole river that runs through Stone Hills, our wildlife sanctuary in Zimbabwe's Matobo Hills. And, as always, Badger threw himself onto my lap for our customary cuddle, while surreptitiously sliding his claws into the side of my shoe, hoping he could whip it off and gallop away with it. He had a special hole in the rocks for all these stolen treasures – plastic bottles, farm tools pinched from the garage, gloves, hats and, best of all for someone with a genetically ingrained foot fetish, shoes – any size, shape or smell.

He was eighteen months old, an age when the mothers of young badgers are thinking seriously of banishing their bothersome offspring into a harsh world, in which less than half of those newly independent cubs will survive. But our Badger was doing fine, after a very shaky start. His mother had been shot by a foreign hunter as a trophy when her cub was around six weeks old. By the time little Badge reached us, he was bony, bloated and dehydrated, and we doubted that he would survive. But survive and thrive he did, and that was our first inkling of the toughness and determination of this legendary little animal.

In those days, our daily routine began with his morning walk that normally lasted a couple of hours. When the sun was high, he'd choose a cave somewhere amongst the koppies to hide out until the late afternoon, when we would catch up with him again, thanks to an electronic tracking device. This would allow us to keep tabs on him for a couple of years, by which time we hoped he would be able to look after himself.

On this particular day, I was doing the evening walk, and, after his boisterous welcome, Badger trotted off along the river, having already decided on in his first port of call. Five minutes later, he was halfway into an antbear's hole, bum up and digging furiously – the same hole from which he had evicted the poor creature on the previous evening. But this time, she wouldn't be shifted. As fast as Badger dug, so did she – showering him with red soil till his eyes, ears and coat were caked with it. This was fun, but when it was clear that the antbear wasn't going to play ball, Badge decided to move on to something more challenging. Giving himself a little shake, he trotted off, tail high, with Mother as always right behind him.

A kilometre or so further on, another hole beckoned, stuffed with dry grass, and this time Badger approached with a little more caution. Working quietly but intently, he began pulling the grass away, till an infuriated rumble from within made him jump backwards. Ah-hah, this was more like it! When the entrance was clear, he pushed his nose inside whereupon, with a roar, an enormous warthog burst out, knocking our cub clean off his feet. Then he tore off into the darkness with a dusty but delighted Badger on his tail.

For Badge, this was turning into the perfect action-packed end to his day. It was by then seven o'clock, and I'd began thinking longingly about dinner: a special one that night, roast beef and even Yorkshire pudding, which Ruthie, head chef at our safari lodge, has mastered to perfection. And Badge was also in for a treat. If he came home with me, which he normally did, he would find half a spitting cobra waiting for him inside his cage – an unwelcome guest we'd recently found lurking in our dining room. Snakes were Badger's idea of gastronomic bliss. He'd pull long white strips off them, then suck them snappily into his mouth like wet spaghetti.

Bites never worried him and head, fangs and tail were consumed with equal gusto. No one knows exactly how, but honey badgers and others of their family seem to have a natural immunity to poisons.

Being a nocturnal animal, our cub wasn't too keen on being locked up when he came home at night, but this was essential for our peace of mind, as he had already demolished the seat of the tractor and ripped up the upholstery in one of the open safari vehicles. And there were limitless opportunities for destruction around the house and lodge for an enthusiastic young Badger with time on his hands.

I called him, and headed for a path that wound homeward through the hills. If Badge didn't find anything too distracting in the meantime, I'd be there in an hour. But he didn't join me, and after ten minutes, I followed the tick-tick-ticking of the receiver to the foot of a tall duiker berry tree. There he was, wedged in a fork about three metres up, pleading for help. Now climbing doesn't come naturally to badgers, as my husband, Richard, captured so perfectly in his film *Honey Badger: Raising Hell*. It takes them months of falling, often on their heads, before they get the hang of it; but thanks to their flexible bodies and the thickness of their skulls, they very rarely hurt themselves. So if Badger was telling me he couldn't get down, perhaps he really *was* stuck. I walked around the tree a couple of times, looking for an easy way up, but there were no low branches within my reach.

The whining got louder, but now the sound seemed to come from a slightly different direction. I shone my torch upwards to find that he had moved to another fork a little higher than the last.

"Badger!" This was ridiculous. "That's it," I threatened. "I'm going home without you."

I strode off purposefully for a few yards, then sat down under a tree to wait, trying to banish the unpleasant mental image of Rich pouring the last of the gravy onto his roast potatoes. There seemed to be some vehicle activity from the Mangwe Road – at this point, only a couple of kilometres away from us. And that was unusual, as it's a quiet dirt track that is generally used only by other farmers in the district. But then it stopped, and all I could hear was Badger. I couldn't possibly leave him there, as well he knew, so I went back and managed to pull one the branches of another tree into a position where I thought he

44

could easily reach it. I called to him, showed him just how to do it by the light of my torch. And he wouldn't budge.

OK. I'd have one last try at climbing up to him, and then I was definitely going to radio Rich and ask him to bring a ladder. So we'd both have a cold dinner. My only option was a slender mobola plum growing very close to the duiker berry, with branches so thin that I didn't think they could possibly take my weight. They did, just, and by stepping up and off them as quickly as I could, I managed to reach one of the lower branches of the duiker berry. With much huffing and puffing, I swung myself onto it, just a few metres below The Most Fearless Animal in the World, who sat there moaning, holding out one limp-wristed paw. Then, by standing on that branch, and using another as a backrest, I found I could reach up and put my hands under his armpits, whereupon he responded by pressing himself tightly into the fork and becoming a dead weight.

I heard a soft chirping, and my torch lit up the enormous yellow eyes of a bushbaby, bobbing up and down behind the leaves. Whenever something entertaining happened on our nightly walks, one was sure to be watching, like some disapproving old lady peering through her curtains at the neighbours from hell.

By this time, Badger was howling, and it struck me that if there had been an axe handy I would have been very tempted to chop the tree down, with or without him. But there was no point in losing my temper, the boy sounded genuinely distressed and from hard-won experience, I knew that gentle persuasion worked better than four-letter words. Climbing onto a branch directly underneath him, I managed to manoeuvre him around so that his backside was facing me. Then I gently winkled out both back legs and put them on my lap, while Badger hugged the tree with his front legs like some frantic Greenpeace volunteer defying the bulldozers.

"Come on, darling," I said in my most encouraging voice, talking him through it as one would to a frightened child, "Just relax and do what I say. Now, down we come."

But having managed to prise one leg free, and then the other, I found that the first one was back gripping the branch as tightly as the tentacles of a hairy octopus. This went on for another five minutes, till I finally had him in my arms, and just as I was figuring out how best to guide him down to the ground, he slid off my lap and made a leisurely but effortless descent all on his own.

"Good boy!" I called after him. And I reckoned I also deserved a pat on the back for my rescue efforts. We were quite a team.

Then in the distance the traffic noise began again, but this time it was louder and there seemed to be more of it. I'd better get back quickly in case there was a drama on a neighbouring farm. It was eight fifteen – if I walked fast enough, I might even arrive back in time for that hot dinner.

But first I had to get myself down, and I could see that Badger had found it a lot easier than I would. I caught hold of the branch above me, and from that moment, things began to happen very quickly. In an instant, the hum of traffic became a roar, and then I felt a needle-sharp sting on the back of my hand. Sometimes, I can put two and two together with impressive speed. Badger had discovered a beehive deep inside the tree and he'd lured me up there under false pretences, hoping that I could help him get to it. And the bees were sick and tired of being bothered. Another sting in the hand had me swinging from branch to branch at a rate that would have stunned the most agile chimpanzee, and then I was off at a run, flailing my arms, with a buzzing line of angry bees in hot pursuit. And there was Badger, loyal as always, lolloping happily along beside me.

"Good on yer, Mum," he was saying. "I knew you'd get them out in the end!"

Bookey Peek
Bookey Peek has written two books – *All the Way Home* and its sequel, *Wild Honey*, both of which have been published internationally. After an idyllic childhood in Zimbabwe's Bvumba Mountains, and ten years travelling the world, she became a lawyer, a profession she was only too happy to leave for a life in the bush. Like her husband, Richard, biologist, photographer and film maker, she is a professional safari guide.

~~~~~~~~~

Honey Badger Facts

Species: Honey Badger (*Mellivora capensis*)

Location: The range of the honey badger is quite broad. They can be found in Sub Saharan Africa, West Africa and parts of Arabia, the Middle East and India.

Habitat: Arid Grasslands and savannahs, but they can also be found in wetlands and forests on occasions.

Behaviour: Honey badgers are mostly solitary. The young will stay with their mother until they are approximately 14 months old. It has been known for honey badgers to congregate in areas where food is in abundance. Their diet consists of mostly small mammals, birds and reptiles and of course honey! Their fierce reputation comes from not being afraid to attack animals which are bigger than themselves, such as crocodiles on some occasions.

Conservation Status: IUCN classify the honey badger as 'Least Concern'.

Threats: Farmers hunting them as they are seen as a pest. Hive traps or gin traps are set and the honey badger is either stung to death by the bees or killed by the farmer. They are believed to be a threat to the livelihood of the farmers and are also disliked due to their fierce reputation.

Action: N/A

For all the above and more, visit Colleen and Keith Begg's website: www.honeybadger.com, which aims to bring you the latest information on honey badgers and to encourage people to appreciate and conserve this fascinating creature.

Closing Circles

By Anne Cleasby

With a wild surge of energy, NeiraKeto burst out of her egg case, and hovered in the water for a second. All around her hung the eggs that contained her multitude of unborn brothers and sisters. The changing colours pulsed across their surfaces as they swayed in the slight current, and as she watched, one tiny, perfect octopus squeezed himself out, leaving the egg case pale and empty. He disappeared out of the cave without a backward glance.

NeiraKeto lingered; she wasn't sure why. Her newly cleared eyes focussed on a pale crater in the dark water beneath her. It was moving slightly. *What was it?* She watched briefly, but couldn't make sense of what she had seen. When understanding did come, it was much later, and far too late for her.

She gathered her new strength and left the cave, allowing the buoyant salt water to help her wriggle and swim towards the light at the surface. Jellyfish thronged in the water, their tentacles spread out to catch the unfortunate, but NeiraKeto was too young to sense her own mortality. Moonbeams shone out across the calm ripples of the sea, calling her upwards, and once she reached her goal, she clung to the top layer of the water, merging with the other plankton. She never understood how lucky she had been; her early hatching meant that the predators had not yet gathered in strength, and she drifted past unnoticed. Her later siblings would not be so lucky; many thousands of them would never live to reach the top of the sea.

She drifted slowly, carried by the winds and the ocean currents, by her small muscular arms and her insatiable appetite for life. She fed voraciously on her fellow plankton, and increased in size, until one day her grip on the surface failed her and she drifted and swam down to a new world, a new life.

The sea bottom was crawling with life, and for a while NeiraKeto was dazed by it all. She had a very strong feeling that she should be looking for shelter, and a home, but it was all so new. She tasted and touched the plants with her suckers, then the rocks, then anything that didn't move away fast enough. Some things tasted good, and she lingered over them. Others were of no interest and she filed them away in her mind. She flattened herself against the coral, feeling the colours change beneath her skin, and watched as an oblivious crab sidled past her. Somehow she knew that she was too small to take it yet, and managed to keep her curious arms under control. If she couldn't eat it, then it could probably eat her, and she had an ancient awareness of where she fitted into the predator and prey relationship. She gazed after the crab wistfully. *One day. Soon.*

After it had gone, she explored the area more thoroughly, establishing that there were several abandoned shells, which looked like they might make promising dens. She selected one in the end, based on its position, size and proximity to food. It was almost buried by a pile of stones and she was pleased by its camouflage. She squeezed into it and wriggled around, then rested for a few minutes before coming out again. She walked around it cautiously, her sharp eyes assessing potential threats, and finally decided that it was the best she could do for the moment. She moved in and made it her home for a few weeks, until eventually it became too small for her. She moved into an abandoned beer bottle after that.

The first time she tackled a crab successfully, she felt a surge of triumph. It put up a wild fight for freedom, but she wrapped it in her eight arms and dragged it under her mantle. She held its jerking body while she drilled a hole in its shell, and injected her toxin. It soon stopped struggling and made a fine meal. Crabs rapidly became her favourite food.

Time passed as NeiraKeto ate and grew, and moved house. Her moves were frequent, as she grew so rapidly. She was always hungry, and now her dens had to be much larger, to accommodate her huge body and substantial arms.

Occasionally she would encounter another octopus; if it was larger than her, she would change direction and try to avoid it. She always succeeded. Smaller versions looked like they would feed her insatiable hunger, and they hurried away from her interested stare.

Once, she found a lobster, trapped in a strange contraption. She walked round the box like cage and touched it tentatively, tasted it with her arms. It didn't taste like food, but it set up no warning signals in her mind either. She threaded one arm through a gap in the thing and touched the lobster. *Definitely food.* It retreated and held up its claws threateningly. NeiraKeto was not impressed. She poked it with a second arm. It reared up in alarm; obviously it couldn't get out of the trap. Her skin rippled with anticipation, and she allowed her body to squeeze through the gap in the side of the contraption. She advanced on her prey.

She had defeated the lobster, paralysed it, pulled it under her mantle and was preparing to eat it, when the prison started to move. She seized the lobster and made a dash for the hole she had come in through. The movement and swaying completely disoriented her though, and she paused for a moment too long. The contraption rose above the surface of the sea, complete with NeiraKeto and her lobster. It swung for a second and then landed with a shudder on a solid dry surface The huge octopus was frozen with fear. Her eyes flickered over the strange environment she found herself in. Two creatures that looked deformed, like upright seals, leaned over the crate, and opened it. The jerky movements they made when they saw NeiraKeto suggested aggression, and she kept as still as she could, releasing her grip on her own lobster. One of them grabbed her by her arm and tossed her away, onto the hard surface; the other one kicked her away with his foot. They both returned to investigating their crates for lobsters.

NeiraKeto lay still, her soft body flattened on the deck, her long arms spread out around her. She could feel her heart rate increasing; the creatures on the boat looked like dangerous predators, she had to get away. For a second, she was stunned by fear and the impact of the kick, then she twitched the tips of her arms and felt around her; tentatively exploring the wooden deck. She could sense the sea below, and when she decided that the two predators were not watching her, she started to move towards the side of the boat, pulling herself along on her powerful arms. The two strange seals turned and started to move towards her, and she grabbed at the edge of the deck, in a final burst of speed. She saw the water below her, smelled the salt and, in a desperate bid for freedom, tipped herself over the edge. She felt the thud of running feet through the deck before she fell back into the ocean. She jetted downwards, gliding recklessly towards the bottom.

Once she reached the sea floor she dived under a large rock, turned round and arranged herself until only her eyes were visible from the sea. She could feel the rapid thudding of her heart, and she sucked water frantically over her gills. She reflected balefully on her experience. She had been lucky, she knew. She was aware all the time, that there were things out there that would eat her as easily as she had consumed the crabs, and if she relaxed her vigilance for a moment, they might have her.

She had a feeling that time might be running out; she had eaten, lived, grown to a size where few of her relatives could threaten her. Now it was time to move on. A sense of urgency overcame her, and she felt the colours move rapidly over her body. *Maybe I'm hungry*, she thought. She was always hungry; that must be it.

She slowly slid out of her new den and walked over the seabed, probing in the sand and silt for crabs, shellfish, shrimps, anything. She tasted everything she came across, but now it didn't satisfy like it used to. She wanted something else, but she wasn't sure what. She kept on hunting.

At one point she saw another octopus, about thirty metres away, and her eyes fixed on it for several seconds. It was big; probably dangerous. *Smaller than me though.* Eventually she turned away and headed back to her den, where she retreated, feeling unsettled.

She sucked in seawater, and expelled it again; rested and repeated her action. Soon the current was carrying a

53

scent from her body; a scent she had produced unwittingly; a scent her restlessness had generated.

She waited, her eyes constantly scanning the sea floor around her den. She knew what she wanted now; she felt drawn to others of her kind, and she knew if she waited long enough, they would approach her. Her instincts told her to stay in her den; to let them come to her. The strong sense of caution she had developed through her life would not let her leave. Something stirred in her mind; she must select the biggest, the strongest of any who might come. It was a dangerous business though; a big male might eat her as soon as mate with her. The timing must be right. She continued to watch.

By the third day, seven large males were visible from her lair. She didn't move, still she watched and waited. She would not venture out into danger; they must come to her. One of the seven eventually made a move and started to walk towards her den. She let him approach until he was several metres away, and she felt anticipation building inside her. *He would do.* He paused for a moment, and then a rush of water swirled around him as the biggest male attacked. NeiraKeto watched as the silt rose around the struggling pair. The smaller was trying to escape now, his arms pulling back, his soft mantle thrashing. Showers of tiny bubbles obscured the battle, but NeiraKeto could see that the smaller one was definitely coming off worst. At any other time he would have been doomed, but feeding was not the highest priority on his assailant's mind, and eventually he wriggled free, leaving the end of one arm with his enemy.

The victorious octopus coiled his arm around the still twitching appendage of his smaller opponent, and played with it for a moment, before casting it aside and moving towards NeiraKeto's refuge.

54

She was inclined to be receptive. This monster had fought for her; he hadn't eaten the defeated one, food wasn't on his mind. She would probably be safe. The thoughts ran through her mind as the victor stretched out one arm towards her. *Safe or not, I'm not going out there.* He could come to her. She remained in the shelter of her den as the male came closer, and his arm reached into her retreat. She didn't attack him, but she wouldn't come out either. She allowed the mating arm into her space, but no more of him.

When the mating was over, the large male left. The others had gone hours ago. NeiraKeto was alone again, as she preferred, as she should be. She rested for a while, and then came out to hunt.

Now she had a purpose again. As she hunted, she examined rocks, crevices, and possible caves. She needed a refuge; she needed a better home than she had ever looked for before. It had to be right. Her future depended on it. She passed her time wandering over the seabed, never staying anywhere for more than a day or two.

After a month of searching, testing, trying out various homes, NeiraKeto found one that would do. It was a cleft between two rocks, adequately spacious inside, and with a small enough opening that it would not be too difficult to defend. *Not perfect, but better than anything else.* She moved in, and spent the first few days pulling rocks and various bits of debris around the entrance. She was satisfied eventually and lay back to wait. The restlessness was gone and now she was happy to be patient.

As each egg was formed and left her body, she grabbed it with the small suckers around her mouth and wove it into an elaborate string with the thousands of identical eggs she produced. Her satisfaction grew as strings and strings of tiny eggs appeared over several weeks. Eventually she had produced hundreds of the strings, each containing hundreds of eggs, and they hung all around her. She surveyed them with pride. *Her babies, her future.* She caressed them, stroked them with her arms, cleaning them, nurturing them. She couldn't bring herself to leave them, and her hunger grew until it felt like a living thing, consuming her, but still she remained. She blew seawater over them, watching intently as the strings swayed in the current.

Her eyes strayed frequently to the entrance of her den, blinking warily as she watched for possible threats to her young. A stray sea star investigated the rocks around the den, and NeiraKeto responded with a surge of rage. *Eat her children? Try to feed on her future?* The sea star died in her arms and its body was deposited outside the den. *I'm so hungry,* she thought, but she could not eat; there were more serious things on her mind now.

Over the months, the eggs darkened in colour, moved, changed, and still she watched them, loved them, cared for them. The tiny occupants grew, became conscious, tested their control of colour changes, and even in her weariness, she watched the tiny flickering with a fierce love. *Mine.* She could feel the weakness in her body now, but it didn't matter. She was still strong enough to protect her young, and to see them on their way. This was the culmination of her short life.

As the strength faded from her body, she was dimly aware of the first of her eggs opening to expel its tiny occupant. She struggled to continue washing her eggs, and she was almost unaware of the incessant movements she made. Thousands of eggs were hatching now, the occupants drifting out of their den on the artificial current she had created. Her eyes were no longer as sharp as they had been, but she watched with a fierce satisfaction as the clouds of almost transparent octopus children left their first refuge. Some of them would rise to the surface, as she had, to take their place amongst the plankton. Her eyes dropped and she focussed on her arm, which now lay limp in the water, its multitude of pale suckers exposed. Before the light left her forever, she had a flash of clarity. *So that's what I saw.* It was her last moment of awareness, before the dark claimed her.

The hundreds and thousands of eggs hatched one by one, and the tiny occupants set out on their individual journeys. Behind them, NeiraKeto's body finally lay still and empty, but around it buzzed her hopes that at least some of her babies would survive to start a new cycle of life.

Anne Cleasby
Anne Cleasby is a scientist living and working in Cambridge. She likes reading practically any form of fiction, but would like to write Sci Fi and Urban Fantasy. She has had a couple of short stories published, and is now working on a novel set in the not-so-distant future.

~~~~~~~~~

Octopus Facts

Octopus: Order *Octopoda*

Species: There are over 200 known species of Octopus; the most widely known is *Octopus vulgaris.*

Location: The octopus has been found in a wide range of oceans at varying depths depending on species, from as little as five metres (16 feet) deep to as much as two hundred metres (650 feet).

Habitat: The octopus is a bottom dweller, living on ocean floors. It tends to live in crevices or holes and move along the bottom of the ocean.

Behaviour: Highly intelligent, solitary creatures they only come together to mate. They can grow up to 3m (10ft) across, but are usually smaller than this. The octopus can weigh up to 25kg (55lb). Females are mature at 1kg (2lb), males, at 1½kg (3½lb). They hunt mostly at night, where they use camouflage and eat crab, crayfish and molluscs. Females can live up to two years, dying after brooding their eggs, while males may live longer.

Conservation status: Not officially determined.

Threats: Commercial fishing of octopuses; on average each year between 10,000 and 20,000 metric tons are caught, seen as a delicacy in some cultures. Octopuses are sensitive to environmental fluctuations. They can also be found languishing in aquariums.

Action: N/A

If you want to get involved in marine conservation projects, the **Marine Conservation Society** (MCS) is the UK charity for seas, shores and wildlife. Find out how you can help by visiting their website www.mcsuk.org.

Delivered

By Pauline Burgess

The cool night smoke filled the young pinto with calm and he began to breathe more easily. Encircled by the black velvet fortress of the mountains, the details all around dwarfed him; the trunks and branches of the tall pine trees, the dark sky lightening to silver on the mountaintop. He moved freely now, divested of his saddle and his rider digging his spurs into his sides to make him go faster. Always faster. He saw a ravine below and made his way steadily downwards, sniffing out the prospect of water. His ears were alert, waiting for instruction, but none came. No gruff voice ordering which way to turn, to run, to stop. Just the flurry of curled branches and the ripple of mountain grass.

That day in April, some six months ago, he had been running with the rest of the team of wild horses. It was strange that they hadn't seen the men coming. Before they knew it they were being chased by Morgans and thoroughbreds and choked with lassoes, gasping and baying pointlessly as the cowboys tightened their control. They were pulled and dragged across the plains for days, nervous and terrified. They'd been given no water. No mercy.

They had reached a settlement and the young pinto, blinded by panic, kicked and reared up, sweat breaking out all over him. His eyes were wild and fixed on the open gate through which he'd come, but the men cussed him and whipped him until he could buck no more.

"Damned pony! I should just put a bullet in him right now!"

"Wouldn't do that Jacob. That pinto's got speed in him. That's what they're lookin' for. Reckon he'll be right valuable if we sort him out."

Billy Wallace didn't give in as quickly as Jacob. He saw dollar signs, but he had common sense too and even a touch of kindness about him. He knew the pony was special. If he could get his younger brother a job with the Pony Express riding this young stallion he'd earn maybe $100 a month. Billy had heard all about it from his cousin in St Joseph, who'd been the first westbound rider. He rode all the way to Sacramento, racing the horse at twenty miles an hour and hardly ever stopping.

The pinto's tail clenched and twitched and his ears moved back and forward. His eyes were wild and fixed somewhere in the distant horizon as Billy came at him with a coiled rope. The horse stood there, looking about, blowing, wondering yet again what was going on. He started to calm a little as Billy whispered and soothed in his ear. He let the man lead him round in a circle, over and over. Every now and again Billy would stop and let him have some water. Then came the moment when the cowboy tried to put the saddle on him. He bucked and reared all over again.

"Told you to stick a bullet in it!" Jacob repeated. "I ain't wastin' time on no wild beast like that. Pony Express wants thoroughbreds anyway. What do you want to go breakin' that pinto for?"

"You need a fast horse – I told you that already! And he's just the right size at fourteen hands high. You need to get out there and earn some money, boy. Ain't enough work to keep us both goin' at Harper's Ranch anymore. Pony Express will be happy to take this horse. I just know it."

The sky was coal black by the time he finished with the pinto. There was a smattering of freckly stars glimmering in the far distance as he started to bed down for the night. The horse had been tethered and fed, greedily swallowing down a bucket of oats shared with a mustang. Billy thought he saw the horses look at each other in a strange way. Almost like they were comforting each other. It was probably just the lack of sleep making him imagine things.

At sunrise the pony felt itself being saddled again. This time he made no attempt to move as the strange object was placed across his back. He didn't know whether or not to trust this man, with his strange ways and his offers of food and water. When Billy swung his legs over and mounted him, the pinto braced a little but found itself waiting on the man's next move. He felt something hard jag into either side of him and he snorted loudly and tossed his head. His tail splayed out behind him, flicking and swishing in the soft breeze. He lowered his head and took some small steps backwards, then forwards, before breaking into a trot and then a canter. The next thing he knew, Billy Wallace was riding him back out across the vast, rolling plains of wind-flattened grass and despite the weight on his back the horse almost felt free again. He galloped as though fired from a cannon, sending up splashes of dust. But all too soon he was back at the camp and tethered once more, grateful to be tied up beside the water trough this time. This routine went on for days, maybe weeks, until Billy was satisfied that the pony was ready for Jacob.

"He's all yours, Jacob. He's still a bit nervous. Unsteady too at times, but if you treat him right he'll do what you need him to do. They need new riders every hundred miles or so, so I reckon if you head to the station a few miles up the creek, you'll pick yourself up a job."

The two men at the station looked the young horse over appreciatively.

"Fine horse, Mr Wallace. Is he fast?"

"Yes, sir! This pinto will run as fast and as far as I tell him. He knows who's master around here."

"You gonna have to cross deserts, plains, prairies and mountains on that horse, in a relay of course. No point pushin' to do the whole thing yerself! But if you *do* see yer way to doin' it all by yerself, well there's more money in it for you. That'll be your decision Mr Wallace."

"That would suit me just fine, sir."

"You know this is a brave and bold project, Mr Wallace. We need the best. Those pony feet are gonna bring the ragged edges of this here nation together."

Jacob was small and wiry enough to suit their purposes as an Express rider, suitably young and 'willing to risk death daily,' so he was quickly despatched on his first run. But the pinto soon realised Jacob was nothing like his brother. He dug hard into him and pushed and pushed him to go faster and faster, barely stopping to relieve the animal's thirst. He rode him so hard the pinto's sweat gelled up into a film across his eyes, blinding him to the hot sun bearing down like a blazing flame. And each time the man reached his destination and delivered his post, the pinto was lucky if his rider remembered to give him anything to eat or drink before he found the nearest saloon and drank himself senseless.

"You stand there, you useless beast! I'm gonna have me some whiskey."

The pinto was well used to this refrain by the time Jacob Wallace had earned a reputation as a drunk. Yet, despite that, it was widely known that he was one of the fastest riders in the Pony Express. The Pikes Peak Express Company was still intent on proving itself and winning that million dollar government mail contract, so riders like Jacob weren't so easily dismissed, even if he did brutalise his pony. No eyebrows were raised when he never even needed a fresh horse. The riders were supposed to change every twenty miles or so like the man at the station had said, but not this one. Jacob's older brother had been right about the pinto's potential.

But with each journey the young pinto became more and more fragile. It wasn't even the racing any more. It was the deprivation; never getting a cool shade to rest in except when the man was at the saloon. Getting just enough food and water to keep it going. Getting lashed at by a hopeless drunk who threatened to shoot him if they didn't reach the next station in time. Horizons stretched out in front of him as man and horse delivered the mochila from station to station, sometimes with as much as forty pounds of mail in it. And that was on top of the weight of a rifle, revolver and Wallace himself. And always, always, another run to do. Another kicking to take.

They were on their way to Missouri one day in August when Jacob fell off in a heap on the ground. He was still drunk from the night before. He'd been drinking whiskey all night in the Eagle's Nest Saloon and playing poker with a few cowhands. He'd even bet the pinto in one game, but despite his slurring his mind had been alert enough to win the game. Now he was none too pleased to find himself prostrate in a stream churned by cattle hooves.

"Son of a bitch! What kinda stupid horse are you?'

The pinto waited for the brute to recover, his eyes pointed blankly into the distance, while Jacob wrestled himself out of the dirt. The cowboy was clearly ready to lash out with his boots again when a searing light blinded him temporarily and he fell back down in a heap. The sunlight burned down on him, but there was something else up there. Something much more dangerous.

He hooded his eyes with his hands and tried to scan the horizon, sensing an enemy. Slowly too the pinto turned his head towards the light, his senses sharpening also. There was a lone figure, sometimes there, sometimes a shadow. The sunlight distorted and dissolved his outline but Jacob Wallace knew. Twitching with hostile excitement he pulled out his revolver and took aim at the sun. The shape was gone. He turned to the right, to the left, ready to fire at anything that moved. Then something came at him. He yelled out. An arm burned his throat. The pinto watched as he kicked out, choking and coughing, the figure's hands over his face. Wallace scratched at the air trying to inhale. He gulped mouthfuls of thick yellow dirt.

Suddenly there were many more of them, dragging Jacob Wallace away, berating him in the rhythms of their own language. The pinto stood motionless. One of the men walked towards him, slowly, carefully. He wasn't frightened. He knew their touch. The

Indian's hands pressed into him like a soothing balm. He spoke in whispers, hushing him with his poetic syllables and focus came back into the pinto's eyes. The man led him gently towards the cooler shade of a tree and fed him some water before he removed his blinkers and saddle and climbed on to his back. The pinto felt himself being led towards the other men where Wallace was astride one of their ponies with his hands tied behind his back.

The group rode out into the plains in silence, treading the land like Braille as their forefathers had done. The contours of the land gave all the direction that was required. They rode their horses as if they were part of them, not masters of them, and for the first time in months the young stallion could take in the land shelving seamlessly to the eastern rim of the sky. They stopped near the boundary of a small settlement, though far enough away not to be detected. Jacob was tumbled off his pony, cussing and spitting. The Indians turned away without a word.

They rode along for a few hours, eventually casting long shadows in the last pale reach of the sun. Travelling further north, the pinto saw the black shapes of buffalo standing out against the grass like ghosts. The land was lusher now, full of obstacles and trees, weaving through tangled thickets of willow and dogwood. The group stopped and the Indian climbed down off the pinto. He slapped him gently on the rear and walked back to the other men.

"Diiya!" *Delivered*

A drizzle came down and the Indians disappeared as if into the liquid sky. The pinto continued to move through the darkening banks of trees towards the ravine. Unharnessed and unrushed, he pricked up his ears to listen for the whinny of fellow mares and stallions. Horses unbroken and free, roaming these plains for over three hundred years. And he was one of them.

Pauline Burgess

Pauline Burgess is a 39 year old teacher of English who spends her limited 'spare' time writing. With a three-year-old in the house, there isn't always the time or the space for this, but she does the best she can. She has had numerous short stories published in anthologies and magazines in Ireland and England, and some of her poems have been published on the N.Ireland BBC website and in a new Belfast anthology to be launched in March. Pauline completed a diploma with The Academy of Children's Writers in 2008 and was recently shortlisted for the Brian Moore Short Story Awards in Northern Ireland. Pauline's story *Traveller's Rest* appeared in the Bridge House publication *A Suitcase Full of Stories*.

~~~~~~~~~~

Wild Horse Facts

Species: Wild (Feral) Horse (*Equus ferus*)

Location: Feral populations of horses are found predominantly in the US and Australia. In the United States the feral population of horses are known as Mustangs, they are the descendents of once domesticated herds from 400 years ago.

Habitat: Mustang horses are grazing animals and therefore are semi-nomadic. They range over semi-arid deserts and have adapted to survive on tougher vegetation than their domesticated counterparts.

Behaviour: Mustangs form small herds with a dominant stallion and a harem of mares and foals. When a colt reaches maturity he will go off and roam with other young colts until they themselves can gather a harem of mares. The herd will have a territory which they graze and will only tolerate other herds on the outer fringes of that territory. The gestation period is 11 months; the mare will go off alone to find a well-hidden location to give birth. The foal can stand just hours after birth and their colourings are the same as the dusty ground until they get older, in order to provide better camouflage.

Conservation Status: Mustangs are considered domesticated and therefore have no conservation status.

Threats: At the beginning of the last century the mustangs were thought to number between 2 and 5 million. Now there are believed to be little over 10,000 left in the United States. The main threat to them is settlers cultivating the land and killing them in their thousands to protect their grazing herds or crops. They are also caught and broken-in for cattle-herding purposes.

Action: N/A

There are a number of horse sanctuaries in the UK. **Redwings Horse Sanctuary** was established in 1984 and today has grown to become the largest horse sanctuary in the UK, working to save horses, ponies, donkeys and mules whose future would otherwise be bleak. Its work has three themes: rescue and rehabilitation, specialist sanctuary care, and prevention through education. Its horse care and welfare hotline receives typically 3,000 calls per year. Redwings currently cares for more than

1,100 horses, ponies, donkeys and mules in its sanctuary sites around the UK, and currently has 500 horses out on loan in Guardian homes. Redwings celebrated its Silver Jubilee in 2009.

To find out more visit:
www.redwings.co.uk
www.redwingsadoptionclub.co.uk
www.youngredwings.co.uk.

The Man Pond

By Gill James

He first saw it at twilight, the patch of brightness that told him there was water down there and it would be safe to land. The reflected light caught his eye, dazzled him slightly. It was a small patch of water, and quite close to the red brick man-nests, but there were grass and trees around it, and he thought, a few moorhens and ducks paddling around.

Fendrak never liked landing. He always put it off as long as he could. In fact, he disliked travelling generally. He'd thought the old lake was going to be his home forever. He shuddered at the memory of the men and their noisy machines.

Land he must though. And water was where he must land. Heart beating fast, Fendrak changed the angle of his wings, spread his webbed feet out and pointed them downwards. They touched the surface. Almost toppling over, he raised his wings ready to balance, managed then to find his sitting position and then glided more gracefully now across to the bank.

He crawled out. It was really almost dark now. Exhausted, he tucked his head under his wing but just before sleep came he remembered Gelda screeching and flaying her arms at the adult human male who had approached them. Why was she still trying to protect the two year-olds? High time they'd found a new flock. But she'd been adamant. The companion of the human male had leapt to his defence and attacked Gelda with that hard shiny tool. Then seconds later she was lying lifeless next to their old nest. The youngsters had fled.

The men came with their big machines. The noise. He remembered the noise. And the lake suddenly empty.

All the others gone. Too late for him to go with them. Too late for him to help Gelda. All he could do then was look after his own needs. So, he had run along the pathway, launched himself into the air and flown looking for water and dreading the landing on it.

He did not like these thoughts. But then sleep came. Blissful, carefree sleep.

There was a frost on the ground the next morning, but the crisp clean air that it brought was reassuring. Fendrak took stock. There was not much activity in the man-nests. Maybe they kept themselves to themselves. There were fish, he noticed in this water. That might be a problem. That might bring the humans here with their dangerous wires. But there was also plenty of weed and other greenery for feeding on – perhaps even for building a nest.

He heard the almost human cry of some passing geese. They flew straight across, though and did not swoop down to examine the water. Had there been one of his kind there before? Would there be another one again? Did they actually perceive and fear him?

It puzzled him a little, how the water came to this place. It didn't seem to be fed by any river or stream. There was an outlet, surrounded by man-bricks, where it might drain away but it didn't seem to doing that. He guessed the water just accumulated here when it rained, which is what it used to do a lot in his old home. That wasn't so far away – he hadn't flown for that long.

There was plenty that he liked about the old place. Never hot enough in the summer to dry up the water and never cold enough in the winter to make it freeze over. And plenty of rain to replenish it. Would it be the same here?

A few humans wandered by during the day. Many of them had dogs that barked with them. Fendrak found himself a corner far away from the man-path, and if one of their unleashed dogs wandered near him, a flutter of his open wings was enough to send them on their way.

It looked as if this spot would do.

The days passed and still the geese flew overhead and didn't drop down to visit him, not even out of curiosity. The moorhens and the ducks still kept their distance but as time went by they ventured a little closer.

There must be another nearby, he concluded. He began to have a sense of a presence and as the time of year approached when the days are almost as long as the nights, when those instincts became sharper, he was convinced there was a female nearby. Then he began to glimpse flashes of white feathers between the straight green rods of the reeds on the other side of the pond. Had she also lost a mate? Or was this just wishful thinking?

She came to him at twilight on the day that is exactly the same length as the night. Her neck, Fendrak noticed, was a little longer and more slender than Gelda's. She moved more gently in the water. In that light that comes as the sun goes down her white feathers seemed almost purple and luminous. She was beautiful.

He sensed a maturity in her and also some sadness. She was, he guessed, an experienced mother and an experienced mate. She too had suffered a loss he was sure.

She swam up to him and stretched out towards him as if she were about to neck him. As he responded, she pulled away and swam quickly. Fendrak felt a familiar old excitement. More exciting perhaps than recent years with Gelda. Their love making had, of course, been perfect but it had also been familiar. This was new.

She swam swiftly and skilfully. He had trouble keeping up with her. She stopped suddenly though and pulled at something on the bank. It was, Fendrak saw, the remains of an old nest. He had not noticed it before. It had been covered by the long reeds that grow on the bank. So, she had lost a mate. And some time ago, by the looks of it. She held out towards him a mat of intertwined grass. He went to take it in his beak, but as he leant towards her, she let the old nest part drop in the water. She stretched her elegant neck towards and rubbed it along his own.

Their love-making was urgent and exciting. It was different from with Gelda. He had to take a little more care with Frayla. He had to hold her head at a different angle from the way he had held Gelda's to make sure she did not drown. He fitted into her in a slightly different way which intensified his excitement. Her violent thrashing matched his own as their coupling came to an end and he knew that they were going to become parents.

The nest building was a pleasant activity. She really did know what she was doing and yet was happy to let him show her some tricks. She'd showed him that she wanted to move to his part of the lake. She'd torn the old nest apart in a frenzied attack but then gave him some bits and pieces which would be useful for the new nest. It was her who led him back to the bank where he always slept and indicated that this was the spot where she wanted to build. Fendrak felt his loneliness disappearing.

She produced three eggs and began to sit on them straight away. Fendrak found the tastiest bits of pond weed to feed her. He had every hope that they would become a happy family.

The days passed. As they became longer, more humans strolled around the lake. Occasionally some of the young males ones would throw stones at them, but Fendrak found he only had to raise himself up on his legs and spread his wings flapping them slightly and the young humans would go away.

Sometimes the humans brought food. It was not like the food that grew around the lake. It was soft and white and easy to digest. You wanted more and more of it even if you were full. It was tempting to overeat but they actually knew better than to do that. And it made feeding Frayla easy. He took his turn, too, sitting on the eggs. Then she would come to him with some tasty morsel in her beak. She would pass it gently to him, letting her beak linger on his for a few seconds and stroking his neck with her own. Fendrak asked himself whether there might be time to mate again and produce a second brood.

Then the young male humans came. Surely they would not do any harm? They were just children, though almost adults he guessed. They approached the nest. Frayla stiffened. Fendrak watched carefully. The youngsters were going towards Frayla. Fendrak sensed her fear. He swam over to the bank and hissed at the youths. One of them growled loudly at him, startling him and making Frayla panic. She leapt from the nest and plunged into the water. The youths started laughing. One of them started kicking at the nest. Fendrak watched in despair as it and the eggs all tumbled into the water. They could build a new nest, but they could not salvage the eggs.

It was a reason to make love again. He was more skilful this time. He had the measure of her. Again as they both screeched silently in their excitement he knew they had succeeded.

They built the nest further along the bank this time. They salvaged some of the old one and found some new materials. There would just be time to raise a family before the cooler weather came.

Again Frayla sat proudly on her clutch. There were four eggs this time Fendrak worked hard to feed her. On the whole, the humans and their dogs left them alone and even remembered to bring some of the white food.

But then the youths came again. This time, they were even nastier. One of them jumped at Frayla and shouted. She hissed back, but the biggest of the youths picked up an old brick and hurled it at her. She jumped from the nest and plunged into the water. Fendrak also hissed but it made no difference. The youths just laughed again. Fendrak saw them take the eggs from the nest. Their hopes of raising a family this season were gone.

He could not stop Frayla dragging herself from the water and back on to the nest. She didn't seem to notice that the eggs were no longer there. He stopped feeding her, tried to entice her into the water, but she would have none of it. He feared she would grow too weak, so he started to bring her the choicest of morsels again.

Only weeks later as the first leaves turned to yellow did she begin to venture from the nest and only when the leaves started to drop from the trees did she abandon it altogether.

Fendrak thought that maybe they should leave, find another body of water. Each time the geese passed over, he would look up, flap his wings and whisper gently. But Frayla ignored him. She seemed tied to this place. And after all, Fendrak hated flying. He felt uneasy but was also glad to stay.

Besides, there was no further sign of the youths. Plenty of humans came by, but on the whole, those with dogs kept their pets under control and they were left in peace. Some brought white food. Fendrak and Frayla enjoyed that. Fendrak knew that they should not eat too much of it. And in fact, as the days became shorter, the humans came less and less and hardly ever brought white food. Besides, Fendrak became aware of two older female humans who seemed to be watching him and Frayla carefully. He sensed some kindness in them.

Perhaps it was safe after all. Life became bearable and almost pleasant as they pottered around on the little lake. There was a good supply of weed and insects here. The rain refreshed the lake and it only went icy at the very edges. They could be content here, Fendrak realised.

The shortest day came and went. Snowdrops bloomed on the banks and leaf-buds swelled on the trees. Something began to stir in Fendrak. He sensed a growing excitement in Frayla too. Maybe this year they could become parents.

As the days became milder, the humans with their fishing wires returned to the lake. There was no sign of the youths, and although the sunnier weather had made Fendrak apprehensive, he began to relax as more and more days went by when the humans just left them alone. Always, though, the two adult females watched them carefully. Fendrak became content.

One day as they fed, Frayla accidentally got a piece of discarded fishing wire caught on her beak. She hissed as she tried to disentangle it from her mouth. Fendrak flapped around her, wanting to help, but not knowing how to. Eventually she was free of all but a little of it, but he could tell it hurt when she tried to feed. Her beak looked sore and swollen. Each day it looked worse. She was eating less and less. She would fade away soon if she could not eat. They might never have a family together. He might be all alone again.

The two female humans now came several times a day. Could he ask them for help? How would he do that? What could they do?

Some more humans came. They had nets and sticks and they looked strong. They started throwing the nets at Frayla. She hissed and flapped her wings. He circled round her and charged at the men with the nets. They waved him away but seemed to speak kindly. They persisted. They even waded into the water and surrounded Frayla. Fendrak now also hissed and flapped as hard as he could, but they mainly ignored him. He even managed to peck one on the arm but he had such a thick skin of clothing that Fendrak knew he could never hurt him.

The two females stood on the bank and watched and seemed to be making soothing noises.

But nothing could sooth Fendrak.

And Frayla, already weak for lack of food, seemed petrified with fear. She suddenly stopped struggling. The net was over her head and two of the men were taking her from the pond. Fendrak watched as they carried her away, put her into their white van and drove off with her.

They had his Frayla. He was alone again. He sat on the water, not moving, stunned. He was aware that the two females were watching him. They said little. As it began to grow dark, they turned away from him and walked away from the bank. Fendrak pushed his head under his wing and slept and forgot.

He awoke to find the sun streaming on to the pond. Where was Frayla? This was going to be a glorious day.

They should share the joy of it. Then he remembered the men and the nets. Frayla was gone. It would be better to die as well. He sank his head into the water, hoping to drown. He couldn't do it though. The urge to breath was too great.

The two human females came and offered him white food but he turned away. He would try not to eat again, to starve himself to death. He didn't want to start again. He didn't want to find a new waterway. He didn't want a new female to come here. He just wanted Frayla back. But the humans had taken her and she wouldn't be back. Every time, though, hunger got the better of him, and he would nibble just enough weed to take the edge away.

He tried to sleep as much as he could, but he could not sleep all of the time. Noises and hunger woke him. But each time as he tucked his head under his wing, he hoped he would never wake again. He was getting weaker and he did sleep more and more. Still he woke every day, though.

On the seventh day when he awoke the sun was already high in the sky but he sensed something familiar and exciting and something of which to be afraid. The white van was at the edge of the lake again. Perhaps they had come to take him. Good. Then he could die, too. He would even swim out and meet them. He tried to edge towards them.

A man jumped out of the van and slammed its door. Fendrak jumped and swam away. He wanted to die but he was afraid of the pain they would inflict on him. He watched from a distance. Another man got out of the other side of the van. The two females were now walking down the path from the road. They shook hands with the two men. One of the men opened the back of the van. Then the two men took out a large cage.

Fendrak suddenly felt excited. It reminded him of how he felt when he first became aware that Frayla also lived on the pond. He had the odd impression that she was nearby again, but how could that be? The men had taken her away and killed her, hadn't they?

One of the men opened the cage and signalled to the other humans that they should stand back. Something white struggled out. Could it be? Surely not? It looked like her, but how could that be?

It was her! She scuttled down to the water, clumsily dived in then gracefully glided over to him and began rubbing his neck. By now, more humans had gathered around the lake. They all clapped. Even the ducks and moorhens seemed to stop what they were doing to stare at Frayla's return.

Oh, he loved her. He wanted to make love to her there and then, but not with this audience. Besides, he knew he was too weak. But she looked glorious. Her beak was completely healed and she was well fed. Her feathers glistened with health. So, the humans hadn't killed her. They'd worked some magic on her and she was fit and well again. He was the poorly one now. That wouldn't last long, though. He would feed properly now.

For four days, they pottered on the lake. They found delicious new weed and beetles and insects and even indulged in some small fish. They had a little treat of white food each day from the two human females who now came several times a day to the lake. They knew, though, not to eat too much and the two humans seemed to respect that as well. Every so often, Fendrak would try to make love to her, but she would turn and swim away. How wise she was! He knew it really. Only when his strength had retuned fully would he be able to make a family with her. But she would rub her neck affectionately along his and he was content and knew that he was no longer lonely, would probably never be lonely again: they seemed to have an aptitude for overcoming disaster.

On the fifth day, after a long necking session, she allowed him to hold her head above the waters as he entered her from behind. This time it was perfect as their excitement rose in harmony and they peaked at exactly the same moment. Fendrak knew that he was a father again and he was sure that she knew she was a mother.

When they were done, she lead him to her old nesting ground in the reed bank. She was right, he was sure. This was far away from where any human could touch them. What did he care if she shared that area with her previous mate? If it mean their family would survive, then so be it.

Frayla produced five eggs. Fendrak was proud. A couple of times he and Gelda had managed seven, but not all of the cygnets had survived. In more recent years there had just been two or three. Five was a respectable number.

Atil was the first to hatch. Then Bella, followed by Callum, Danik and Esmee. Though he'd got through the alphabet twice with Gelda, Fendrak still always found it an exciting moment when the first one pecked his or her way out. It had always been a male, the first one, in the broods he'd raised with Gelda and Frayla seemed happy to carry on the tradition.

They were ugly of course, at first. The moorhens and the ducks came and stared. They had young, too, but their young just looked like smaller versions of themselves. No one can ever look at one of Fendrak's children and believe that one day it will become a graceful swimming bird that actually belongs to the Queen or King of England. Atil, Bella, Callum, Dana and Esmee started off like all cygnets – white and fluffy and clumsy. Then they became grey and fluffy and clumsy. Then the fluffiness gradually disappeared.

The greyness would eventually turn to white. They would be short-necked for a while but eventually they would become as elegant and as handsome as their parents, though they would remain unsure of themselves for a while yet and would need Fendrak and Frayla to guide them. In the end they would even lose their clumsiness.

The humans came to stare at them. Then, Fendrak and his family would put on a little show of behaving how swans are supposed to behave. They would swim in a straight line: Fendrak, Frayla, Atil, Bella, Callum Dana and Esmee. More humans would now bring the soft white food. Sometimes, though, they would just bring too much. Then Fendrak and Frayla would guide the little ones away.

Fendrak was charmed by his new family. They were all so different. Atil was the serious one considered everything he did very carefully. Bella lived up to her name, and even through her grey, fluffy, clumsy state, anyone could see that she was beautiful – perhaps even more beautiful than her mother. Callum was the one they had to watch. He'd been the first to go tippy-up in order to feed but had forgotten to hold his breath and Fendrak and had to pull him back up by the neck. Callum always wanted to try new things before he was ready. Dana was practical and wise beyond her days and Fendrak already guessed that in a couple of years time she would be the first that he and Frayla could happily encourage to join another flock. Esmee was timid and needed looking after. She, he guessed would be the last to go or might even be one of those swans who never left the parental flock. Flock! Maybe he and Frayla would breed again next year and there would indeed be a small flock of swans on this small lake. Sweet indeed.

One day a small human came with, Fendrak supposed, a grandparent. As far as Fendrak could tell, the child was younger in human terms than his five were now and the adult much older than he and Frayla. The humans had white food with them. Today's treat, then. Fendrak lead his family to the bank where the humans stood. But as the white food hit the water, Fendrak realised that something was wrong. There were blue spots on it. He remembered vaguely a long time ago white food with blue spots and Gelda's very first cygnet, Almo, dying. This stuff was dangerous. And of course, bold as ever, Callum was making right for the first pieces.

Fendrak scuttled out of the pond and hissed at the humans. The child whimpered and the adult pulled him towards her. They backed away.

Frayla seemed to understand and was now circling round Callum, trying to stop him eating the spoilt white food. It would be impossible, Fendrak, realised, with Callum, but maybe they could stop the others coming to any harm.

Suddenly there was a large splash behind him. Fendrak turned to see a fully-clothed young male human diving to towards the spotted white food. Callum was pecking and hissing at him and Frayla was hissing and flapping her wings. The other four cygnets just sat and watched and the ducks and moorhens had also stopped what they were doing to see what was going on.

Fendrak realised what was happening. This wasn't one of the youths who had been here before to destroy their nest or steal their eggs. This youth was collecting up the poisonous food. The child and the grandmother had wandered back to the road now. That danger was over. And on the bank was one of the females who visited every day, her hand over mouth and concern on her face. The youth was no doubt with her.

Callum would hurt him soon if he didn't do something, Fendrak realised. He slid back into the water and guided his family away. Frayla seemed a little puzzled at first but then she and all of the cygnets, even Callum accepted without question. Soon they were all happily feeding on the delicious weed which grew on the east side of the pond.

The youth, Fendrak noticed, had collected all of the poisonous food. He had got out of the lake and he and the older female were now laughing. Yes, he did look silly, even for a human, with water dripping from his clothes. They usually take most of them off when they go in the water.

The sun suddenly came out from behind the dark clouds overhead. A faint breeze rippled the surface of the water and gently tickled Fendrak's feathers. It seemed like a sign that all would be well from now on.

Fendrak was pleased to see the child and its grandmother join the two females in visiting the lake every day. They all seemed to be friends now. Only sometimes did they bring white food and never any with blue spots.

Fendrak realised something else. This was a man-pond. Humans had made it for some reason. That's why there were red bricks at the side. But they didn't need it anymore and they'd left it for the swans and the ducks and the moorhens and everything else that could live in and around it. Those men who had come and taken Frayla away had been trying to help and they had helped. She would have died if they hadn't come. The youths hadn't been back since the two females started coming.

Yes this was a man-pond, but it was a fine place to live and the humans were keeping an eye on them and keeping their distance. Frayla swam up to him and rubbed her neck along his. He felt the excitement growing. Was there time this season to raise another family? He looked at the light. A little weak, perhaps. Well, there was always next year.

Fendrak was at home.

Gill James

Gill James writes fiction for children and young adults under the name of Lian Childs. She writes non-fiction and short fiction for adults under her own name. She works as a lecturer in Creative Writing at the University of Salford. She lives opposite a disused millpond, home to a small family of swans.

www.gilljames.co.uk

~~~~~~~~

Swan Facts

Species: Swan (*Cygninae spp.*)

Location: The mute swan can be found in Europe and North America.

Habitat: The mute swan inhabits both natural and man made water bodies. They can be found on shallow lakes and ponds, slow flowing clean and weed rich rivers and streams or on reservoirs and gravel pits etc..

Behaviour: Other species are migratory but the mute swan is essentially sedentary. The mute swan will build up nests like mounds in hidden out of the way areas. Cygnets start learning to fly at 60 days. The adult birds will go through a period of flightlessness when they moult in

July/August time. The cygnets mature around 2-3 years, but tend to stay with their parents, who mate for life, until they nest again. The young have been known sometimes to stay through the second clutch too. The mute swan is largely vegetarian, surviving on pond weeds and other aquatic vegetation, but they have been known to eat small aquatic invertebrates and amphibians such as tadpoles, frogs, small insects and worms.

Conservation Status: The IUCN Red List classifies the Mute Swan as 'Least Concern'.

Threats: Lead poisoning from discarded fishing weights and shot is the most common cause for concern. Entanglement with fishing wire and other pollutants is also a threat to them.

Action: N/A
The Swan Sanctuary is a charity dedicated to the care and treatment of swans and waterfowl with an established reputation not only in the British Isles but worldwide.
To find out more about swans visit www.swanuk.org.uk.

All Things under the Sky

By Mandy K. James

The afternoon sun relentlessly cooked the plains to within an inch of brush fire.

Lencho edged a little further into the scant shade of a Thorn tree and tried to remember when the last rains fell.

It must have been at least two moons ago. He recalled that the elephants had come and the Impala had been thick on the ground. He and his family had snatched them from the waterhole as readily as apes pick ripe fruit from trees.

Dinner on the hoof had been so easy that even he had ventured out. As head of the pride, Lencho normally preferred to let his mates do the hard work. Now, most animals had moved on, as the water hole was as dry as matchwood.

He licked his great paws and raised his head to gaze with amber eyes across the veldt. Partially opening his mouth to draw the smell of the world over his olfactory organ, he tasted the air. He could detect not even the faintest sign of water, and the cloudless sky stretched without end.

In the distance, a handful of Zebra pawed the earth and picked at clumps of withered grass, whilst a depleted herd of Wildebeest struggled to keep standing. Lencho shook the dust from his mane and lowered his head again.

If the rains don't come soon we'll have to move on again. Ageing Wildebeest and a few bony Zebra won't feed us much longer.

A golden lioness materialised through the shimmering heat, moving closer on silent paws. Settling by him in the shade she said, "You seem lost in thought today Lencho, what worries you?"

"The same thing that has worried me for a good time now Alika, we have no water and no prospect of rain. No water means no prey, and we ourselves must drink soon. If we don't, I fear for our family, we have lost three already remember."

The pride numbered Lencho, his brother Chionesu, three lionesses, Alika, Dalila, and Tiaret and seven cubs, aged from two years to six months. The pride was small, but easier to move and defend. Lencho was all too aware that the time would come when he would be too old to fight off challenges to his leadership. The sound of wandering young males roaring at dawn and dusk made his blood run cold.

Nevertheless, he knew that this was the way of things and he must do his best.

Lencho and Alika observed the little ones at play. The eldest was Jubari, an adventurous male who had already found himself in a few scrapes. When Jubari was a very young cub, one of these scrapes had involved Lencho rescuing him from a hungry hyena.

His mother Dalila had warned him countless times to not wander off on his own, but Jubari rarely heeded advice. In a while he would feel the call to strike out on his own or with a brother, and then eventually take over his own pride. Lencho was concerned about his reckless nature however. *That boy is so much like I was at his age it's uncanny, he has guts and determination, but he's still too wet behind the ears to make it alone just at the moment.*

Watching the young male slapping down his brothers and sisters with an already powerful paw, Lencho decided that it was time to have *the talk* with him, the same one he'd had with his own father.

The sun eventually switched off her oven, the moon and stars filled the heavens, whilst the musicians of the insect world tuned up for their nightly concert. The pride had fed on a relatively plump Zebra, and were now grooming the remnants of supper from their blood stained faces. An atmosphere of contentment descended.

Jubari however, still full of energy bounded over to Lencho.

"Did you see me leading mother and the others to bring down that huge Zebra, father?" he yelled inches from Lencho's nose.

"Don't yell at me boy, and don't exaggerate. You hardly led the hunt, and let me tell you, that Zebra was far from huge," Lencho said cuffing Jubari gently.

Undeterred by this put down, Jubari continued "Yes, ok, but I did help didn't I? Mother says I'm a fierce hunter. What do you think?"

"I think you are too vain, reckless, and inexperienced to even think of yourself as hunter, fierce, or otherwise."

Jubari felt his temper flare. He *had* helped secure the kill tonight, and he was definitely the strongest next to his uncle and father. How dare Lencho talk to him like that? He began to walk away, but then without thinking, launched himself at his father, sinking sharp claws into his rump.

Lencho let out a furious roar, shook Jubari off, and clamped his teeth onto his windpipe, pinning him to the dirt. Realising his mistake, the youngster went limp and immediately submitted to the anger and might of his father.

"I'm sorry father," he managed to gasp as Lencho relaxed his grip slightly.

"So you should be!" Lencho roared into his face, his eyes blazing like the noon day sun. Unsheathing his claws, he landed a sharp blow across Jubari's head. Jubari screamed in pain as his right ear received a nasty cut.

"You ever try to challenge me again Jubari and I'll kill you, do you understand?" Lencho growled menacingly, still towering above his prone son.

"Yes father I understand... I'm sorry" he whimpered.

Lencho let him up, and then he lay back down again. The rest of the pride seemed to release a collective sigh as they realised the conflict was over. They went back to their grooming, and Jubari prepared to slink off to lick his wounds.

"Not so fast, boy. Come here and sit by me."

Jubari did as he was told, but fearing another attack sat as far from him as was polite.

"Come closer lad, I won't hurt you. I think you've learned your lesson for now," Lencho said, trying not to smile at his son's terrified expression.

The two lay side by side listening to the night. Lencho licked his paws and shook his great dark mane. Jubari copied, him shaking the first few tufts of hair sprouting from his neck.

"I see you have the beginnings of a mane, boy. You soon will feel the need to leave us behind and eventually lead your own family."

Jubari bristled with pride. At last his father had noticed he was growing from a cub into a lion. "Yes father. That's kind of what I was trying to say earlier..."

"You need to become less reckless, impulsive, and cool your temper before you leave," Lencho interrupted, "but most of all you need to know the way of things. There are many dangers in the world."

"Oh yes father I know, there are the large creatures like the Elephant who can be an enemy at certain times, particularly when they are protecting their young and the Rhino..."

"Stop Jubari. This is the time for me to speak and for you to be silent for once," warned Lencho sternly. Jubari nodded and settled quietly next to his father.

Lencho yawned, stretched and began.

"The creatures of which you noted, such as the Elephant and Rhino, are, as you say, sometimes our enemy, though the most dangerous creature in the world walks on only two hind legs."

"Two hind legs? I've never seen such a creature."

"No Jubari, that's why I'm telling you, and unless you have a genuine question, remain silent please. If you interrupt every sentence we'll still be talking tomorrow night."

The young lion sighed and nodded.

"As I was saying these hind leg walkers are our greatest threat. They carry a stick like thing in their paw which they point at creatures. Next is heard a thunderclap and the animal is dead. Sometimes there is blood, sometimes not. They do not even have to walk very close to their prey, they just point the stick."

Jubari was awestruck by this information and had to bite his tongue to keep from speaking.

Lencho continued: "They also have the power like the sun to create the great burning. It is legend that when the night is cold, these creatures can make the great burning to keep warm. This is mighty powerful, *they* are mighty powerful, and what's most frightening is that they are growing in number all the time." Lencho said this last sentence in a grave whisper. The whisper made Jubari shudder with fear and he crept nearer to his father.

"Are you frightened son?" asked Lencho.

"Yes father, I am. I do not like the sound of the hind leg walkers. They must be very large and have powerful jaws."

Lencho laughed mirthlessly. "They are small compared to us. If I walked on my back legs I'd be taller, and my jaws could snap off their head in one bite. No their power lies in their sticks, the great burning, and the creatures that carry them away like lightning across the veldt. Even if they lost their sticks and we gave chase, we could never catch them so fleet is the creature they ride on."

"How many legs does it have father?"

Lencho decided that this was a sensible question.

"That's the strange thing Jubari. It has no legs, eyes, or tail. It roars as it moves on moon shaped stones, churning up the dust in great clouds just like the giant herds of buffalo."

Father and son sat in silence for a few minutes. Jubari found the information both terrifying and exciting. Part of him wanted to see this hind leg walker more than anything. Another part of him would rather die than face such a danger.

"Have you ever seen this creature father?"

Lencho gave an involuntary shudder. "Yes I have. In the last few years I have spied him from afar many times. Once he came too close for comfort. I was out hunting and hiding in the tall grasses. My ears were suddenly pained by the crash of thunder and I saw a Zebra fall dead a little way off. I crept nearer and saw three hind leg walkers lift the body onto the fast creature and gallop away. They didn't see me thankfully."

"They might not kill our kind, just Zebra perhaps," Jubari ventured.

"If only that were true, boy. It is not, sadly, and I'll tell you how I know. Legend has it that one of our kind was captured by them. My father told me what I'm about to tell you now, and you must pass it on in turn to your sons."

Jubari made himself comfortable and concentrated hard.

Lencho shifted position, took a deep breath and began.

"Many years ago, there were no limits to our hunting grounds and the hind leg walkers had only a few dens here. Now their dens are increasing. There are many barriers of stone and sharp vine that sometimes kills an animal if they touch it. Our hunting land is smaller because of this, but we have tried to keep away from their dens. In the old times the dangers were not known, and a few of our kind wandered too near to the dens. They were seen, and the killing sticks took two of us and wounded another. This one was not too badly hurt but couldn't run away. They threw him in a small pen with sticks driven round him in the ground. He couldn't escape and the sticks were too hard to bite through."

Lencho stopped for a second and said, "Now Jubari, what I am about to tell you is upsetting but you must hear it. When you have heard it you will never forget it."

Jubari looked at his father and for once was at a loss for words. He didn't want to hear it but he knew he must.

"The two dead lions were skinned and their coats adorned the bodies of the hind leg walkers. One of the heads was

91

set on a sharp stick and shook at the pen, taunting the wounded one. They made strange sounds like hyenas, and drank liquid from shiny objects. They jabbed the wounded one with sharp sticks and cut his great mane about. They fetched blood along his back, and all the time howled and drank. They did not eat the flesh of the dead ones, and since that time they have been observed sometimes killing animals and leaving them to rot on the plain."

Jubari could stand it no longer and he leapt up crying,

"What are these creatures who would take the life of another for no reason, to kill but not eat? I will find these hind leg walkers and kill them all!"

"Silence Jubari! Have you learned nothing so far? You wouldn't stand a chance against them. Even if all of our kind joined together, we could not beat them."

Jubari hung his head and tried to shake the anger from his body. He felt sickened by what he had heard but knew it had to be learned. That was the way of things.

Lencho continued.

"The wounded one was kept for two days with no food or water and the sun burned down mercilessly. The captors would occasionally poke him and kick dust into his eyes. He thought he would soon die, but then on the third night the miracle happened.

A young female hind leg walker came to him, and they communicated without words. They looked deep into each others eyes and somehow they connected. She told him that not all hind leg walkers were the same, and that one day we would co-exist peacefully. She said that all things under the sky have a place on the earth. He told her that our kind kill to survive and only take what we can eat at one time. She said that she was sorry that some like her killed for fun, took the land which all creatures need, and built barriers. She said they were very greedy. She also said that we were the king of beasts and should be admired and respected. Unfortunately some of the hind leg walkers wanted to trap us, and put us in pens only a few paces long and wide to show the world how powerful they are. This was a thing she hated and despised and would fight against forever. Her father was one of the captors and she must fight against even him.

He said that she seemed logical and sensible, and much like our kind. She explained that one day the cruel hind leg walkers would be beaten, and the killing sticks would be replaced by flashers which just take our reflection, not our lives. The female then gave him meat and drink and begged him to warn our kind of the dangers of hers. She said that we must live as we have always done. We should set an example, so that one day they may learn from us. She then released him back to freedom. It took him many days to recover, but he got back his strength and was able to pass on the message."

Jubari sensed that Lencho's story was done and decided it was safe to ask a few questions.

"That is an incredible story father… but how do we know it is true?"

"Because, Jubari, the captured lion was your great-grandfather, and it is legend. Legend teaches us the way of things, and we live our lives by it."

"How will we know if the hind leg walkers we may see are good like the female, or bad like the ones who captured great grandfather?"

"We do not, Jubari, and that's why we must always avoid them when we can."

"I think it is fitting that all creatures under the sky have a place on the earth. It sounds like it should be the way of things."

"Yes Jubari, it should be the way of things. I think you have listened well tonight, but now I'm tired, the dawn is approaching and a new day waits."

In the following weeks as the rain clouds gathered, Jubari wandered further from the rest. He was missing for a few days at a time, until one day he did not return.

Dalila started long into the night wondering after her wayward son. Lencho knew he had left them and he felt proud. He lay down next to Dalila and nuzzled her ear.

"Don't worry, Dalila, he will be safe. We have taught him well," Lencho said.

The next day, the rains came.

Mandy K James

Mandy K James has had a passion for writing and storytelling since she was knee high to a grasshopper, but because she has to eat, she has a day job teaching. She writes every spare moment and although she finds teaching rewarding, she dreams of writing full-time. She has written two-and-a-half novels and numerous short stories. Four of her stories have been published online and one as an audio story, but this is her first success in print. She is very proud to be included in a book which promotes such a worthy cause.

~~~~~~~~

Lion Facts

Species: Lion (*Panthera leo*)

Location: Lions were once found throughout Africa and much of Asia, but today live in just scattered areas of Africa and the Gir Forest in India.

Habitat: Known as the 'king of the jungle', the lion in fact prefers open savannah country.

Behaviour: Big cats must defend their home-range or 'territory' from others living together in groups called 'prides'. The females hunt prey co-operatively, while the males defend the territory, their magnificent manes and roars intimidating rivals.

Conservation Status: The IUCN classes the Asiatic lion (population 350) as 'Endangered' and the African lion (population as few as 25,000) as 'Vulnerable'.

Threats: Zoos, circuses and other captive facilities, human population growth, habitat loss, and depletion of prey species. Another reason is trophy hunting; nearly 600 adult lions, mostly males, are legally killed every year.

Action: Born Free Foundation has sanctuaries in South Africa, Malawi and Ethiopia which have rescued lions from lives of misery in poor captive conditions. In addition, Born Free has a lion conservation project which aims to research and protect lions in their natural habitat.

To find out about adopting a lion with the Born Free Foundation visit www.bornfree.org.uk/give/adopt-an-animal/lion.

Jia Ting

By Diane Reeves

Clutching my tender muzzle in an attempt to quell the throbbing, I slumped onto my haunches and rolled backwards into the spiky shrubbery of a large rhododendron bush. I found myself staring through watery eyes at the variegated green of the canopy above, surrounded by a myriad of deep pink blooms, still with my paws attached to my smarting snout.

As I carefully extracted myself from the enveloping branches, I caught a flash of his creamy white *Yue*[2] as he scampered adeptly up the great trunk of a nearby camphor tree. I didn't need to see him to know where he was; the mocking tone of his clucks and chuckles bounced around the trees as if to goad me into chasing him, but I'd had enough.

It was always the same. We'd start off playing amiably enough, but he never knew when to stop, and I would invariably end up landing in an undignified heap, nursing some minor injury, whilst he cantered off laughing into the forest, oblivious to my predicament. It was as if a

---

[2] *Yue* The crescent moon shaped marking on the chest that gives the bear its unofficial name.

yaomo[3] took possession of him and the nipping, biting, tumbling and thwacking became overpowering, sending me scurrying into the undergrowth to find MaMa Moon.

Then, when his calls of "Mei Li, come and get me" failed, he would come lumbering back to find me full of remorse at the pain he'd unwittingly inflicted. Brothers!

On the whole, MaMa preferred not to become embroiled in our petty bickering and would always scold me for telling tales on Xiaobo. "Mei Li" she would say, "you are my dark beauty and Xiaobo is my little wrestler, I am doubly blessed. Be thankful and remember; *Jia Ting* – Family – is everything."

Even if he was a galloping meathead, I could never stay mad at him for long. As I scratched my rump against the gnarled trunk of a cypress, I could see the fern fronds and bamboo canes shivering a few metres in front of me. Three, two, one…

"Rrroooaaarrr," Xiaobo exploded from the bushes like a giant puffball fungus and barrelled towards me, his huge ears erect and a massive grin on his face.

I smothered a snigger as I side stepped at the last minute, causing him to hurtle into the tree and crush his snout. *Touché!* Make no mistake; I was the brains of the outfit.

"Where were you?" Xiaobo grunted as he fondled his grazed nose. "I found the best hiding place but you didn't come, and I waited and waited for hours upon hours, till I was weak with hunger and couldn't wait anymore."

"You exaggerate, Xiaobo, you're led by that huge belly of yours." I prodded his round tummy with my paw

---

[3] Yaomo Demon

and smiled. "Well, it must have been some hiding place, because I couldn't find you anywhere!"

"Yeah, might use that one again, right near the termite nest too." He smacked his long tongue around his slavering mouth. "Tasty!"

Oh yes, last in the queue for the brains, that's for sure!

Whilst he could never be accused of being a genius, his other talents more than made up for it, and we had all eaten well on many an occasion thanks to his remarkable fishing skills. In the cooler months, when fruit and nuts were less plentiful, MaMa would take us down the mountain to the Tanshui River to catch carp or freshwater catfish.

I was never fast enough to catch anything other than a chill and, even if I did get lucky, my clumsy paws were no match for the energetic wriggling fish. As often as not I'd forage around near the river banks looking for an easier meal, perhaps a dim-witted mikado pheasant or even a fresh carcass, whilst Xiaobo seemed to charm the fish from the water with such ease and dexterity it was embarrassing. The occasional thwack on my head heralded the arrival of a 'pity fish' which just added insult to injury, but I appreciated the gesture and never passed up a free meal.

This afternoon, MaMa padded watchfully between us, ears pricked, stopping periodically to survey the area and sniff the air, half-heartedly chewing on any fish which Xiaobo pitched her way. She was always tense near the river, on account of the proximity to the village. "Humans are no friends to us Moon Bears, you must keep your distance; our lives depend on it."

Of course, Xiaobo and I didn't understand. Now that we were older, MaMa allowed us a bit more freedom to roam and once, when she was snoozing in the shade away from the stifling heat of the afternoon sun, we had sneaked down to the river to observe the humans from the safety of the dense undergrowth. Watching the little ones jumping and splashing in the water, whooping and squealing, we remained puzzled at how their scrawny hairless bodies could be of any danger to us. We could crush them with one swipe, incapacitate them with one bite, what was so threatening about these puny stick-creatures?

Nonetheless, MaMa patrolled the banks alert to every noise, occasionally tut-tut-tutting in warning when she mistook the innocent rustling of a Taiwan partridge or the skittering of a grass lizard as something more sinister. Finally, sated from our fishy lunch, we heaved our engorged bellies further uphill and slumped deep under a rocky ledge obscured from the sun where the air was fresher.

Xiaobo was asleep within minutes, half propped up against the dark grey rock, all four paws wide open, shamelessly exposing his generous undercarriage and snoring gently. He was just about the same size as MaMa now, who slept less peacefully next to him crouched on her front with her head resting on one curled paw, her eyes twitching as she snuffled sporadically. *My family – Jia Ting.* I curled up between them and drifted happily into slumber.

The loud dripping of heavy rain woke me from what had obviously been a long sleep; the sun hung low, like a giant red jujube fruit in the darkening sky, and I could hear the distant whooshing of fast running water. A misty haze was rising from the tops of the cypress trees as the cool rain extinguished the heat in the branches, and the air smelled vaguely fruity but tasted of salt.

MaMa was standing near the edge of the ridge, her front legs strong and rigid, claws extended, glossy black fur swept back by the breeze to expose her white Yue, her snout raised to inhale the messages brought by the new wind.

"I'm hungry." Xiaobo half yawned and half growled beside me.

MaMa swung her head round towards us. "Tut-tut-tut." She paced up and down the ledge sniffing in different directions.

"What is it MaMa?" I padded slowly towards her drawing in the air around us, trying to catch the scent of anything unusual.

"Just rain, my beauty, wet and heavy but just rain," she replied, not looking at me.

To satisfy our growling stomachs we headed off into the forest to forage; there would be plenty of ripe mangoes washed down by the driving rain, sugar apples too and perhaps the last of the season's sweet lychees, my particular favourite. Within minutes our fur was drenched and heavy, and it was difficult to see through the curtains of rain. The forest floor was unable to soak up the huge deluge of water leaving deceptively deep mud pools everywhere, and making our progress slow.

Although the sun had all but disappeared, the thunderous clouds were threaded with thick peach-coloured veins; night was closing in and the downpour showed no sign of easing. Xiaobo splashed happily in the dirty brown puddles, swiping at the juniper bushes hoping to disturb a few juicy insects but having to make do with the bland berries that impaled themselves on his claws. MaMa and I looked for something more substantial.

When it became apparent that our quest was to be, quite literally fruitless, we hauled ourselves up into the sturdy branches of a huge sprawling alder and constructed a makeshift nest for the next few hours, hoping that the torrent and the escalating winds would ease. They didn't.

Before long, the mighty trunk of our provisional shelter was trembling against the relentless assault of the howling gales, and the rain continued to hammer at our backs. Tree boughs flailed around, assorted projectiles from branches to birds' nests, even a Chinese green tree viper were hurled from the skies to land in soggy thumps below.

Clinging to the tree, my claws dug into the bark to gain as much purchase as possible, I could hear the macaques in the high trees above us screaming in alarm. A small shrieking bundle plummeted past me, and the baby macaque hit the ground with a sickening thud.

"Tut-tut-tut, tut-tut-tut." My heart pounded in my chest, and my claws ached from holding on so tightly. "Tut-tut-tut." MaMa's mouth was open and her impressive teeth bared, drool glistening in the occasional lightening which lit up the inky sky. Her voice was smothered by the roaring in my ears which sounded like huge breakers crashing on the shore. Paradoxically, the scent of the sea was carried by the storm and, despite my fear, my belly groaned for the delicious flesh of a sea bass, or succulent Formosan Salamander.

Xiaobo's wide eyes and frozen posture told me his panic mirrored my own, but I could offer no words of comfort; a tutting, chattering distress call was all I was capable of. To see Xiaobo so petrified intensified my own fear and, shamefully, I turned my face away and evacuated my bowels.

By sunrise, the cyclone winds had subsided, leaving the debris of the storm all around. It was still raining but nowhere near as heavily. Xiaobo and I exchanged a meaningful glance which needed no explanation; I stretched my arm around the tree trunk to reach him and he licked my paw reverently.

"Climb down carefully, my brave ones." MaMa ventured first, ready to break our fall in case our legs gave way, and both Xiaobo and I clambered unsteadily but safely down the great alder to the squelching ground below. Nudging us gently, sniffing us and nibbling our ears, MaMa established that, other than our frayed nerves, Xiaobo and I were unscathed. She looked each of us in the eye and pressed her front paws together, claws touching end to end as if in prayer. "You are no longer children, my little heroes; you have learned of Mother Nature's fury and have survived her great wrath." There was an almost respectful tone to her voice. "Come, my little adults, we need to eat and build our strength."

Typhoons were nothing new to our island, but Xiaobo and I had never experienced anything quite as ferocious before. Nonetheless, we *had* learned that the aftermath brought with it an embarrassment of riches, an abundance of food on which we could feast until our stomach bulged to bursting.

Everywhere, the unfortunate victims of the previous nights tempest were strewn about, bird carcasses half floating in mud filled crevices or slumped humiliatingly amongst the shrubbery. "Mei Li, here, look!" Xiaobo called, holding up the bedraggled remains of the baby macaque.

"Mm... I think I prefer something more... mature," I replied, grasping at a tortoise snake dangling from a nearby branch. My stomach rolled and I drew in a deep steadying breath as I acknowledged a flash of compassion for the macaques. But I am a bear, a mighty courageous and almost adult Moon Bear, and we do not live by fruit

and nuts alone, so I tore the head from the brown pat-
terned snake between my paws and savoured the meaty
and welcome flesh as it hit the bottom of my needy belly.

Having gorged on all manner of small mammals, beetles,
grasshoppers, fruits, berries and nuts, our slippery journey
through the forest smorgasbord brought us to the edge of a
clearing. The rain continued unabated, rivulets of brown
slurry cascaded down the hillside and over the sides to
form tiny muddy waterfalls.

A small pangolin, shell-shocked from being un-
earthed from its burrow, scurried by, scrabbling to keep
his balance on the waterlogged earth. On any other
occasion Xiaobo would have pounced on it, flipped it up
on its back, tossed it around in his paws and enjoyed
'playing ball' with it before forcing it to uncurl and
sinking his great fangs into its soft underbelly. But, with
our stomachs uncomfortably full, he and I stood and
watched as it skittered into the greenery.

MaMa had wandered a short way ahead of us, a little
further towards the edge of the hillside, where her
considerable weight had caused her to sink into the sludge.

"Mei Li, Xiaobo! I'm stuck, help me!" She was gig-
gling, a little embarrassed I think, but there was an
anxious tone to her voice as she struggled to extract
herself from the mire, lifting one paw then another and
trying to jump free only to be sucked back in.

Not daring to look at Xiaobo who was, by now, rolling on his back and laughing so hard that tears were
forming in his eyes, I took a step towards MaMa, still not
quite sure how I was going to help.

"Tut-tut-tut, take care Mei Li, you're no use to me if
you get stuck too! Xiaobo, stop laughing and help your
sister!"

103

Xiaobo grumped as if trying to clear his throat and attempted to right himself, but immediately dissolved into another fit of the giggles and slumped to the ground with a splattering thump.

A mighty vibration underfoot stopped me from moving any further. I froze, reflex causing me to wrinkle my nose, curl back my lip and let out a faltering growl as I shot MaMa a wide-eyed glance. Suddenly, now looking quite sober, Xiaobo appeared at my shoulder. Dropping onto his distended belly with a sorrowful groan, he attempted to slide closer to MaMa, his powerful forearms outstretched to meet her similarly extended paws. He couldn't reach.

Writhing in the viscous mud, Xiaobo edged nearer inch by inch. The earth trembled again, somehow feeling much closer now. My eyes darted towards MaMa who lay collapsed on her front, her fatigued limbs struggling to keep up the effort of reaching for her son.

I was startled by a deafening noise behind me, an unnatural sucking slurping sound accompanied by more violent tremors. As I turned, I could see a torrent of glutinous brown liquid hurtling towards me from above, uprooting huge trees and washing down boulders as if they were acorns. My mouth opened as I spun my head back to face MaMa but it was so dry that I could form no words, no warning.

"Run! Mei Li, run now, as fast as you can. RUN, RUN!"

I ran.

I shall never forget the stricken look on her face as long as I live. Xiaobo didn't see it coming, but the last thing he saw was the white fear in his mother's eyes and he must have sensed his destiny. The tremendous speed of the mud flow took them quickly. They never stood a chance.

Although logic told me that there was no miracle great enough to have saved them, my empty heart ached with such intensity that I continued to search for them for many long weeks. The thought of living without my beloved MaMa and my annoying, heavy-handed, numb nut of a brother was, at times, too much to contemplate so I trekked and scoured the landscape to seek that which I knew in my spirit I would never find. The guilt of my lone survival weighed heavily upon me, the days seemed long and the nights; alone, cold and silent of snoring, were even longer.

MaMa had been so proud that we had survived Mother Nature's great fury when, in fact, the storm had been merely a temper tantrum, the mudslide just another brutal weapon in her cruel arsenal. In a final act of altruistic mother-love, I had been saved. How I wished that MaMa had been selfish that day.

My lonely quest took me to parts of the island I had never visited before. Without fear or care I would slosh through rice paddies, amble across open plains, wallow in secluded hot springs and wander the shoreline gorging on betel nuts, figs and the occasional scarlet land crab.

Occasionally under cover of darkness, I would skirt one of the villages to take an easy kill, maybe a domestic fowl or even a newborn piglet. Perhaps a more experienced bear would not have courted such peril, but I could think of nothing worse than the hellish life I had been forced to endure.

It was on one of my predawn raids to a remote hamlet on the east coast that my naivety was brought home to me. The air was still and humid, and the beginning sounds of the forest waking could be heard in the distance as I silently crept between the plum blossom and magnolia trees which surrounded the collection of ramshackle wooden shacks on stilts. I had learned the basic patterns of human behaviour and knew that they mostly slept during hours of darkness, rising only after dawn. All was quiet.

Watching, waiting, I peered out from the obscurity of the dark foliage of a rhododendron, scanning for any sign of movement, for light flickering inside the huts or human voices signalling their awakening. All remained still.

The black sky had faded to charcoal grey when I made my calculated move. As I stepped noiselessly across the litter strewn yard behind one sprawling assortment of shacks and lean-tos, I paused to sniff the air. Ignoring the overpoweringly sour and yeasty human stink, the unmistakable scent of fresh chicken wafted like a comet tail beneath my dripping nostrils. Heading left, I could see the corroded wire enclosure ahead; the gate looked flimsy and I knew it would take no time or effort for me to gain access. I took a further few steps, all the while my ears twitching and my keen eyes inspecting every shadowy crevice for danger.

A rooster crowed raucously and I shot up clear of the ground and let out a deep impulse snarl. I hit the ground running and, in three giant galloping leaps, I dived for refuge into a nearby conifer. The amber sun was crowning on the horizon and the light was growing quickly. If I was to eat I would need to make my move. The pounding of my heart was still pulsing in my ears but under it I could hear something else, like a growl or rumble. No, a sort of... groaning!

Beyond the rusty chicken pen was a larger compound containing what looked like a number of smaller confines. At first, they appeared empty but then I heard the pitiful groans again, wretched whimpers and weak growls from within the wires. I could just make out a dark and indistinguishable shape within each one and felt oddly comforted by the vaguely familiar musty, earthy smell emanating from the area. Although I was intrigued, curious as to what could be housed here, there was also a whiff of something bad, an underlying evil stench which I couldn't ignore.

It was almost light now and the rooster was crowing incessantly. I had missed my chance for breakfast and decided to return to the forest and make do with what fruit I could scavenge, a few crunchy stag beetles and juicy grasshoppers or maybe I'd get lucky and find a full honey-bee nest. Just as I turned to leave, a blinding light washed over the yard as if a white ball of fire had been tossed into the sky.

Another low growl escaped from deep within my hammering chest, I couldn't hold it in. For an instant I was sightless in the harsh glare but quickly regained my vision in time to see a human, an adult male, appear from a doorway. He shouted to someone inside and then bent down to pick up a heavy basket which chinked and rattled as he did so. Although I was crouching in the shadows, I felt certain that the man would see me, if he hadn't already heard me. Recognizing the *firing stick* leaning up against the wooden doorframe, I flinched as I watched the man grab it. I waited for the bang, but he merely slung it nonchalantly over his shoulder by its strap. He didn't seem to notice me; his eyes were focused on the compound.

From my dim hiding place, my eyes followed the human's towards the stack of metal behind the chicken coop and, in the briefly illuminated scene, before the light was extinguished; I saw what it meant to be truly damned.

By the time I'd stopped running my pads were bleeding, my joints ached, my fur was soaked with perspiration and my lungs were convulsed in agony. I can't tell you how far I ran that morning, but the coral sun was high in the bright blue sky by the time I tripped over a broad vine and collapsed into a shallow forest stream.

"Humans are no friends to us Moon Bears, you must keep your distance; our lives depend on it." These words rang around my head, suddenly finding resonance. *"Run! Mei Li, run now, as fast as you can. RUN, RUN!"* MaMa had rescued me once more.

I could not imagine why these bears, scarcely recognizable as my brothers and sisters but for the dull pale Yue on their chest, had been so cruelly incarcerated by the humans. The decaying stench of malevolence clung to my nostrils; the anguished pain in their feeble voices pierced my ears. As my shallow breathing gradually deepened, I closed my tired eyes but, despite my exhaustion, sleep would not come. Haunted by their dull milky eyes and gaunt faces, the vacant expressions and their stolen freedom, I sobbed like a cub until night closed in around me.

Awoken as usual by my insatiable, yawning belly, my first thought was for the desperate plight of those bears now many miles away. I licked my swollen, blood stained pads and immediately felt overwhelmed by shame; such an insignificant discomfort compared to what I had seen in that place.

Driven by hunger, I heaved myself up and padded a little further downstream to where I knew the salmon would be leaping. My fishing skills had not improved but, at this time of year, my chances of a good meal were much enhanced since the fish seemed to compete to be eaten, hurling themselves from the water with aberrant zeal.

All around me the forest was bursting with life; a small flock of Formosan blue magpies cackled gutturally to each other as they hopped around the woodland floor, as pretty brown and yellow shrikes twittered contentedly in the branches above. Mesmerized by the graceful interplay of a couple of Paris peacock butterflies, their iridescent green swallowtails fluttering on the breeze and flashing their vibrant aqua markings, I seemed to be viewing my bright and beautiful surroundings with new eyes.

It grieved me more than anything that I could not help those poor bears. The bleak scene was indelibly imprinted in my mind, although I had glimpsed it only briefly. From what I had seen, I feared that any help would be too late.

The only thing I knew for sure, here amongst the rich and plentiful flora and fauna of my island, was that I was free. A Moon Bear, young and healthy and free to roam, to bathe in hot springs and fail to catch fish, to climb trees and catch bugs, and to sleep anywhere I pleased. MaMa had saved me once and I had not appreciated the sacrifice, believing a life without her and Xiaobo was worse than death. I now knew different. Having been granted a second chance, I vowed not to waste it this time; freedom is a gift to be cherished and I would embrace my liberty and live as Mother Nature intended, as all Moon Bears should.

The odour hit me before I saw anything; a musky tang, not unpleasant, becoming more pungent as I approached the river-bend.

Stood up to his haunches in the rushing water, a large bear, perhaps a little older than I, was snatching up one salmon after another with embarrassing ease as each leapt from the stream. I watched for a few seconds as he took a careless bite from one fish and launched it onto the bank, immediately preoccupied with another as it erupted from the water. Glancing up briefly, he grunted innocuously towards me before returning to the job in hand. Taking this as permission, I approached the half-eaten fish on the bank, turned my back to him, a little humiliated if I'm honest, and tucked in.

Thwack! A wet slap on my rump and a thud on the ground next to me signalled the arrival of another fish. This time it was whole and still flapping. I turned to acknowledge the gesture and saw that he was grinning broadly.

The resemblance to Xiaobo was not lost on me but there was something else, something I could not define, a sort of... presence.

"I'm Jiang, it means River." He said. "I guess I was born to fish. Want another?"

Not waiting for a reply, he hurled another wriggling Salmon my way and it smacked me right between the eyes, making me stumble, much to his amusement. Jiang laughed a lot, I learned.

That set the pattern, two for him one for me, and we fished like that for most of the morning. After we'd both had our fill, we wandered together through the trees and collapsed against the trunk of a broad cypress. The heat of the midday sun was unavoidable but the dense canopy shielded us from the worst of its brilliant intensity, where we snoozed under a moving dappled blanket of sun spots.

I watched Jiang as he grunted gently in his slumber, his paws twitching and his legs shamelessly akimbo; he even slept with a smile on his face. It was only then that I appreciated that I had been alone for

110

too long. My chest contracted at the thought of my lost family, but a strange warmth spread from my softly churning belly to the tips of my extremities as I gazed at Jiang. Snuggling a little closer I drifted into an easy sleep; smiling.

Jiang and I spent the next few days together, meandering aimlessly through the hemlock and spruce of the mountain terrain or the palms and fruit trees of lower altitudes, depending on how the mood took us. Interested only in food and each other, we slept where we dropped, with our stomachs full and our hearts overflowing.

I learned that Jiang, an only cub, had parted from his mother in early spring when he was almost 2 years old, just before she gave birth to twins. It was our custom for adult males to live mainly solitary lives, and certainly not to stay around new cubs, but his mother had prepared him well.

He showed me some useful hunting skills, like how to stay downwind of prey and remain hidden until ready to pounce, retaining the element of surprise despite our bulk. Following a number of unsuccessful attempts shortly after MaMa and Xiaobo died, I had considered the Taiwanese serow to be a troublesome delicacy not worth the injuries which generally accompanied the hunt, but Jiang taught me how to avoid their sharp horns by ambushing it from the rear, and seizing its neck to immobilize it before it could do any damage to our soft spots. I never did learn how to fish though.

For my part, I showed him the best termite mounds and how to harvest honey without mistaking a wasp's nest for that of the more docile honey bee. After a hunt I would rake my claws through his tangled fur in the gentle warmth of the late evening and groom him free of fleas and ticks whilst the russet-red sun went down on the horizon. It was bliss.

All too soon, the day arrived for us to go our separate ways, as we both knew it would. There was no sense in prolonging the inevitable; it was always to be this way for it is *our* way, the way of wild bears. Nuzzling each other briefly, we groaned our mournful farewells and tramped away in opposite directions into the greenery. After a few heavy steps I stopped and turned, but the forest had swallowed him whole. He was gone.

On a similar day, many months later, when the sun was mild and the breeze gently whispered through the leaves, and a lone laughing thrush chortled to an unseen mate somewhere in the bush, I dozed peacefully against the granite wall of a secluded outcrop.

A rustling of dry leaves and a cracking of twigs nearby alerted me and my eyes snapped open, though I remained stock still. My ears rotated and located the source of the noise, the stifled clucks and chuckles escaped from the forest and I could see the bamboo canes and fern fronds tremble a few metres away from me. Three, two, one…

"Rrroooaaarrr." He exploded from the bushes like a giant geyser and rocketed towards me, his huge ears erect and a massive grin on his face. Bracing myself for impact, I scooped him up into my arms as he landed clumsily on my feet; my son.

"You're so mean, Xiaobo, I'm telling MaMa." Mei-Hui, his sister, came scampering unsteadily into view, her bright eyes rimmed red, her little paw clutching her snout. "MaMa, look what Xiaobo did to my…"

Scooping MeiHui up with my other arm, my heart squeezed as I looked from one to the other. "Now MeiHui, you are my wise and beautiful one, and Xiaobo is my little wrestler, I am doubly blessed, be thankful and remember; *Jia Ting* – Family – is everything."

Diane M Reeves
Diane is 45 and lives with her husband of 24 years, daughter aged 15 and Golden Retriever. They live near Ormskirk, Lancashire. Born and raised in Inner-City Liverpool, she is the youngest and only girl of three. A civil servant for twenty-five years she has come to writing only recently. This is her first short story, dedicated to Aimee, the one thing in life she says she managed to get right.

~~~~~~~~~

Moon Bear Facts

Species: Moon bear (*Ursus thibetanus*)

Location: Found throughout southern Asia, from Iran to Japan. Each bear will have a home territory of up to 13sq km (8 square miles).

Habitat: Moon bears prefer heavily forested areas in hills and mountains, and are found in tropical rainforests, temperate broadleaf and tropical monsoon forests.

Behaviour: Moon bears are 'crepuscular' – active at dawn and dusk. They often hibernate between November and March, and can migrate in warmer months to higher altitudes, descending to lowlands in colder months. Moon bears are usually solitary except during the breeding season, though little is known about their reproductive behaviour.

Conservation Status: There are around 25,000 moon bears. The IUCN Red List classes the moon bear as 'Vulnerable' meaning the species 'faces a high risk of extinction in the wild in the near future'.

Threats: Bear bile is an ingredient in Asian medicine and is extracted from living bears. There are more than 10,000 moon bears held in horrific conditions in China and Vietnam.

Action: Animals Asia has campaigned tirelessly to end the cruel practise of bear bile removal and rescued hundreds of bears in China. The Born Free Foundation is supporting their work to create a rescue centre in Hanoi, Vietnam, and to promote herbal and synthetic alternatives to bear bile. At the sanctuary, the rescued bears will receive expert veterinarian treatment and enjoy nutritious food, lush natural foliage and swimming in cool water.

To find out more about moon bears visit
www.bornfree.org.uk/animals/moon-bears.

Those That Are Left

By Sally Angell

A sound pierced the strange-smelling darkness with such an ear-shattering echo it seemed her skull would explode. At the open window, Lisa gulped in air that was heavy with the scents of creatures. The howl reached a pitch, hollow as her stomach; lonely as the vast plains outside.

During breakfast at the Lodging House next morning, Tris and Todd, Lisa's colleagues at the independent TV company, introduced themselves. They were that new breed of television directors, with short haircuts and sharp suits. The two young men shook her hand in turn.

"Ms Taylor."

"Lisa," she corrected.

As they headed out to the site, some of the general cameramen gave her a friendly wave. They were standing alongside in the jeep, next to their equipment.

As Lisa and the crew followed a winding track up to the shrubland, the excitement grew. Silhouetted beyond vegetation, a huge dark grey shape loomed against the deep Kenyan sky.

They'd reached the end of the track. There was a clearing ahead.

"*Loxodonta Africana*. African elephant. Female." Tris said, reading out a text on his mobile phone. Amazing he could get a signal.

"Cow." Lisa informed him of the correct term. She crept forward, keeping the creature in view. "Wow!" What a magnificent animal. Lisa had her own camera, with a super lens to capture the most detailed and powerful close-ups. It was a present from her father,

"Ready?" That was Tris. "Right. You go in now."

"But —"

There was no itinerary, then, no actual directing. Tris and Todd stood back, already red-tinged and glistening in the heat.

"The internet said it was the rainy season in Southern Kenya at this time of year," Tris gasped, gulping from his water bottle.

Someone dancing about to Lisa's right said he was Bob Health and Safety. "Don't go too near, ma'am. Not more than a hundred metres."

Lisa took up her position inside a group of shrubs. She lifted her mike in her left hand and gave the date and location. With her right hand holding her camera funnel, she shut one eye and focused on the scene through the viewfinder. She saw the animal close up for the first time, and nearly dropped the camera. The elephant's gait and shape were such a shock. The cow looked to be with calf.

Lisa stopped still. She was vaguely aware that Todd had seen her freeze.

"What's the matter? – Oh sorry, Ms Taylor – Lisa. We didn't know if we should tell you."

Lisa was stunned, but what else did she expect from the media world? There was no privacy. Everyone knew your business in this industry. They'd get every angle.

Probably why she'd got the job. Run, she wanted to warn the animal, run now before they get you. Before you know it, you will be watched and controlled for their purposes.

When Lisa was offered the chance to work on the documentary, *Elephants at Risk*, it was like stepping into a dream. Bereft of her mother very young, she'd found an affinity with animals. They were undemanding and nonjudgmental. Her father loved to tell the story of how, when he looked for Lisa as a little girl, he'd usually find her in the company of her non-human friends, and her explanation: "Well, animals are nicer than people."

Lisa pulled back her shoulders. She was here, doing work that she loved. *Get on with it.* She inhaled slowly and lifted her equipment again. She watched as the huge creature moved slowly. She must be very near her time.

"Stop!" An Afiikaner woman, in shorts and a broad hat, was striding towards her. Lisa looked round for an interpreter, but Tris shrugged. There wasn't one.

"Rose." The woman addressed Lisa, adding a surname with a lot of Bs and Os, and waving what looked like an identity card. "Call me Rose B. I'm from *Wildlife Protection.*" Oh good, she spoke English.

"Lisa Taylor."

"You cannot do this."

Lisa started to explain that they had permission to film here.

"No, no. Not this way. Tara, she has been separated from her kin," Rose said. "Others in the herd were supposed to be transported here, also."

Lisa caught her breath, mentally replaying that guttural night cry.

117

"What's the hold-up?" Tris was looking annoyed.

The authorities did want the elephants to be filmed to show how they thrived when living free from captivity, Rose explained to Lisa. But the forest which was their natural habitat was not accessible to the public. This area of grassland, here, was a place where wildlife could live freely, in similar conditions to those they were used to.

"We didn't mean to cause distress to any animals," Lisa apologized.

"It's the authorities. Trust them to get it wrong." Rose B was adamant that she could not let them continue. She made a call on her radio, speaking rapidly. The other elephants will be here by four o'clock this afternoon, she told the crew. Tris and Todd did not look pleased. Such a delay meant they would be behind schedule. They only had four days to get filming under wraps.

Lisa left them and accepted a lift into the nearby village. There, she sat in the tea-house in the shade, drinking some strange-tasting brew, and tried to clear her head. She should not have let the star of the show's condition to get to her. Women had to be professional, and not let their personal life affect their work. From a selfish point of view, while it wouldn't make up for the loss of her own baby, she had hoped that working with the animals she loved might ease the ache inside her. But it was the plight of the African elephants, themselves, that had driven her to undertake the project; to show their need for freedom to live unharmed and naturally in their native surroundings.

Lisa arrived back at the film location by mid-afternoon. Not a moment too soon. The rest of the herd had been released into the reservation, and something extraordinary was happening.

Lisa hurried into position and let the film roll, as Tara's extended family found their bearings, and the emotional reunion began. The huge creatures stomped and flailed, their massive ears high and flapping, discharge pouring down from their foreheads as they stampeded towards each other. Lisa had to smile. Not a lot of families she knew would be so ecstatic at a gathering of close relatives! It was amazing. Lisa zoomed into a close-up of her main subject. Tara's body was vibrating with energy.

"That's Teresia, the matriarch," said Rose, who was standing behind Lisa. Mother and daughter were rubbing against each other, making almost purring noises.

"See those two bulls over there?" Rose pointed. "One of them must be the father." Neither male was showing much interest and stayed at a distance from the celebrations.

"Not so different from humans!" Rose joked, and Lisa laughed with her.

After that, the project really began. The work was long and tiring, but to Lisa it was totally absorbing and satisfying. She felt privileged to observe her subjects as they found food in the grassland and shrubs, interacted with each other, particularly the females, slept standing up, and made trips to the watering holes. The other wildlife living in this area was also fascinating. She watched a buffalo lumber along behind a tree, and followed the movements of other smaller unfamiliar creatures and birds.

By the last full day, the main filming had been completed. Lisa did some packing in the morning. She would miss this lovely place, the sense of time being suspended, of space and land and possibilities.

A hooter blared outside the window. Someone was shouting. Lisa threw on jeans and top and grabbed her filming bag, her hair still wet from the shower. Bob was waving from his van. Lisa jumped in the back, and they roared up the track to the reservation. Bob ran to the security hut, his accommodation for the duration of the shoot.

"She's about to drop," he said, reappearing with a short man whom he introduced as the wildlife doctor for the region, who'd been called as soon as Tara showed signs of being ready to birth.

"Awesome!" Tris and Todd whistled and high-fived. This was a scoop. Considering the long gestation period for pregnancy in the elephant population, it was obvious from their faces they couldn't believe their luck.

Lisa took up her usual vantage point for capturing the most immediate images. This was not to be missed, so she prepared to wait. As long as it took. The crowd had drawn back from the edge of the grassland. Lisa felt a subtle change in the air. She pulled her fleece tighter round her. Bob had commented on the darker colour in the sky, the sharper feel of the air.

"Rains won't be long."

As quiet settled over the plains, Lisa sensed the frisson of expectancy, her heart racing. To catch this special moment would be the scene-stealer of the whole production. But at the same time she wondered: *Are we exploiting these creatures, especially now, exposing this most private of experiences?*

Tara was rearing up, her head thrashing from side to side. Lisa wished she could soothe the distressed creature.

A couple of handlers were restraining Tara, so that the wildlife doctor could get closer, and a tranquillizer dart calmed the writhing body.

Cramp shot up Lisa's left leg. Tris came towards her, carrying a mug of tea brewed in Bob's hut. Lisa eased herself into a position that was more comfortable, but still allowed a clear view of the clearing where Tara lay. She sipped the hot sweet liquid, remembering that particular pain, the uncertainty of an unknown experience. The giving of life.

Then it was happening. Lisa focused the camera, trembling with excitement and fear for the animal. The lurch of Tara's body, the twist and cry, the creature slithering to the ground.

Silence. Stillness.

Everything stopped. Lisa wanted to run forward but couldn't move. The world spun around her. She could hardly see or hear. Make it breathe! Make it live! She lived again that terrible sense of time suspended. Her own loss. Long minutes. Surely too long...

Then the wildlife doctor's voice, from far away, "It's a female."

And a cry.

Lisa was jolted back to catch the calf's first stirrings on camera. With each of the small creature's movements, its life affirmed, she felt stronger herself.

Tris and Todd, who had looked stunned and stupefied, exchanged glances.

"Name?" They queried simultaneously. Lisa gave a wry smile. They were so going to milk this. But then, anything that would catch the attention of, and raise awareness in, audiences back home of this endangered species was surely a good thing.

"Jumbo?" Tris suggested.

"Dumbo." Todd's offering.

"How about Nellie?" As everyone groaned, Bob burst into a rendition of the well-known lyric – "Nellie the elephant packed her trunk and said goodbye to the circus…"

"Tika!" Lisa cried. She didn't know where the name had come from, but it seemed right for the new, young, shiny life that Tara was clasping in her curled trunk.

Everyone nodded.

"Tika it is, then," Tris said.

Lisa forgot about her packing, and concentrated on getting a record of those first few hours, observing the growing bond between mother and calf.

And as she experienced their closeness, and the calf's increasing strength and hold on life, Lisa thought about her baby, but something shifted. Somehow she started to heal.

*   *   *

"I can't work this machine." Mr Taylor was fiddling with the video recorder.

Lisa shook her head and focussed on the television screen, her whole body tense. "It's OK dad. A box set will be out next month."

The presenter was introducing the documentary. Lisa stood up and paced about. She never like watching herself on screen; was always self-critical. As the titles, and faces of the crew, came up, they looked strange, as if the filming had been a long time ago.

There it was – the habitat. And there she was, each day showing the autonomous practices and sensibilities of Tara and the rest of the herd.

And then that long lens moment. Lisa hadn't breathed in case her hand moved, as the new life spontaneously suspended and then was expelled to the ground. And there it was, on screen.

"Superb shot!" A rush of pride warmed Lisa. Her father didn't part with praise easily.

The closing credits rolled. It was over. The clearing was empty.

The rest of the story, not for public consumption, unravelled in Lisa's memory, to its conclusion.

That last night in Kenya, wound up emotionally and overtired, Lisa had found it impossible to sleep. She could not shake off the sense of threat. It might be that she was reliving her own loss and couldn't believe the calf had been delivered safe and well. But she couldn't rest. She pulled her fleece round her shoulders and slipped out of the front door of the Lodging House. It was eerie picking her way up the now familiar track, in darkness punctuated with just a comma of moon.

A couple of warthogs scurried across her path and disappeared. As she neared the shrubland, the usual dungy smell creeping into her nostrils, her heart constricted. What was going on?

Lisa had a vague idea that Tris and Todd had gone off on some late night drinking party. She felt in her pocket, and went cold. Her mobile wasn't there.

A huge vehicle was parked on the edge of the grassland, Lisa could only make out the shape of it. Figures, in orange outfits, were moving about in the dark – what a stupid colour to choose for a clandestine operation, Lisa remembered thinking later. As her eyes adjusted and made the darkness seem less dense, she could also make out a large shape nearby. Tara!

As the human figures moved swiftly, a chunk of moonlight showed something being pushed towards the truck. Tara seemed to be collapsed on the ground. As the cage was lowered down around Tika's frantic little form, Tara's head lifted.

Lisa's mouth mimicked the cry that shook the animal's great body.

"NO-O-O-O-Oh!"

The separation of mother and child was more than Lisa could bear. She almost lost consciousness.

Shots rang out.

The locals denied any involvement in the incident.

"It wasn't us, Miss Taylor."

"Who was it then? The press out to get a story, to pre-empt the release of the programme to get in first?"

She should have known. *You can't trust people. They let you down.*

It was Rose B who solved the mystery, when she arrived early next morning, as the crew were preparing to depart.

"The kidnappers belong to an underground organization that the government hasn't been able to infiltrate, that kills adult elephants for ivory, and steals calves. Those particular culprits are under lock and key I'm glad to say. Thanks –" Rose stretched out a hand "– to this young lady."

Lisa found herself enveloped in a warm hug. The flare gun was in the jeep, kept nearby for supplies of bottled water and other supplies, and on autopilot, she'd just grabbed it up and fired. In the blackness, the men didn't realize it wasn't a real firearm, and prepared to take off without their quarry. The local police were alerted and caught them on the boundary of the reservation. Tara and the calf had not suffered any real injury.

"Result!" Rose B had beamed, and waved as the project team drove off down the track, until they could no longer see her stalwart figure through the dust.

Lisa smiled at the memory as she switched the television off.

Worlds away, over oceans and continents, the wind blows across plains as the elephant herd makes its majestic way back from the watering hole. The calf, Tika, already independent and capricious, prances off on her own to explore.

Tara lifts her head, and looks about her in the space and stillness. The quiet is punctuated by the sounds that she understands, that throb through her being. She listens to the rhythms of the language, of the place, and the life, that is hers.

Sally Angell

Sally Angell writes fiction and poetry for children and adults and she's had a number of short stories published by Bridge House. In her writing she likes to explore the truth and reality of feelings, the originality of language and the possibilities of words. She is delighted to be included in *Gentle Footprints* because she believes it is the right of all creatures to live in as free and as natural an environment as possible.

www.sallyangell.firecast.co.uk

~~~~~~~~~

Elephant Facts

Species: African savannah elephant (*Loxodonta africana*)

Location: African elephants are found in 37 countries south of the Sahara, but are extinct in much of their former range.

Habitat: African elephants live in a variety of habitats including open plains, grasslands and woodlands, needing a large home range to find enough food and water.

Behaviour: African elephants are intelligent, sensitive creatures. They live in close-knit families, led by a dominant female. Up to 4m (13ft) high and 6 tonnes, these massive vegetarians need 200kg (440lb) of grass and 225l (50 gallons) of water each day. African elephants may live for 70 years.

Conservation status: Classed as 'Vulnerable'. Just 400,000 remain, and elephants face a high risk of extinction in the wild.

Threats: Habitats are destroyed for human developments, and thousands are slaughtered for their ivory tusks. Elephants are also exploited in zoos and circuses.

Action: Born Free Foundation funds anti-poaching units, fights the ivory trade, cares for rescued baby orphans, and tackles captive exploitation.

To find out how you can get involved with elephant conservation visit www.bornfree.org.uk/give/adopt-an-animal/african-elephant.

At the time this book went to print, one hundred elephants were still killed every day for ivory. So when you go abroad, please don't support this trade. Visit www.bloodyivory.org and act now.

I Am Wolf

By Debz Hobbs-Wyatt

"I Am Wolf."
Nose pressed to earth
Along edges of night
A million scents
Yet only one
The smell of human

"Ja Volk." *I Am Wolf.*

These are the words scribbled in the pages of a journal. These are the words pressed into the cold air of a wood cabin. And these are words that were spoken by the Russian the first time she saw her. Amy Greene was there to witness it. She was there to witness a little girl in jeans and a striped sweater that didn't quite fit. She was there to witness a little girl who folded herself into the corner of a room with her hands and knees pressed to the floor. And she was there to witness a little girl who raised her head and howled her sorrow, caught in the glare of a million camera flashes.

"Ja Volk," she said. They were the only Russian words she knew.

From a window a pool of silver moonlight bleeds out across a bed where a rucksack lays open, spilling its residues: a coca cola can, an empty box of panty liners and a copy of *Little Women*. On the bed is a child's toy, a stuffed animal. Amy stands in the doorway, her journal clutched to her breast. She watches shadows move in the blackness behind the glass.

"Ja Volk," she says. As she speaks a single tear rolls along her cheek. And as she turns away she whispers a name. It's the one they gave the Russian, "Volchitsa." It means *Female Wolf.* And somewhere in the Alaskan wilds something calls back.

Pulling out a chair, wood scraping wood, Amy sits down and runs her fingers along the edges of the journal, stuffed with newspaper clippings. She turns the pages slowly, carefully, pressing her finger along the crease. Then she reads the first headline.

Russian Wild Child raised By Wolves

A seven year old girl, unnamed, was res-cued last night just outside the rural village of Kostino, 250 km north of Moscow. She is believed to have been living with Grey Wolves.

It was the headline Amy Greene had read that day as she sipped her Starbucks mocha. It was the headline splashed across every major newspaper that spring morning, and it was the headline that buzzed around the office at the *New York Sun*. What it meant to Amy was people had someone else's life to dissect. That was until her boss, Jonathan Pitt, had appeared in the doorway. Amy had turned away, looked at her computer screen, read more headlines

"Family denies that Russian Wild Child is Eba Volvotino missing child abandoned by alcoholic father in 2002. The search continues."

Amy had felt Jonathan's stare stretch out across the office, thought about him in her apartment, the smell of him on her things. Then she'd squeezed the thought between her fingers until it was gone.

"Wolf Child will be moved to a Moscow centre for a program of re-humanisation. Director, Vladimir Baikov, claims, "It will take some time to adjust. The child has to be socialised. But we are optimistic she will make a full recovery."

Office gossip hissed like urban snakes. Amy glanced at the group gathered at the photocopier, Claire at the centre of it all, Claire who she thought she could trust. Then she looked back at her screen.

"Moscow psychiatrist and linguist, Boris Glebov, formerly from the Tverskaya region, unveils plan to teach the Russian girl to speak. He claims the first word they'll teach her will be 'Volk.' It means 'Wolf.'

The door to Jonathan's office was shut but Amy could still hear the whispers, could still feel Jonathan watching, his stare perched on the edge of the blinds.

On the table, clipped to the moonlight bleached pages of Amy's journal, is a photograph. It's the Russian, she's on all-fours, her head tilted back, her nose lifted skyward. There's another underneath it, it shows her face, close-up. In the text are a million adjectives: de-socialised, dissociated, uncivilized, uncultured, abandoned, speechlessness, but the one that sticks is 'disconnected'. It's the word that's printed underneath the first photograph. And it's the one she remembers.

She remembers holding the picture, sitting there that day watching the office snakes and she remembers how she knew then what she had to do.

"I want to cover the story," she'd said. "I could use a trip to Moscow. Besides you owe me."

She remembers Jonathan's face, his red tagged cheeks, the photograph of his wife looking at her from the desk, where piles of papers were stacked in neat rows.

"I thought we weren't gonna talk about it," he said.

"Who's talking about it?"

She watched him root around in a drawer, thinking time. Men always needed thinking time.

"You know I'm the best person for it."

He'd snapped the drawer shut and looked right at her, "Okay. The press conference is Friday. You'll need a photographer." Then he added, "I'm sending Mark Zander."

She'd stared at Jonathan, watched him shuffle papers without looking up.

"You're sending Mark?"

He was the guy she'd wasted three months of her life on. He was the guy who asked too many questions. He was the guy who said he loved her when he hardly knew her.

"You're sending my fucking ex?" she'd said.

"You want the gig or not?"

At the door he'd said something else. "You're like her, you're like that girl."

"What's that supposed to mean?" she'd said.

"You figure it out."

The flicker from a gas lamp casts shadows across wooden walls as Amy thumbs through the pages of her journal. Next to her, a laptop sleeps, snapped shut. It's another vestige of who she was and not who she is. Pink plastic edges the moment. She reads on, black coffee in a mug grows cold.

Outside the wind pushes its breath to glass and rattles at the door. Alaskan pines creak and somewhere an owl calls. It's a sound she knows, a sound she's learned to tell time by. She belongs to the night now. But not just any night, she belongs to this night.

She closes her eyes, imagines the blackness before it comes, before it presses against her, before she folds herself into it. She rests her head against the pages of her open journal. She thinks about Russia, about Mark Zander. She half sleeps, half listens, but mostly she waits.

Mark acted like he'd bagged himself the best gig in town, like the trip to Moscow was winning the state lottery. He hadn't changed, he still looked at her with puppy dog eyes, same barrage of questions. Like why she moved to New York and why she twisted her hair round her finger like that. And why she wouldn't look for her mom.

She'd dumped him because he asked too many questions. It had started out okay. It always starts out okay. He seemed different but then he wanted her to meet his parents.

"A trip to Vermont," he'd said. "They're gonna love you."

"To play happy families?"

She still remembers the way he looked at her. "What is it with you?" he said. "All we want is to know you."

"No," she said. "You don't."

That's when she told him her dad dropped dead of a heart attack when she was four and her mom was an alcoholic she hadn't seen in ten years.

He'd looked at her like she was kidding. No one kids about stuff like that.

Then she told him she was screwing the boss. At the time it wasn't true.

"Sex is sex," her mom used to say. "But as for love, love messes with your head. No one wants damaged goods."

On the way to the airport Amy had picked up a book, *The Wild Wolves of Russia* that she read while Mark pretended to sleep. There was a photograph, a caption underneath it, '*Canis Lupus*, largest wild canid'. She remembers staring into its eyes and she remembers wanting to cry but not knowing why.

'Wolves live in packs of seven to nine animals. They develop strong social bonds many of which last a lifetime.' After she'd read it she'd teased her journal from the seat back, started to scribble. She wrote '*Canis Lupus* has an erratic relationship with human beings.'

Amy reads it now, the same words scribbled on the page in front of her. She stands up, carries the mug of coffee to the sink. She watches the black liquid as it drains away. Then she pours another. As she crosses the room, holding the mug with both hands, she thinks she sees them, eyes like Christmas lights watching through the trees. Then she thinks she doesn't.

The first full day in Moscow was the day of the unveiling, Amy's first encounter with Volchitsa. A ton of photographers and journalists, a little girl in a corner. The saddest cry she ever heard.

She thinks about it now. She remembers searching for the right adjective, the one with punch, the one that would make people understand. But she always came back to the same one. Pitiful.

She says it now. She says it out loud to the wooden walls. She draws it out, "Pit-i-ful." She says it as she looks at the clipping with the photograph Mark took that day, Volchitsa with her head raised, howling her pain. She remembers how Mark's eyes misted as he clicked away with his fancy digital camera. How they never spoke about it on the way back to the hotel.

That night Amy told Mark she was going out.

"Don't wait up," she'd said.

She got wasted. Some guy with a moustache and blue eyes had taught her Russian drinking games, slamming vodka shots and telling his friends he was with the "Pritty American, yes?" She told him she was there to cover the story on the wolf girl, even got out her tape recorder.

"So what do the locals think?" she'd said.

"Is fraud," he'd said. "Many stories like this. They make money."

"Cry wolf?" she'd said. He just stared at her, no understanding in his eyes. Then she left.

So there she was in a hotel room in a strange city where strange voices lifted from strange streets but everything was the same. Except for that memory of a little girl crouched in the corner of a room. Amy had pressed play on her tape recorder, "Is fraud." Rewind. "Is fraud." Rewind. Rewind. Rewind. The sound of Volchitsa's howl. Pit-i-ful.

That night she'd fallen asleep with the machine pressed to her cheek. She'd floated away on a vodka tide, pushed her tears into hotel linen.

Next day she woke up with red marks on her cheek, laptop grinning pink across the hotel room and four voice messages from Mark.

"Just making sure you made it back okay. It's 12.30."

"Still making sure. It's 1 am."

133

"Okay, so you're either dead in a ditch or you're having way too much fun. It's 2.15."

And the last one, "Don't forget, we meet the Russian's doctor at midday."

Health Fears For Russian Wolf Girl

After her release from hospital last week, Russian Wolf Girl, known to the world as 'Volchitsa,' has been moved to a centre for rehabilitation. Her doctor, Ivan Gordieva, said yesterday, "She refuses to eat, but she has to learn to trust us." Child Psychologist, specialist in abandonment, Viktor Kopul said, "Who knows what horrors she's seen. Children like her have to learn about love. It takes a long time."

They'd spent three days in Moscow speaking with doctors, linguists, speech therapists, child psychologists and sociologists. They all smiled for the cameras. They all said the same thing. "Kids like her never turn out normal."

"I thought she was learning Russian," Amy had asked one of the translators.

"She know two words," he'd said.

She'd wanted to ask him, "You don't speak wolf then?"

On page six of her journal are the notes Amy made from *Bernstein: A Short History of Wolves*. She'd come across it an American bookshop in Moscow.

'The wolf uses a range of sounds to communicate,' she reads, blowing waves across the top of her coffee. 'But many believe the true spirit of the wolf is in its howl. Wolves howl longest when separated from their pack.'

She'd tried to imagine Volchitsa's forest, wolves with their heads lifted across a Russian moon. She'd imagined Volchitsa waiting for them to call back. It's what she used to think about when she couldn't sleep.

Amy agreed to have dinner with Mark on their last night in Moscow. She'd been a jerk. He deserved better. But there'd been another salvo of questions.

"Do you ever think about your dad?" he'd said.

"I've only got one memory of him."

And the whole time he'd watched her, Okroshka dripping from the end of his spoon. He said it was like Gazpacho but she opted for a hamburger.

"You ever thought about looking for your mom?" he'd said.

"You ever thought about shutting up with the questions?"

"People *do* care," he'd said. "But you never give them a chance." As he spoke he raked his spoon through his Okroshka. And then he said, "What happened with Jonathan?"

"He said he wanted to leave his wife. I told him to fuck off."

"You're scared."

"What do want, Mark? You want me to fuck you for old time's sake?"

"What are you so afraid of, Amy?"

He'd leaned across the table, his fingers reaching for hers. She hesitated, her hands pressed against wood. Then she pulled away.

"I'm afraid of deadlines," she said. "I need to email the story to Jonathan."

As she stood up to leave he looked right at her, "We're not all the same, Amy," he said. "Everyone deserves to be loved."

She'd thought about what he said as she worked on her report supping vodka from a bottle. She thought about her mom and she thought about Jonathan, about his wife. Mark's words in her head, "We're not all the same." Then she pushed it away, looked back at her screen. She added a quote from one of the Russian's care workers at the 'Centre,' Lolita Daletsky, "We plan to introduce Volchitsa to other children. She needs her own kind."

Then Amy had typed, "They should give her back to the wolves, then."

She deleted it.

Amy turns the pages of her journal and reads what she copied from *Bernstein*. 'Wolves form strong parental bonds.' Then she stares at a photograph of a mother playing with its wolf cub and the caption, 'Adults play for hours with their cubs. Most learning is facilitated by imitation'.

On the bedside table is a photograph of her mom and dad. It's the only one she has of the two of them together, taken in the backyard at the house in Albany. She remembers how she used to hold it in her hands, stare at it until their faces dissolved.

"I'm in the lobby," Mark said to her. "The taxi's here."

Amy had woken up with piles of papers spread out on the floor, a list of titles, one called, 'The Biology of Wolves' ringed in red ink.

"I'm not leaving," she'd said.

"You want me to change the flights?"

"You'll miss the taxi," she'd said.

"What do I tell Jonathan?"

"Whatever the hell you want."

As she hung up she heard him say, "You gotta take care of yourself, Amy."

Then she'd opened the laptop and looked into the Russian's eyes. "Dis-con-nect-ed," she said.

Amy looks up from her reading, presses her feet deeper into faux fur slippers, feels the warmth against cold toes, she wonders if it's time yet. She unpacks the bag of groceries that have been sat on the table since this morning, slowly placing things in the cupboard. The man from the village drops by once a week. He has a key. Amy hardly ever sees him. He was there the day she arrived. He'd looked at her, at the pile of books on the table, a map, a chart of animals tracks. Then he'd looked at her things, old hiking boots, pink waterproof coat, binoculars.

"Research," she'd said.

"You'll need the right clothes," he'd said. "It gets cold even in the summer."

And she'd thought about being a little girl in a place where demons hid in kitchen cupboards inside glass bottles.

"Mustn't forget your coat, Amy," her mom said. Except she never did. She just wanted her to. It wasn't the same.

Amy was the kid who never ate breakfast. The kid who stuffed dirty shorts into a gym bag, because she hadn't figured out how to use the washer. And Amy was the kid who went out without a coat.

The man had told her. "You want anything special, you call me or you leave me a note, okay?"

"Sure," she'd said.

"It gets lonely up here," he'd said.

After four weeks in Moscow Amy's credit cards were maxed out, her inbox was jammed with emails from Jonathan and her cell phone was cut off.

"You think this is funny?" Jonathan had said.

"Get your ass home."

"I thought you hated animals,"

"Stop sending me this stuff, people have forgotten about the Russian,"

"She has a name," Amy wrote back.

"I thought you flunked at science, what's with all the biology shit?"

"Fuck you," she wrote back.

There was one from Mark Zander. All it said was "When you coming home?"

Wolf Girl Hospitalised With Common Cold

Volchitsa the girl allegedly raised by grey wolves, was rushed to a Moscow hospital yesterday. Already malnourished, the wolf girl is said to be suffering from a common cold. A spokesman at the hospital claims, "She has no immunity to even the most common human viruses." Since her removal to a centre for rehabilitation four weeks ago, Volchitsa's health is said to have steadily declined.

It would have been easy to get lost in Russia. Would have been easy to sleep with the first guy who called her his 'Pritty American' for free vodka and rent. Would have been too easy.

It was amazing how fast everything could unravel.

Amy saw Volchitsa two more times after Mark left. She'd stood at the back of a small pack of reporters all holding up tape recorders and pointing cameras. It had made her think about Mark, about what he was up to.

Volchitsa had looked up from a corner with bared teeth. "Wolf Caught In Headlights." It was a headline she'd never write.

"Will she ever stand?" someone had asked in a British accent. "Will she always walk like that?"

"Why doesn't she eat?"

"Does she really think she's a wolf?"

"Get her a dog."

And Amy had a thought, a moment of transient imaginings of a little girl standing upright running with a poodle at her heels.

"Will she ever behave like a human?"

Amy had turned around to see who'd spoken: an American, all wide eyes and white teeth.

"It is our hope," the doctor said, "she will learn to be human. Yes."

"But what if she doesn't want to be human?" Amy had said.

Amy sits back down at the table. Next to her journal is a copy of *Learning to be Wolf* by Adams, Hobbs and James. She picks it up, lifts it to her nose, sniffs. She lets it fall open in her hands and she reads the passage she's underlined.

'Socialisation begins at birth. Understanding this sophisticated and highly complex social system is the key to understanding the wolf.' Her eyes dart sideways to the photographs in the journal. One is Volchitsa, next to it is one of a female wolf, ears pressed back. Underneath it says, 'Expression of Fear.' She looks from one to the other, stares at the eyes. They look the same.

'Each wolf assumes a particular role within the pack. This role may change as the wolf matures and develops into either a strong, decisive individual or a more submissive follower.'

"Who were you, Volchitsa?" she says. "Who *could* you have been?"

Wolf Girl Continues To Worry Doctors

After recovering from a cold that had her hospitalised last month, the Wolf Child, Volchitsa from Tverskaya, continues to worry her doctors and carers. Dr. Ivan Gordieva said yesterday, "The only thing she's responded to since she came here is wolf song played into her room. She spends most of the day pacing." Despite efforts to feed Volchitsa by a tube she is still losing weight. "We have seen her bite the tube out with her teeth," one of her carers claims. "We're trying to avoid sedation," her doctor said this morning. "But we may have no choice."

The last time Amy saw Volchitsa she had been moved back to the 'Centre,' the place government officials had gone to great lengths to point out *wasn't* an 'orphanage.' She called first, cleared it with someone who spoke broken English, almost imagined him saying, "You Pritty American, yes?"

She'd flashed her ID and a man in grey who'd looked her up and down, said something she didn't understand to his co-worker and gave her a visitor's badge. Next to them, on a table, was a Russian newspaper, the face of the American pop legend looking back at her. He was the reason no one else was there.

Pop Icon dead at forty-five: shocked world in mourning.

Volchitsa was folded into a foetal position on a bed with a tube taped to her nose. The bed was pushed up against a white wall, curtains pulled halfway across a window made of frosted glass. The carer, a young woman in a uniform, stood in the doorway.

"Sedated?" Amy said and the carer just looked at her. "She doesn't move?"

"No close," she said. "You stay."

"What's that?" Amy had said, pointing towards Volchitsa.

The side of her face was pressed to the pillow, and in her arms she was clutching onto something. It was grey.

"Feed tube," the carer said.

"No that," she said, taking a step closer. The room smelled of soap and shit.

"No close," the carer had said.

"I want to see," Amy said, taking another step.

That's when Volchitsa opened her eyes and that was the moment the world fell away.

It was a connection. A moment when time might have stopped. Amy was close enough to see her hair. It was cut short. Her face was clean. She was staring back at Amy, she was seeing her. Amy smiled, but nothing registered. She watched her fingers dig into the grey thing, pulling it towards herself with soft jerking movements. That's when Amy realised it was a stuffed animal. It looked like a dog.

"You stand at door," the carer said.

But Amy didn't move.

She stared at Volchitsa, at the way she blinked slowly, no expression, but tears ran along the edges of her thin face. She was staring back at Amy. She kept on staring back. Then she closed her eyes and pressed her cheek into the soft fur of the stuffed dog.

That's when Amy cried.

She hooked her bag over her shoulder, where it had fallen across her arm, and turned to look at the carer. Then she walked back towards the door. She wanted to turn around, to see Volchitsa one last time, to see her holding onto the stuffed animal, seeking comfort in the artificiality of it all. Jesus she wanted to take a photo and show the world. But what she did was walk away and what she heard was the pit-i-ful whimper of a wolf cub. It was the sound that followed her into the corridor where her footsteps clanked against shiny floors, faster, louder, hands pressed to ears until she had smothered it. But it was there. It would always be there.

Amy didn't need to speak wolf to know what Volchitsa was saying:

She didn't look back. Amy didn't look at the guys who stepped aside as she marched by, dropping her visitor badge in the face of the pop legend on a crinkled newspaper. She didn't look back when she got to the door, pushing it with both hands, almost falling into fresh air. And she didn't look back when the taxi pulled away.

"She needs to go home," she'd said. "She needs to go back."

The driver had looked at her through a glass shield. "Please repeat slow," he said. "I not understand."

She'd looked away.

If she could have she would have taken her, right then she would have bundled Volchitsa into her arms and taken her with her. She would have set her free along the

142

edge of the forest, and she would have watched her walk away, on her hands and knees, back to who she was.

Amy was still crying when the taxi pulled up at the hotel and when she threw the last of her things into a pink bag, and dumped empty vodka bottles in the wastebasket. She was crying when she called Jonathan at home. In New York it was the middle of the night.

"Who the hell is this?" his wife said.

"Put Jonathan on."

"What?" he said.

"I need your credit card details," she said. "I need to get home."

"Call the embassy."

"Please," she said. "Please, Jonathan, help me."

She remembers the silence, the way she pressed the phone to her face listening to him breathe. She remembers closing her eyes, pushing the words out, "I was scared," she told him. "I'm sorry."

"Okay," he said.

On the flight home Amy had dreamed about her dad. It was the memory of him standing outside the tent he'd built her in the backyard at the house in Albany.

"One day we'll go on safari," he'd said. "See all sorts of animals." And then he'd scooped her in his arms and said, "If you could be an animal, Amy, what would it be?"

So Amy traded one set of city lights for another. Bag over her shoulder, one in her hand and a stack of mail under her arm, she'd turned the key and stepped back into her old life.

A light blinked red on an answer machine. A message from Jonathan. "Call me when you get this." And a

PS: "My wife left me." She held her finger to the button, skipped through a ton of messages, mostly the credit card company. There was one from Claire. "What's going on? Call me when you get back." And the last one was Mark. "Hey, just checking you got back okay."

She pressed delete and went to Sam's for coffee.

Over the next few weeks Sam's Deli was the place Amy went to disappear. She'd pick at pretzels and white chocolate muffins, listen to songs go round on a loop. She'd make endless notes in her journal. She'd sleep late, ignore the phone, send emails to Jonathan in the hope he'd run something about the Grey Wolf. He never did.

Mark called several times, left messages, offered to take her out for pizza but she never called back. She thought about asking him to the State Zoo. There were wolves there. She wanted to see them but it was the haunting image of a little girl, clutching onto a stuffed animal that stopped her. If she looked into their faces she was afraid she would see the same thing.

She'd read something in a brochure from the New York Society Against Captive Animals. She wrote it down. 'Displacement behaviour as a measure of anxiety.'

She looks at it now, scribbled near the back of her journal and she thinks again about the last time she saw Volchitsa. She closes her eyes.

Life went on, going to Sam's, being invisible, breathing in and out until finally everything fell apart, the way Amy always knew it would. There was a message from Jonathan on the answer machine. He'd called before, usually late at night, usually saying, "can I come over," usually deleted. Except for the one last week when he said, "My wife's taken me back." Then a moment of silence and, "Amy, I'm sorry too. You deserve better."

But this time all Jonathan said was, "I guess you heard about the Russian."

Amy reads the headline now.

Russian Wolf Girl Dies In Captivity

It says everything.

They called it a virus. They mentioned malnutrition. Didn't matter. Words on a piece of paper. They all knew the truth but no one would say it.

Mark gave Amy the money for the trip. She said she needed to get away.

"You've only been just come home," he'd said.

"Volchitsa died."

"Yes I'm sorry."

"Don't be. She's out of her misery."

"Where will you go?"

"Maybe I'll look for my mom."

And when she said it she might have believed it, for a second.

"I'll bring the money over," he'd said. "We'll go out. Think of it as a send-off."

She would have said no, mail it to me, but she figured she at least owed him that.

There wasn't much more about Volchitsa in the newspapers, just a comment on page six of the *New York Sun* the day she died. Amy looks at it now, runs her finger along it. She feels the ache in her throat.

The Wolf Girl's doctor, Ivan Gordieva, said "It's a terrible tragedy. We did everything we could to save her."

She shakes her head. "No everything," she says.

Another piece was printed four days later about her funeral, with a photograph, not much bigger than a postage stamp. It said they took her body back to the village of Kostino where they buried her in a patch of earth near the forest.

"Small mercies," Amy says. She says it out loud.

Propped against the far wall at the end of the wood cabin is a picture, unframed, it's the one Mark sent after Volchitsa died. It's called *Eternal Souls*. Artist unknown. The painting shows a wolf paw print and a human footprint together in sand. Underneath it says, 'The Wolf guards the path walked by the dead. The Wolf and the Human whose souls have come together on earthly soils shall forever walk together.'

When Amy looks at it now she catches a tear on the edge of her finger.

Mark took Amy out for pizza the week before she left. He didn't say a whole lot, just kept watching her, like there were things he wanted to say but couldn't, half spoken sentences killed by a waitress fetching a refill or Happy Birthday sang to the kid at the next table. She'd finished her pizza, chased salad around the plate with her fork and said she didn't want dessert.

"I guess I'm not hungry," she said.

"You've lost weight," he said.

And later he walked her up to her apartment and when he handed her the envelope of cash it was like he wanted to say something then, but all he said was, "Call if you need more."

"I won't need more," she'd said.

"Okay, then call when you get back." Then he added, "I hope you find your mom."

146

He'd reached for her hand, held in there for a second before he let it go and turned around. "We all deserve to be loved," he said. And she'd wanted to say, "Maybe I got it wrong about you. Maybe my mom got it wrong about love." But instead she watched him walk away, the word thank you frozen on silent lips.

Amy trails a finger across the photograph clipped right at the back of her journal. It's a young male wolf. She traces the shape of his face; stares real hard into his eyes and imagines the warmth of him, the smell of him. She imagines it so hard she drowns in the ache.

"I get it now, Volchitsa," she says. "I'm sorry what they did to you."

She closes her journal and walks back to the bedroom. She brushes against the rucksack where the coca cola can sticks out of the top, and her copy of *Little Women*, well thumbed, spine broken. She looks at the photograph of her mom and dad on the bedside table. Then she picks up the stuffed animal from the bed and presses it to her cheek.

"I'm ready now," she says. She moves to the window, presses her face to the glass. "Ja Volk," she says.

Wolf Woman still missing In Alaskan Wilds

The search has been called off for Amy Greene, the 26 year old New York reporter that went missing from near Cantwell, Alaska last month. It was local warden, Tom Greer, 43, that alerted the police when he discovered her groceries had not been touched in a week. He said yesterday, "The wilderness is no place for a city girl. They come here for the solitude but in the end it drives them crazy." Amy Greene is believed to have been doing research for a book about Grey Wolves. "She asked me lots of questions about them," claims Tom Greer, "she wanted to know the best place to see them." Amy Greene's good friend, Mark Zander, 27 year old New York photographer, is still in Alaska and refuses to believe Amy could be dead. Spokesman for the Alaskan Wildlife Society said, "Without the right equipment, with winter approaching, Alaska is a dangerous place to be." Warden Tom Greer added, "The girl didn't even take her coat, we found it amongst her things."

"I won't give up," Mark Zander said last night. "All I want to do is find her and bring her home."

I lift my head, nose eclipsing silver
Bear my soul on an icy breath
I Am Hunter
I Am Hunted
But never Slave
For I am Wolf
And I am Free.

Debz Hobbs-Wyatt

Debz has two passions in life – animals and writing. To date she's had six short stories published and is seeking an agent for her novel *Colourblind*. She's currently working on her fourth novel *While No One Was Watching*. She lives in North Wales where she works full time as a writer, as well as the publicist and editor for Bridge House. She is absolutely thrilled that her idea for an animal anthology came true!

www.debzhobbs-wyatt.co.uk.

~~~~~~~~

Wolf Facts

Species: Grey wolf (*Canis lupus*)

Location: Inhabits a small and fragmented portion of its former range across Eurasia and North America.

Habitat: Wolves have thrived in many different habitats including temperate forests, deserts, mountains, tundra, taiga, grasslands, and even urban areas.

Behaviour: Wolves are pack animals. The number of individuals that makes up a pack depends on the size of the territory. There is a very strict hierarchy with wolves. At the top there are a dominant male and female known as the Alpha (male and female). The Alpha pair mate for life and tend to be the only breeding pair in a pack. The lowest ranked wolf is known as the Omega and is submissive at all times. The order of the pack decides who eats first. Wolves communicate through body language and each wolf has its own unique howl. The howling helps to establish and mark territories and discloses the location of the pack to any lost members.

Conservation status: Despite the fragmentation of its habitat, as a species the grey wolf is regarded as being of 'Least Concern' for extinction according to the International Union for Conservation of Nature. However, many wolf populations are in dire need of protection.

Threats: Habitats have become fragmented and human-wolf conflict has become significant in some areas leading to persecution and extermination as perceived threats to livestock and pets. Wolves are also often hunted for sport.

Action: Born Free Foundation supports Turkish NGO, **KuzeyDoga** which is undertaking research into the grey wolf populations of the Sarikamis Forest National Park in North East Turkey, where they are threatened by hunting, persecution and habitat fragmentation.

If you want to get involved with wolf conservation in the UK, check out **Wolf Watch UK**.

Wolf Watch UK is a wolf rescue sanctuary which in 2010 celebrates 30 years of rescuing wolves from zoos, wildlife parks and other places where their situation has become untenable through excess breeding, dominance fights or closures. The sanctuary is a membership organisation that includes behavioural and conservation education, conducting its own distance-learning course in order to further those aims. Their website address is www.wwuk.org.

'We are proud to support the good work done by *Gentle Footprints.*'

An Ugly Penguin

By Phil Thomas

Part I

Fire Island was their destination. The light reflecting off
the sea before it reminded him of how the setting sun lit
the crystals in the rocks around the Reykjanes cliffs.
Across this shimmering vision less than 10 miles from the
coast, anvil-shaped Eldey – Fire Island – stood black and
proud against the horizon. He would share Eldey with the
five other oarsmen in his fishing boat, as well as the
proceeds from the catch. Today was different, however.
Today the catch would not be of fish, but of birds, and
more lucrative than any haul of sea creatures that so
occupied the lives of the men of Keflavik.

Sigurdsson had been specific about some things, as
Sigurdsson often was. But you didn't question him. For one
thing, the merchant was probably the richest man in
Reykjavik, and therefore in the whole land, made rich by the
people he knew in England and Denmark and by the things
he collected for them. Things that made little sense to collect.
Small animals, mostly, and birds. All dead, of course. He'd
seen Sigurdsson loading them into jars of alcohol. As well as
trophies for wealthy foreigners, he collected people. A small,

select group he trusted to carry out instructions. To be in Sigurdsson's circle was to be in a place of high profile and considerable profit. It was a place Ingeman Mikkelsen and his two friends wanted to be. So they rowed towards Eldey with the instruction still loud in Mikkelsen's head: "Bring me some geirfuglar – as many as you can carry."

In Mikkelsen's youth, snaring geirfuglar had been fraught with danger. Back then they roosted on the Geirfuglasker islands, rocks with sheer cliffs that only collectors tried to reach and fishermen shied away from. He heard tales of how British explorers landed there and clubbed them for food and sport. But an underwater volcano caused Geirfuglasker to sink and the birds fled to Eldey, an island closer to the mainland and easier to land upon. Fishermen went there occasionally, but there was easier profit to be made from cod and shark.

With the June sun on their backs they rowed to the far side of Eldey where the cliff rose less steeply from the sea. The scream of thousands of sula rang from the rocks where they nested and the sea boiled as they dove for fish. The fishermen headed for a nook in the rocks and stopped rowing as they pulled into calmer water. Black cliffs clouded with birds towered above them. With clubs in their hands they climbed onto the rocks and over seaweed and tethered the boat to a prominent stud of rock. Mikkelsen pointed upwards and they went, picking their way through flapping wings and snapping beaks. They randomly clubbed birds and left them where they lay. When they reached a ledge they paused to look for geirfuglar, and when they saw none they plotted their next steps. They split into two groups; Mikkelsen went left with his two friends and the other fishermen went right.

They followed the ledge and climbed higher, the sea glimmering below them. As they closed on the summit

Mikkelsen saw something and he led his companions to a hollow in the rock where a geirfugl pair were nesting. He stopped a few feet away and repeated Sigurdsson's instructions, and ordered his friends to put down their clubs. The geirfuglar sensed their presence and started squawking. Mikkelsen lunged forward and one of the birds ran from the nest, as fast as a geirfugl could ever run. Its tiny wings were useless out of the water and it scrambled ungainly over the rocks, still squawking, occasionally falling, as Mikkelsen chased it. Behind him the other bird ran in another direction, chased by one of the men. The third fisherman stooped to find a solitary egg in the nest, but it was broken. He stamped on it in disgust. Mikkelsen, his arms spread, herded the bird into a dead-end. Careful of its powerful bill, he grabbed the frantic creature just below the head, holding it so it couldn't nip him. He got hold of the neck lower down with his other hand and twisted, feeling the snap. The bird was silenced at once, and it went limp. Rather than carry it out by the neck he cradled the deadweight, as per Sigurdsson's instruction. He took it back to the nest where the second bird already lay dead. The sight of the smashed egg brought an angry cry from him, but his friend told him its fate had already been sealed.

They returned to Keflavik with the solitary pair of birds, having searched the cliffs for more but finding none. It came as no surprise to Mikkelsen, who had come to learn during the year that geirfuglar had become less prominent on Eldey. That they had a pair was pleasing enough.

Sigurdsson was delighted. Mikkelsen rode to Reykjavik at once with his prizes wrapped in calfskins, and when he arrived at the grand wooden house close to the cathedral the merchant was at the door, waiting for him. Mikkelsen marvelled at the luxuries of Sigurdsson's house

– a wooden floor with rugs, glass windows that made the most of Iceland's long summer light, a real fireplace, and chairs with the softest cushions. On his previous visit Sigurdsson showed him a lamp that worked from shark liver-oil, and he told Mikkelsen that Europe had great demand for shark oil to light the city streets. Sigurdsson knew the waters around Iceland teemed with Greenland shark; in his quiet way he was telling Mikkelsen to purchase a larger boat and fish for shark. It was with the money Sigurdsson gave him for bringing the geirfuglar that Mikkelsen would do just this.

Sigurdsson's eyes lit up when he unfolded the calf-skins and showed him the two birds. Immediately the merchant went into another room and came back with two large jars half-filled with fluid. He took the stoppers from the jars and into each he carefully eased a bird. Mikkelsen had no idea why he did this, and Sigurdsson chose not to offer an explanation. Instead, with the birds strangely magnified in the jars, Mikkelsen waited for Sigurdsson to drop a cloth bag bursting with rigsdaler coins into his waiting hands. He thanked Sigurdsson and left.

While in Reykjavik, Mikkelsen sought the advice of a shipwright for the construction of a sailing boat. He could not fail to notice the large decked vessel anchored in the harbour, but what he didn't know was that it was this ship that would take Sigurdsson's geirfuglar to Liverpool, as well as a shipment of shark liver-oil. Sigurdsson paid the captain to ensure the glass jars were delivered safely to another merchant in England, a man called Edward Cranham.

When the ship docked at Liverpool many days later, Cranham sought out the captain and collected the jars. He travelled by carriage to Shrewsbury and delivered the birds to Henry Smith, a taxidermist of some repute and especially skilled in mounted birds. Smith had never seen birds such as

154

these before, and he questioned Cranham about their origins for some considerable time. Cranham paid Smith well for the mounting of both birds. The taxidermist, pleased at how well the undamaged specimens had been preserved in alcohol, started to prepare arsenical soap he would use to treat the skins. He removed the birds from the jars and put them in sealed cases to dry. Cranham, who had no interest in witnessing the man's work, told him when he would call to collect the finished items and bade him farewell.

Smith wasted no time. Once the specimens were dry he set to work on the first bird, plugging the nose and throat with cotton wool, breaking the wing bones and lying the bird on its back on a table. He made a series of incisions and carefully removed the skin without disturbing the plumage. He soaked a cloth in benzoline and rubbed the feathers clean. Then using the second bird as a guide, Smith created a false body with wires and eased this framework into the skin. When he was happy with the shape he packed out the skin using sawdust as tow and then sewed the skin up. Working from the second bird again, he created false eyes using coloured glass. Happy with the bird's appearance, he placed the bird in a dust-free cupboard and began to work on a mount. Using Cranham's information of the bird's origin, he sought some rocks from the local stonemason and created a miniature landscape on which he envisaged the bird once may have stood.

Cranham returned several weeks later to find the birds mounted and cased in large glass domes. He was delighted with the workmanship and surprised at the final size and weight of the creations. A plaque on the wooden base of each dome bore the following information:

Geirfugl (Garefowl), Eldey, Iceland, June 1844

At this point the two birds went different ways. Cranham sold one to a collector working for a natural history museum in Paris. The second he delivered in person to the man who had funded their capture. He took a carriage to Henbrook Hall, a fine country mansion in the rolling hills west of Ludlow. There he was met by the butler, who helped him carry the heavy dome to the drawing room where Charles Hamilton-Fairfax kept the most treasured specimens of his collection. Cranham set the dome down on an oak table and covered it with a silk cloth. Then he sat on a sofa and waited. The tick and pendulum swing of a grandfather clock held his attention, but only briefly. Instead he admired, not for the first time, the various animals that adorned the room. Deer heads, foxes, Highland stags, an otter, a young springbok from Natal, various birds in glass cases, a spectacular Bengal tiger rug with the best head feature Cranham had seen. He luxuriated in how nature's beauty could be so wonderfully celebrated and preserved. Cranham could not afford such extravagance but understood why men should desire to collect such things. It allowed for a better appreciation of the world's great natural wonders.

Hamilton-Fairfax, ruddy-faced, bustled into the room, barking orders at someone as he did so. Cranham got to his feet and straightened his jacket. He saw the covered glass dome in the corner of his eye and felt a frisson of excitement run through him. Although he always enjoyed unveiling such items for his clients, and found clients' enthusiasm appealing, there was something extra special about the bird he had delivered this time.

"Awfully sorry, Cranham, this will have to be fast. Stay for tea?"

"I must return to Shrewsbury, but thank you."

"So," Hamilton-Fairfax said, eyeing the large item on the table, "let's see."

Cranham pulled the cloth away, revealing the glass dome and the stuffed bird within it.

The estate owner's face lit up and he clapped joyously. "Splendid! What a clumsy-looking creature. Like an ugly penguin. How truly wonderful."

"I understand it was once classed as a penguin," Cranham said. "However, it's now known as garefowl, or geirfugl as the Icelanders call it. Its English name is the great auk."

"I trust it will be valuable."

"Of course. In fact, I hear there hasn't been a single live sighting since this specimen was captured."

"Good work," Hamilton-Fairfax said. "And now I must go. The wife simply will not countenance my love of nature. She can't bear me admiring my collection!" He shook Cranham's hand. "My accountant will reimburse you. Would you mind putting the bird with the others?"

"Of course."

Hamilton-Fairfax left the room without another look.

Cranham carefully lifted the dome and placed it on a sideboard where other stuffed birds gazed from their mounts. He turned it until it gave the most pleasing view to the room, and for the first time he gave the specimen his full attention. Its white breast was a startling contrast to the black back, and the white patches nears its eyes were equally distinctive. The webbed feet reminded him of the park ducks he sometimes took his children to feed. But the thick, grooved bill seemed to belong to another bird, while the wings were more like flippers and looked comically small.

"An ugly penguin" was an apt description, he thought.

Something puzzled him then. It was only when he folded the cloth and put it in his breast pocket that he realised what it was – the tick of the grandfather clock was missing. He looked and saw the pendulum had stopped.

Part II

The parcel came with a note. "What do you want this for?" it said, and then, "It's been too long. I worry about you." It was signed: Lab-Rat.

Richard smiled, despite himself. He pulled the DVD disc from its sleeve, popped it into the player and then flicked on the TV. His finger hovered over the play button on the remote control. Was he ready for this? He hesitated a moment longer, then went to the drinks cabinet and poured himself a whisky. He looked at the grandfather clock as he always did when he stood at the cabinet, as if willing it to hurry time along. How could it? He hadn't wound it for years. There was a thick layer of grey dust on top of the still pendulum. Next to the clock on the wall was a photograph of him as a young, eager scientist. He was standing behind a large transparent tank. At the centre of the tank stood a bird, penguin-like, but with a large, grooved bill. He'd looked at the picture enough times – why would watching the video be any different?

He sat down in a well-worn armchair and pressed play on the remote. A homemade movie title appeared on the TV, "The Early Years" and then a second, "Audubon's First Press Conference." A reporter stood outside a building, which Richard immediately recognised as the University of Iceland in Reykjavik. The reporter talked about a "momentous occasion" and then coverage switched to a large room filled with press, their cameras and microphones trained on the stage at the front. In the middle of the stage was Richard, or a younger version of him at least, dressed appropriately in lab clothes. He stood alongside a large, rectangular object covered in a plain green cloth.

"One hundred and seventy years ago this month," he announced, "Icelandic fishermen unknowingly killed the last pair of great auks that ever lived." He paused, partly for effect and partly because he turned to check he held onto a tassel of the cloth. Camera flashes zapped his face as he added, "But today, here, the great auk finally lives again."

He pulled the cloth away and no one in the press conference remained seated. There were gasps, and then general applause. The great auk stood haughtily in the centre of the glass enclosure. It looked as though it was posing, proud of its triumphant return, untroubled by the chain around its webbed feet.

"We've called him Audubon," Richard said as the applause subsided, "after the man who gave us the most understanding of this magnificent creature."

There was rush for the stage as cameramen and reporters sought a closer look. The bird became agitated when cameras flashed around the glass. Richard tried to push the reporters back and others ran in from the wings to help, but there was a general melee on the stage and the glass tank was obscured. The TV view bounced around as the cameraman fought his way through the crowd to the front, and suddenly the auk was in view again. Its tiny wings flapped uselessly and it stumbled around in a circle, the short chain keeping it away from the glass walls. The tape around its beak that prevented it from making any noise was obvious to see.

He paused the DVD and wondered, not for the first time, why he had to call it Audubon. He took a drink of whisky and restarted the video.

When order at the press conference was restored a few moments later, Richard began to explain the cloning process he and his team had pioneered. For the first time, he said, they had been able to use degraded DNA from poorly preserved skins and taxidermists' mounts dating from the 1800s. The surrogate was a razorbill but the genome had been modified several times after earlier DNA samples failed. Audubon was not the first auk born, but the first not to die of a lung infection days later. After many months of tests and monitoring, Audubon appeared to be a healthy, young adult great auk.

A woman stepped forward on the stage, announcing herself as Jessica Beiderman. She said they'd learned so much from Audubon. First, and not least, about the sounds a great auk made. Nineteenth century explorers documented appearance and sometimes behaviour, but rarely sound. She referred to a projector screen showing pictures of Audubon's development. She played a recording of the auk calling and shrieking and made a joke about the tape on his beak. Jessica was off-camera now, because the view was trained, fixated, on the great auk. The bird was calm again, and seemed to look straight back at the camera.

"Audubon," he said, and managed a smile.

He caught just one of the questions as he skipped through the remaining coverage of the press conference.

"Given the element of doubt in building the DNA, surely this is just your 'best guess' at what a great auk actually is, or was?"

"It's an approximation, yes," Jessica said. "However, nature isn't perfect."

The press conference video finished but the DVD went on to show TV news reports from countries around the world. It included cuttings of newspaper and magazine articles, where initially the headlines were about awe and excitement and fascination. There followed a short series of clips from chat shows and discussion programmes. In these various people from scientists to pressure groups criticized the ethics of the great auk's cloning. Finally the montage ended with a prolonged excerpt from the BBC, reporting on Audubon's death. It was Richard who explained the circumstances. "We don't understand," he said. "It's almost like he didn't want to be here."

He paused the video again, suddenly feeling exhausted. He sought relief by looking through the window. It gave a view of fields with welts of snow hiding beneath hedgerows. Right on cue four sheep wandered in from a gate, paused as if waiting for others, then buried their heads in the grass. He smiled and raised his glass in a silent salute.

And so the video went on, charting the return of the great auk. Audubon's death had been a green light for others to take up the challenge. A laboratory in Sweden announced it too had created a cloned great auk using DNA from a guillemot. Then a scientist in Scotland claimed to have created a pair that was breeding. Other great auk programmes appeared, with each geneticist claiming their creation was more healthy and authentic than the last. The DVD included clips from a documentary that used hidden cameras to follow the first successful mating of a great auk pair and the birth of their offspring. Richard smiled as the youngster stumbled round the nest in a way not dissimilar to the adults. He watched part of a children's wildlife show featuring great auks in captivity in London Zoo. "They're ugly penguins!" a child declared to camera. Then a pair was brought back into the TV studio, beaks taped up, and assembled children patted them as though teddy bears.

The second anniversary of Audubon's death was marked by a ceremonial release into the wild. A camera crew followed scientists to Eldey, where the last great auks of the 1800s were known to have lived. It was little more than a stub of rock off the coast of Iceland, now home to a huge colony of gannets. Someone lifted up the trapdoor of a cage and two great auks stumbled out, squawking loudly. The camera stayed with them as they stood uncertainly on the rock. Richard felt a lump in his throat when he first saw the report. Now, years later, it brought a tear to his eye, too. He knew what was coming.

Hidden cameras followed the auks' progress on Eldey. Incredibly the gannets left them alone and thanks to regular boat patrols around the island, they were allowed to breed successfully and without disturbance.

The DVD ended with a wildlife programme focused on the great auk. It showed scores of them nesting in another sanctuary site, on St Kilda in the Outer Hebrides. They braved harsh winters and battled with each other. Like penguins they mated for life. They cared for their young with a moving, single-mindedness. They were attacked by skewers and chased in the water by grey seals. On land they were clumsy, ugly-looking creatures, but in the sea they became sleek and powerful swimmers. They looked like they were flying.

The disc stopped and ejected itself, and he took another drink of whisky. Outside it started to snow. He made a fire. When he finally had healthy flames lapping up the soot-stained chimney he poured another whisky and sat down again. He found another remote control, this time for the TV hard drive, and pressed play. He'd recorded the news bulletin from the previous evening. Behind the newsreader was a picture of the great auk.

"Attacks on people in Iceland have increased four-fold this year, as scientists believe the original DNA of the cloned bird created a far more aggressive version than the original."

The report cut to an outside broadcast where a reporter was standing at the foot of the cliff. Although he didn't announce his exact location, Richard recognized it as Eldey. The reporter was wearing gloves, arm guards and thick overalls.

"When they were first reintroduced to Iceland there were just six breeding pairs of great auk. Today it's estimated there are more than a million, three times the human population. Flawed DNA programming meant numbers grew far faster than anyone originally expected. And yet that's not the main problem." He demonstrated by holding his arm towards a great auk nest. An adult bird lunged for it, grabbing it in its beak several times. The reporter clearly had a problem freeing it. "They're incredibly strong," he added, stepping carefully away from the nest again. "Without this protection I'd need hospital treatment now."

The report showed still images of a young boy with cuts on his legs. "This boy was attacked yesterday while playing in his garden. The attacks are so frequent they're putting pressure on hospital services. And tourism chiefs claim visitors are staying away from the island because of great auk attacks."

"There was massive interest in the great auk," an interviewee said. "And it's fair to say Iceland's tourism did very well from it. But now our hotels and spa resorts are half empty because people don't want to worry about attacks and tetanus when they're on holiday."

The reporter explained poison had been ruled out for the culling programme because it could affect other species. Cattle prods and sharpshooters using quick-acting poison darts were the preferred methods.

Richard stopped the recording. The fire crackled in the hearth while beyond the window snow fell silently. The light from the fire played on the walls, on the bookcase, and on the photograph of him in a lecture theatre at the University of Iceland with his last-ever creation chained to the floor of a glass tank.

From the bookcase he retrieved John James Audubon's *Birds of America*, volume seven, the book that had inspired him to research the great auk so many years ago. He flicked to the page he wanted and left the book open on his armchair. Then he took the press conference photograph down from the wall, removed the backing and pulled it from the frame. The frame was used to draw a box around a line drawing in the book. Using scissors, he cut the line drawing out and then placed it neatly into the picture frame. He put the frame back together and hung it on the wall.

Next, he brushed dust off the phone handset and dialled a number. It was answered after three rings. "Jessica Beiderman."

"Hello Lab-Rat," he said.

It could have been five minutes since they last spoke, not five years. They agreed to meet. "Thanks for the parcel," he said finally. "It's just what I wanted."

He took the press conference photograph and threw it on the fire. He didn't even watch it burn. Instead he stood in front of the picture frame and its new contents. He was satisfied as the rising flames temporarily gave the room a much brighter glow, and pleased, in particular, at how they lit the line drawing inside the frame, and how it seemed to bring alive the eyes of the two great auks, as one stood on a rock and another paddled in the sea towards it. He used the moment to wipe the dust off the grandfather clock's pendulum and wind the clock using the little key. With the clock hands moved to what he thought was the right time, he gave the pendulum a push and it began to swing. He stood back again, calmed by the clock's lazy tick and the sight of the beautiful drawing. As the flames faded he was further comforted at how it seemed more light in the room remained.

Phil Thomas

Phil Thomas is a professional copywriter and a member of the Chartered Institute of Public Relations. While working as a journalist in the North West of England he researched and wrote a book on the history of Wigan Rugby League Club's ancestral home, Central Park. He now writes press releases and marketing literature for businesses, as well as short fiction stories for pleasure. Phil has had several short stories published and is currently working on his first novel. He lives on the Isle of Anglesey in North Wales with partner Wendy and their border collie, Bryn.

~~~~~~~~~

Great Auk Facts

Species: Great Auk (*Pinguinus impennis*)

Location: The Great auk was found in the north Atlantic in the cold coastal waters around Norway, Greenland, Iceland, Ireland, Great Britain, Canada and the north-eastern United States. The great auk migrated south in the winter with evidence found as far south as Florida and Gibraltar.

Habitat: The great auk's nesting colonies required rocky islands that had a natural slope down to the water. The great auk only left the Atlantic waters for land to breed.

Behaviour: The great auk was a large flightless bird that was slow and awkward overland, and used their wings to help them traverse rough terrain. They were excellent swimmers and could dive to depths of 76m (250ft). It is believed that the great auk mated for life. They only laid one egg a year, between late May and early June. The pair would take turns in incubating the egg.

Conservation Status: Extinct

Threats: The main reasons for their extinction were believed to be because they were hunted significantly for food, eggs, and down feathers to make clothing etc., and then later as specimens for museums and private collections.

Action: N/A

Although Phil's story is fictional it is based on real events that led to the extinction of this great bird. It is too late to save the great auk, but if you want to help stop other birds going the same way support the **RSPB** (The Royal Society for the Protection of Birds). Visit www.rspb.org.uk.

The Last Big Cat

By Marilyn Fountain

Across the valley the first tinge of amber – dim yet as candlelight, but growing stronger – foretold the dawn. Despite the complete stillness of the air, dead leaves of beech and chestnut were dropping silently and with unexpected violence, spreading a fresh veneer over the splintered floor of Middle Wood. The year was turning, yet still the nights were not long enough for any nocturnal animal to find water, because there was no water left to find. It had been the driest summer on record. Wild creatures of the woods and moors, fields and hedgerows, had been born, lived and died without knowing the sweetness of rain in their nostrils, the light feeling of springiness underfoot, the taste of soft water on their tongues. The ditches had drained before the July heatwave. The dew ponds had evaporated by the end of a baking August. Where once there had been fields, this year the harvesting of poorly yielding crops had left acres of concrete-hard deserts. There had been no rainfall since April.

The big cat had not drunk water for many days. The lure of human activities, of their garden ponds and lawn sprinklers and drain spouts, was becoming more and more irresistible. Then the circus had arrived, the noise

167

patterns of voices and vehicles, the clang of steel scaffolding and the high billowing outline of tented canvas just away and below Middle Wood, triggering a half-forgotten response, drawing him back to this particular place. His actions dictated by opposing tensions of fear and thirst, the cat had not come this close to civilisation for many months. Now, as the sun rose, he stood hesitatingly on the edge of Middle Wood, as black and still as one of the ancient timbers that had fallen before any villager now living could remember. Curling his lip and wrinkling his nose to taste the air, the big cat lifted his angular head to the sky. Some of the migratory pink-footed geese, who'd arrived to find their usual over-wintering freshwater lakes bone dry, were taking to the air again to try further inland. Small confused squadrons of unfamiliar individuals, splitting and reforming, attempting to forge a cohesive unit, passed over the big cat's head. His eyes, coal black pin-prick pupils within glowing emeralds, followed the birds chaotic progress and lingered on the spot where they dissolved into the amber arc on the south-eastern horizon. As silently as the falling leaves, as the rising of the sun and the lifting of the night, the big cat turned around and dissolved back into the woods.

In the village, a man called Jackson was standing at an upstairs window, his binoculars trained on the landscape. Like a bird honing in on its prey, his line of vision travelled along the temporary perimeter fence erected to guard the travelling circus, up the pale gradient of the dry field, its ridges now baked hard into the landscape, and to the abrupt edge of Middle Wood. The faintest of movements held his attention. The barest shifting of a shape, black against black.

168

"You're there," he murmured intensely. "I know you're there all right."

On Jackson's single bed covered with a grubby, crumpled duvet, were pages, neatly clipped over the course of the summer months from the local newspapers, their headlines in sensational typefaces: *'Is There a Big Cat Loose in Woodthorpe?'*, *'My Close Encounter with Big Cat'*, *'Bigger than a Labrador'*, *'Are our Children and Pets Safe?'*, *'Woodthorpe Big Cat Sightings; the Myths and the Evidence'*. This last article had been written by Jackson himself.

For three days each September, the circus set up in a fallow field close to the village. The chosen site this year was a low lying saucer of usually boggy land, a natural amphitheatre between the village and Middle Wood. There were two more performances to give before it moved on again; its annual route round the southern and eastern counties as reliable as a mediaeval pilgrimage. Business had already been good this time. Nothing deterred the paying customer more than bottomless fields and rain dripping through slits in the canvas and down the back of the neck. The Indian summer was all the encouragement the villagers and townsfolk had needed to maintain a 'make hay' philosophy and deny the arrival of autumn by a trip to the circus.

Circling the giant marquee, articulated vehicles and domestic caravans were parked. The first signs of human life in the new circus day came from one of them. The top half of a white door swung outwards and George leaned over and breathed in a lungful of stale summer-warmed air. He lit a cigarette, exhaled the smoke and, through narrowed eyes, watched the sun swell like a pink chrysanthemum bloom. The only other signs of life seemed to be the small groups of geese careering overhead. George wouldn't have known – or wondered – if it was nature or conditioning that led him to wake and rise early. There was no need to get up at this hour, now there were no longer any animals for him to clean out and feed and water. He had no work to do until the afternoon, when he'd parade around the town in costume, drumming up business for the evening performance and his own part in it. But he dressed in character as soon as he rose, before he could think himself out of it.

Leaving the caravan door open, he sat down on a three-legged stool in front of a small mirror and began applying the dramatic face make up of white, black and red. Until a year ago, for every day of his working life he'd been Gorgieou the big cat trainer. For the last twelve months he'd been Georgey the Clown – in appearance at least. The oversized mouth he now drew was an exaggerated echo of his own down-turned lips.

He dressed quickly, carelessly, in a loud blue-checked suit with comedy orange daisy buttonhole, oversized black boots and a bowler hat with a detachable rim. He didn't keep a full length mirror in the caravan. He was ready. The dread that built in him before the preparation drained away in resigned submission. There would be no escape today. George would not be running away from the circus today.

After quickly tidying the caravan, he stepped outside as far as the perimeter fence and looked round. No-one else in the company had stirred. There were no sounds of life from the village or the countryside. Usually at this time of the year the farmers would be digging in the stubble or the muck, or drilling winter wheat or peas, but the iron-hard ground had defeated them and their vehicles.

Directly in front of George the dusty-grey land rose gradually in iron ridges to a strip of dense woodland, a block of dense colour in a broad, pale sky. It was a scene not unfamiliar from dozens of other places where the circus had set up. Yet there was something about this place, something familiar, which stirred his memory, forcing him to think back. Yes, it was here, a year ago, that he had first become Georgey the Clown. And Georgey the Clown, previously Gorgieou the big cat trainer, allowed himself to wonder what happened to the last big cat.

The circus owner had told him to shoot it. George had gone into the back of the lorry, locked the door behind him, and looked into the eyes of the big cat. When he'd pulled the trigger the cat, used to the sounds of comedy bangs and whip cracks, had not panicked. Much later, George had returned, unlocked the van and opened the cage to the night. *Could it have survived*, George wondered, *all through the long hard winter, a delayed, reluctant, abbreviated spring, and now the endless summer drought?*

After sunrise, the cat had gone to ground in Middle Wood and was dozing in an abandoned fox's lair deep underground, below the exposed root ball of a gale-torn beech tree. Noise disturbed him from time to time, but not sufficiently to cause him to move.

Later that morning a dog walker found the remains of a muntjac deer, which the big cat had killed and eaten as much for the moisture of its blood as for its meagre flesh. Jackson inspected the visible evidence with the zeal of a medieval witch-finder. To an eager reporter he gave his expert opinion, that expertise consisting mainly of what he'd read and seen on the internet.

While the big cat slept, Georgey the Clown walked the town, handing out advertisements for the evening's show. The other circus performers rehearsed their acts and tested the safety equipment. Jackson stripped down, cleaned, and reassembled his hunting rifle. The sun crossed a cloudless sky, sucking every last droplet of moisture from the ground. Another day had passed without rain.

"Aren't we lucky," the circus-goers agreed, crossing the fields in tee-shirts and sandals, and buying cans of drink from stall by the gate before they went in. "This time last year we wore weatherproofs and Wellington boots."

Patrons took their seats as the music started. The sun slid away and the sky darkened. Deep in the perpetual blackness of his underground lair, the big cat stirred and inched out towards a tunnelled twilight. Under the overhang of the exposed tree roots, he sat and cleaned his fur meticulously. Afterwards his tongue was coated with particles of sand and dust and bone dry earth. By the time Georgey the Clown had thrown his first bucket of water across the ring in the big top, the big cat had begun to weave his way around a well trod circuit of ditches and dew ponds, seeking water.

Early the next bleached, dry morning, Jackson's eagle eye was caught by a flash of colourful movement from the circus field. He trained his binoculars outside the perimeter fence and tried to make sense of why a clown at… Jackson looked away to consult his watch …at six-forty a.m. would be placing a pink plastic bucket on the ground, then staring across at Middle Wood for some moments before making his way, shoes flapping like flippers, back to one of the caravans. He couldn't have known that George had bought a local newspaper while he was in town and read the big cat stories. Jackson's gaze moved across the parched earth to the line of trees. After some moments he hazarded a guess, and knew in his bones he was right.

The big cat had returned to the den long before dawn, only sleep now easing the discomfort of chronic thirst. As the circus day gathered pace, some of the villagers travelled to the nearest town hall to discuss what should be done about the big cat. While they met with town councillors and a representative from the police force, Jackson had loaded his rifle. Weighed down with surveillance equipment, he made his way over the field to Middle Wood, clambered up the ladder constructed against the largest oak tree on the perimeter, and onto the gantry from where deer were sighted during cullings. He didn't have to be at the meeting to hear the pussy-footed arguments going back and forth. As far as he was concerned, there was only one remedy, and that was to hunt the alien beast down and destroy it. From his elevated position on the sighting platform, Jackson surveyed the landscape and imagined himself in what he liked to think of as a more natural bygone era when the hunting of boar, bear, stag and wolf had been unexceptional and routine.

The daylight faded suddenly but without fuss. The sounds of the last night's performance of the circus reached a crescendo, then faded away. The still air became increasingly mild and heavy. Like a hesitant ghost, a full moon hovered, pale and ringed with a thin sliver of mist. Nothing stirred. Jackson yawned. At least he was fortunate with the weather, he thought.

In the sanctuary of his caravan, George stripped away his clown persona and redressed in his old animal trainer outfit of black sweater and trousers. He'd not worn them since that night a year ago. He was surprised to find the gun was still in the trouser pocket. He switched off the light before opening the caravan door. The creaking of the hinge could have come from a tree, if there had been the slightest movement of air to create it. Jackson put down his ham sandwich and raised his night vision binoculars.

Earlier, the big cat had crawled from the lair and exited the woods from their eastern boundary, away from the village. He had travelled across unfamiliar territory that night, taken greater risks, and still not found any water to drink. Having no inherited memory of the land, some deeper instinct guided the big cat away from recent man-made footpaths and onto tracks established by animals on the move over the centuries long before the days of crop cultivation, these tracks re-established by their descendents after the modernisation of strip fields to prairie farming. Badly dehydrated, thin, with energy diminishing, the big cat had returned to Middle Wood. The sounds and scents of the circus had drawn him back again. But he had waited for silence before making his move. Now the big cat stood on the south-eastern fringe of the woods with his attention focussed on the circus field below; not seventy-five metres to one side of the ladder above which Jackson sat, his night vision binoculars trained on the same spot.

From a heap of brooms and tools left out behind a storage unit, George selected a galvanised bucket. The hooks at the ends of the handle clanked within their loops. George filled the bucket with water and carried it over to the plastic bucket by the fence. Only evaporation had caused the level to drop. The untouched surface was covered in dust; George could feel the grittiness on his fingers when he drew his hand away. He tipped away the stale water. It didn't penetrate the rock hard earth, but rolled over the surface like an elongated slug. As George refilled the plastic container, the galvanised bucket clanked again.

The big cat's ears pricked. He associated the sound with drinking water and his reflexes were responding. For the first time since he'd been released from captivity, the cat moved forwards in the jerky, cowed manner of the show ring. George sensed rather than saw or heard the cat's approach. He straightened up and moved slowly backwards. Jackson was alerted by the sudden change in George's body language, and aimed his rifle at a puppet-like shadow creeping over the moonlit dust.

George whipped the pistol from his pocket and fired it once into the air. An infinitesimal division of time later, so close to the first shot that ear witnesses would later swear they heard just a single crack, Jackson pulled the trigger on his hunting rifle. Yet a full second before both reports the big cat had stopped, turned and fled. Instinct and conditioning had collided in a chain reaction. The big cat's instinct to maintain independence had proved stronger than the conditional satisfaction of his thirst, and had saved his life – for now.

Disappointment and a sense of anti-climax washed over both men. Jackson climbed down from the gantry; George went back into the circus caravan to prepare for the morning exodus. The big cat had already dissolved back into the landscape it had begun to make his own. Just below the south-western horizon, rain clouds were forming. Just before the next dawn, it would begin to rain.

Marilyn Fountain

Marilyn Fountain has been making up stories for as long as she can remember. Her publication credits include the Mail on Sunday's *You* magazine, *Women's Weekly* and *Take A Break*. She is an animal loving vegetarian and enjoys walking her dog in the Norfolk countryside – particularly when it is raining. Any royalties from this story will go to the Born Free Foundation.

~~~~~~~~~~

Black Panther Facts

Species: Black panthers are commonly melanistic leopards with a recessive gene that causes dark colouration.

Location: Black leopards have been reported from areas of south-western China, Myanmar, Assam and Nepal, as well as parts of southern India. They are less common in tropical Africa.

Habitat: Melanistic leopards are most commonly reported in mountainous and densely forested areas.

Behaviour: Leopards are solitary, nocturnal animals and during the day rest in thick brush or in trees. It is thought that melanism may act as a camouflage advantage under certain conditions, since the leopard is more common in regions of dense forest where light levels are low.

Conservation status: The leopard as a species, which includes melanistic leopards, is classified by the World Conservation Union as 'Near Threatened'.

Threats: Although leopards have the widest range of any species of cat in Africa and Asia, their habitat has become fragmented and their range decreased due to habitat loss and hunting.

Action: Born Free Foundation rescues leopards from lives of misery in poor captive conditions from Africa and Europe, raising awareness and providing lifetime care in spacious natural habitat sanctuaries in Africa.

To find out how you can help to protect big cats in the wild visit www.bornfree.org.uk.

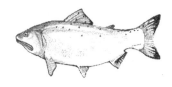

Liberty and Acquiescence

By Mark R Smith

Naktek Head

There was the tiniest stirring, the smallest movement in the cold gravel bed of the Naktek River. Minute shavings of ancient stone, chilled by the fast flowing meltwater from the interior, gave way, micron by micron, to the birth wrigglings of thousands of alevins. Each carried their own yolk sac with them and none who wished to live raised their heads above the gravel. Here they fed on their yolks and waited.

Liberty had only the haziest memory of this time. The constant roar of cold water above his head. The wriggling of his brothers and his sisters. The cycle of light and dark as day gave way to night and day arrived again. He knew that he grew and as his yolk sac shrank he gained in strength.

Then he was hungry. He remembered that. And he remembered that he had lifted his head marginally clear of the gravel and smelled his way to his first meal. He had made it from alevin to parr. He now darted from gravel bank to river bank and back again, making the most of his cunning camouflage, to search out tiny larvae and succulent fresh water insects. He twisted and turned among his kin, still myriad in number though he also sensed many had failed to join him in his new adventure.

As Liberty became hungrier and reached for the larger grubs he began to sense the flow of the water and swam easily downstream. There were always hundreds of family around, but he found himself swimming more and more with Acquiescence, his own blood brother, whose silver head was never far from his shoulder

"Look at the size of that!" exclaimed Liberty as he indicated a plump fly drifting downstream above them. 'Your turn. Go for it!"

Acquiescence slipped invisibly through the water, altered his trajectory upwards at the last minute and took the fly in the briefest instant. "That was good", he said, as he rejoined Liberty in the safety of a shadowed dip in the bed of the stream.

As they continued on their journey, the brothers became inseparable. They had other brothers and sisters, of course. In fact they had hundreds. And cousins too; ten thousand times ten thousand. But the two growing parr now swam everywhere together, until the river suddenly slowed and the water deepened and darkened.

Beaver Pool

"This is odd," said Acquiescence. "Nothing's moving. There's no flow to go with any more. Where to now?"

"Interesting," said Liberty. "I think this means that we could, if we wanted to, go back the way we have come."

They tried going back and found themselves stuck at the point they had entered this new world. Here there was a gentle flow of water into the middle of a much larger pool. From there, Liberty found that he could branch out in any direction he liked. Acquiescence followed him, and together they discovered new worlds.

They could go wider. They could go deeper. They could go further. Liberty found a tiny gap between a latticework of sunken twigs into which he could squeeze and rest. "Come in here," he called. "It's a great place to hide. And the food just drifts on by ready for me to grab it and eat."

Acquiescence liked it too.

The light of day was only just beginning to fade when each of them noticed a gentle flow of water back upstream to the point they had entered the pool. The flow became stronger and they had to wedge themselves against the submerged trellis of twigs as water they had never tasted before shivered through their gills.

"I wonder what's going on?" said Liberty. "Let's go and see."

"Are you sure it's safe?"

"Let's find out," said Liberty as he ventured out of their lair into the pool. "Look at this. If I allow myself to float to the top, I go inland. If I swim downwards the flow is cooler and brings me back to where I've been. It's a circle. And – wow! The pool's getting bigger! I can see things below me that were on the bank when we arrived. See how far we could go."

"Be careful," said Acquiescence. "Who knows what will happen if we go too far."

That night they sensed the water recede and the clear pure mountain water refreshed the pool again.

The next day it rose and fell twice more and they explored a little more each time. Tide by tide they began to welcome the new water from the other side of the twigs as their gills became accustomed to its salty thickness.

Days turned to weeks and as each day shortened the flow of cool clear water from the mountains began to lessen. They ate copiously from the riches of the pond and from what the tides bought in, and grew strong. Early one morning Liberty's chewing was interrupted by a strange sound. He caught the silvery eye of his brother and they listened. They could hear an incessant gnawing. Sharp incisors tearing heartwood out of a giant tree not far from the bank. Then a creaking and splitting, a crack like a loosened boulder hitting the bedrock of a mountain stream. Then there was silence but the rising sun was being shut out. They looked up and saw leaves, twigs and branches descending from heaven. As the sky darkened to inky black the first twigs hit the surface. Seconds later they were followed by the thunderous crump of a huge trunk hitting the water, sending shock waves pulsing over, through and under the water. The pool became a maelstrom.

"Hang on tight," screamed Liberty. "We're getting out of here. The tide is coming up. We can get over the dam. I don't know what's out there but it can't be worse than this. Our whole world's been turned upside down."

Open Sea

"Keep going," yelled Liberty. "I can smell some of our cousins out there. If we get into a group we'll be safer. They clearly had the same idea we did."

"I think I can smell Ferocity and his crowd. And there's Beauty. She's calling. Over there, over there."

Hundreds of young smolt were gathering in the lee of a shallow bank of sand in the estuary. Liberty and Acquiescence, Ferocity and Beauty were joined by

181

thousands of cousins they had never met before. There was safety in numbers. And numbers they had. As the next dozen tides rose and fell their school swelled to over fifty thousand rapidly growing and changing smolt.

"Did you know," said Liberty, "that Beauty was never in Beaver Pool. She never saw the tree come down. She says she's been here seven tides longer than us. You know what that means don't you?"

"What?" said Acquiescence.

"It means there are literally thousands of fish here who we've never met; fish who came down the river earlier or later than us. Fish who waited in other pools. Some even came straight into the estuary. They said it was a total shock to the system."

"There must be a huge number of us," said Acquiescence. "I don't think I've seen the open water now for three tides; just fish as far as the nose can smell."

They stayed together in the estuary, eating and growing, growing and eating. Barely noticed changes day by passing day slowly prepared them all for the call of the ocean. They turned from smolt to salmon.

"It will soon be time," said Liberty. "Time to explore a world we could never have dreamed of."

"Can't we stay here?" said Acquiescence who seemed to be maturing just a little slower than Liberty.

"I'm not staying here and letting Ferocity see all the sites first."

"But what's it all for? What are we going to see? More water? More plankton? It's not very exciting is it? And frankly – would it really matter if I didn't come? There are thousands of us in this estuary alone, and I hear a whisper from Beauty that there are hundreds of schools up and down this coast. What difference do I make?"

Deep Den

With measured tread and muscular grace Ursula eases herself down into her den. She is pregnant. All summer long she has feasted on the abundance of the lower slopes. Berries and roots at the beginning as she waited for the fish to come up to the falls. But they had come as they always did. Succulent and sleek, almost leaping into her mouth, she had gorged for days.

She is fat and full and ready for bed. When she wakes next year she will introduce two sons into the snow. She will train them well.

Deep Ocean

Deep pacific peace settled in the dark ocean.

Liberty made his way to the edge of the shoal, not for the first time, and stared out into the deep blue width of ocean. Above him the water lightened into an electric blue. Below him the blue darkened to thick impenetrable black. His head flickered as he sensed something on the current.

"Herring", he whispered to the fish around him. Acquiescence was just able to hear, as he stayed further from the open water, protected by the shoal around him.

"Herring, herring." The whispered message rippled through the shoal in seconds.

"Come on brother," said Liberty as he flicked his tail and pointed the way for Acquiescence to follow.

"I'm coming, I'm coming, give me a chance," said Acquiescence as he fought past several dozen other fish and struck out behind Liberty.

"They've still not seen us. Speed is our weapon. Take them by surprise."

Liberty fixed his pearly eyes on a herring at the edge of her own shoal, opened up his throttle with several rapid flicks of his tail, powered into a dive and opened his mouth just as the herring spun around in alarm. Too late. Liberty's teeth tore into the flesh behind the herring's gills and ripped a huge gash down and back to her belly. Acquiescence followed up with a sharp clamp of his teeth on her head and she became another snack on the brother's journey.

They swam through rough seas and calm, through currents warm and cold. They ate well and widely. Liberty loved the herring. Acquiescence preferred the pilchard. The shoal shrank a little as they travelled. Herring and pilchard were smaller than they were but shark and tuna and marlin were bigger. But even after four years in the deep ocean there were still too many fish to count when a very strange feeling came over Liberty.

Naktek Calling

He noticed it first when a large shoal of plump and slow moving herring came within a whisker of them. There was a collective twist of sleek silver and herring exploded away from the salmon in a starburst of fins and tails. Acquiescence snapped his jaws around a particularly fat fish and ate his fill. For the first time in his life Liberty didn't really feel hungry. He noticed that Ferocity had not joined in either.

"Not hungry?" said Acquiescence, spitting out the gristle. "Most unlike you. What's going on?"

"I don't know. I just don't feel like food. And I've been thinking."

"Dangerous," said Acquiescence. "You told me not to think too much."

"I know I did. But don't you ever wonder what it's all for? We eat, we breathe, we swim, we eat some more. Where's it all leading? What's the point?"

"The point is we're growing, getting bigger and stronger."

"But why? I'm very big and very strong now. Almost as strong as Ferocity. I get to eat the best herring – but so what? And look around you. What do you see?"

"Fish?" said Acquiescence with a mischievous look in his eye.

"Exactly. Hundreds and thousands of fish. And across this vast ocean there are billions. What is one fish worth? What I am worth? Who cares about me?"

"Well I do," said Acquiescence.

"Thank you," said Liberty. "And I care about you too. But what happens next? I think we're missing something. There must be more to life than this?"

The next day three cousins also stopped eating and the day after that even Acquiescence began to lose his appetite and sniff at the ocean currents.

"What do you smell?" said Liberty.

"I don't know exactly but it smells very familiar, though it's as faint as a squid at twenty fathoms."

"It's as if something were calling me," said Liberty. "Something I can't resist. Let's follow the smell. It could be just what I've been looking for. It could be the answer. Come on."

Even as Liberty led Acquiescence towards the smell, Ferocity and many of the others were already calling their companions together and setting off. The shoal that had been following the herring, shadowing the shoals of pilchards and tracking the ocean floor for baby squid, now stopped eating and headed for home.

The Roaring

Mile after mile Liberty and Ferocity led the shoal and Acquiescence and the others followed closely. Each mile the faint whiff of home became stronger until Liberty tasted a drop, just one drop of clean fresh water. He stopped.

"Did you feel that?"

"What?" said Ferocity.

"Keep very still. Can you taste it now? There are drops."

Ferocity wriggled a little but kept as still as he could.

"I can taste it too," he said. He swam slowly forward and tasted the drops again. "It's home water," he said. "This is our destiny. This is what we were born for. This is our great God calling. If we follow the smell, if we taste the water we can swim all the way to heaven."

"I'm sure it's worth trying to find out what's going on," said Liberty. "So I agree we should carry on. But I think swimming all the way to heaven sounds a little bit over the top."

"Nonsense. Can't you taste it? It's the taste of home; it's the taste of heaven."

So the salmon ran. Some followed Ferocity in the hope of heaven and some followed Liberty, excited to see what they might find. Many just followed the others. Acquiescence kept close to Liberty's shoulder.

Liberty's back began to ache a little, the flow of the river increasing. The water was now much shallower in places and poured fast over the rocks. It was an effort to swim and he hadn't eaten for several weeks. Acquiescence seemed to be finding it equally hard. Some distance ahead they could hear a roaring. As they approached they came upon hundreds of their cousins swimming back and forth.

Each of them would swim with the flow and then turn, pause, and with a desperate and rapid beating of their tails accelerate towards the roaring water ahead and leap into thin air.

"What's going on?" said Acquiescence.

Ferocity pondered for a moment and then confidently turned to his shoal and said: "Beyond the roaring and the spray, above the rocks and the spume, a reward awaits those who make this final great leap of faith. Keep the taste in your gills. If you fail, go around again. Never give up. Heaven will be your reward."

"How do you know that?" said Liberty, dodging out of the path of a huge salmon powering towards the roaring waters. "How do you know there isn't another roaring after this one?"

"Because the smell and the taste have led us here after weeks of fasting. This is surely the time of glory. One more leap of faith."

"Well, I'm going to do this with the least energy I can," said Liberty. "I may need to do it again on the other side."

"You won't make it without faith," said Ferocity.

"You may not make it with faith."

As Liberty approached the roaring, looking for a way from level to level, trying to calculate flows and speeds, he saw on the far bank, outlined against the snow, three shapes. As he focussed carefully he could see that one was large and the other two smaller. They were dark brown and ambled on all fours to the edge of the roaring water. He watched as the large shape made for the centre of the roaring and took up station on a large rock over which some of his cousins were trying to leap. Several hit the rock and slid back downstream to turn round and have another go. One salmon made it past the large brown shape, leaping elegantly and smoothly from the raging torrent and landing in a pool beyond the rock from where it wriggled to safety upstream.

"I'd avoid trying to jump near that brown shape," said Liberty, having to shout at Acquiescence over the noise of the roaring. Even as he said this they watched, horrified, as the shape extended a long arm and snatched one of their cousins out of the air and pinned her to the rock. She screamed in agony as four sharp claws tore the scales from her side and then the brown shape's enormous jaws crushed her in death.

Liberty and Acquiescence exchanged a nervous glance and moved nearer the edge of the river to look for a way up.

"If you doubt heaven is over the roaring water, why are we still trying to make it?" said Acquiescence.

"Because I'm not going all the way back to the ocean for more of the same thing day after day. There's something in me that has to see what's round the corner. I want to know what's going on. What's it all for? Who knows what we might find up there? I don't think it will be heaven, but there must be something. We all feel it. It's pulling us on"

"I suppose it is," said Acquiescence, sounding less than fully convinced.

Liberty had found what looked like an easier passage up the roaring water where it ran slightly less menacingly. There were three small pools, each a little higher than the one before. Together they created a slippery staircase upwards. The only problem Liberty could see was that it was very near the edge of the river where one of the two smaller furry brown shapes was stamping and splashing.

"If we do this together I think we stand a better chance," said Liberty. "I'll take the outside near the bank.

You swim just inside me. Remember – you don't need to go flat out but you do need to get up the next two steps quickly after the first. Each step is not too big, but staying in the little pools on the way up isn't an option. You must keep moving."

They moved away from the roaring in order to get up a modest speed, because the first jump was the largest. Turning upstream they could see the smaller brown shape ambling among the pools. Liberty knew now what this muscled monster was: a great grizzly bear. But he also knew he and his brother were fast and sleek and that this was their best chance. Their tails twitched and then began to beat sideways faster and faster. Soon, Liberty's whole body was rippling with rhythmic grace as he aimed himself at the first jump, Acquiescence immediately to his left and just a little behind.

To the bear, on the edge of the stream they would have appeared together: Two elegant silver-pink salmon arching upwards out of the maelstrom below. He waved an ineffective paw but missed them both and, in an instant, Liberty and his brother had landed in the first pool up the staircase.

"Two more leaps," shouted Liberty, and immediately bent his back hard and flicked his tail, heading for his next jump. He made it before the bear even had a chance to regain his young balance and landed safely just one step away from the top.

"Jump. Jump now," screamed Liberty from the higher pool, but Acquiescence could not hear over the roaring of the water. "Keep going. You must keep moving. Jump. Jump."

A little dazed and very tired from the first jump Acquiescence realised that he had to hurry. He collected his

189

thoughts, reversed as far back in the small pool as he could and set off with a flick of his tail for the jump up to join Liberty. The bear had had time to recover and was now staring at the lower pool waiting for the next jumper. As Acquiescence leaped clear of the pool he almost passed the bear's shoulder, but the grizzly creature had time to spin around and knock him upwards. He shot up in the air and, like a stricken aeroplane, stalled in flight and collapsed to the river below. He almost made it to the next pool but landed hard on a flat boulder just short of his objective. The bear moved fast, taking advantage of the stunned fish. He danced his back legs in a slippery jig and managed to stamp a leathery foot on Acquiescence's tail fin. Suddenly Liberty leapt vertically out of the pool. The young bear was so pleased he made a grab for Liberty, missed, and lost his balance. Acquiescence was free.

"One more leap, brother," bellowed Liberty. "And quickly. Stick with me."

Liberty, undamaged and bigger than Acquiescence, called all his muscles into one co-ordinated ripple of effort and set off for the final jump. Acquiescence knew what he had to do but his tail was damaged, and he was still stunned from his fall. He swam after Liberty but he fell inches and inches behind. Liberty leapt first and rose in a slow arc, sun bouncing of his shiny sides. He almost hit the bear, who opened his mouth, baring rows of ripping teeth, and snapped them shut. On thin air. Liberty splashed into the higher reaches of the Naktek River and turned round quickly. Liberty's leap had distracted the bear and Acquiescence avoided it entirely. His leap was less powerful than Liberty's and he took off just a little too soon. His spring into the air was too steep, and although the sun splashed its orange glow over him too, he fell with

190

a sickeningly cold thud onto the rocks, just short of the upper reaches.

Liberty watched as the bear reacted swiftly and pinned his brother to the rock. This time his paw thumped down and held Acquiescence squarely across the middle of his back. Acquiescence attempted to swim but all that happened was that his head and tail thrashed back and forth like a propeller. He remained pinioned to the rock. Lazily the bear bent his head low and inspected his catch. Acquiescence struggled just once more but then gave in as he saw the ripping incisors heading for his neck. The bear bit away his lifeblood in one crunching clamp of his jaws and his twitching body slackened and died.

Liberty could do nothing but watch from the higher level. He saw cousins pass him heading further upstream. He saw many die. Some were eaten but many simply failed the jump and drifted back, exhausted, to be picked off by bears and eagles, or just to drift downstream and rot in forgotten stagnant water. He looked from a distance again and marked the spot where his brother had died but he knew in his heart he would never see it again. The Naktek still called him upstream.

My End is My Beginning

This was not heaven. He had not seen Ferocity since the great roaring. This was actually very hard work. This was grinding on when all your strength was slipping away. He had eaten nothing since the ocean. He couldn't face it. He just had to press on, if only to discover what all this life had been about. Further falls had held him up, sometimes for days. He had narrowly escaped a swooping eagle and for many days, bears had lined the river waiting for fish to give up the journey. But he would not. He was determined to find out what all this was for.

And then, five hundred miles inland, he smelt something new. Wriggling forward, exhausted, he saw Beauty, Ferocity's sister, slip over the shallows to a bed of gravel. He followed. Slowly and with supple waves of her curvaceous tail Beauty began to dance for him. And as she danced the gravel immediately behind her began to stir and the rippling current carried small pieces away. He watched, entranced, as her sinuous efforts cleared a large shallow hollow in the gravel. A stream of tiny pink translucent pearls began to appear and to settle into the bed of the stream. An overwhelming urge took hold of Liberty as he smelt the sheer power and pull of the chemistry in the water. His sleek flesh was full of all the pulsating seed of countless generations before him. This was what it was all about. Not heaven, but an encounter so deep and so visceral that he didn't care if he died in its completion. He swam hard over to the hollow and emptied himself of the last dregs of his energy, spreading his seed over the pink shimmer below.

Drained and shattered beyond his wildest imaginings, he swum slowly but gracefully to a quiet, sweet pool, lay down on the gravel, felt death steal up to him and softly acquiesced.

Mark R Smith
Mark R Smith has been writing seriously for a year. He has had a story published in Spooked by Bridge House and is also working on a novel about singing, sinning and redemption. He would love to see some of his poetry published but thinks it might not be funny enough yet. He is intrigued that he has written the only animal story in Gentle Footprints about an animal that most of us consistently eat!

~~~~~~~~~~

Salmon Facts

Species: Salmon is the common name for several species of fish of the family *Salmonidae.*

Location: Salmon are found in both the Atlantic and Pacific oceans as well as inland lakes such as the Great Lakes.

Habitat: Salmon exist in both freshwater and saltwater habitats.

Behaviour: Most salmon are born in fresh water (rivers or streams), travel to and live much of their lives in salt water oceans, and return to fresh water to spawn. There are, however, some salmon species that live their entire lives in fresh water.

Conservation status: According to the IUCN, both the Atlantic Salmon and Pacific Salmon are classed as 'Least Concern'.

Threats: As salmon swim upriver to reach spawning areas, the damming of rivers is a significant threat. In addition, habitat loss, disease, overfishing and reduced food availability pose threats to salmon.

Action: N/A

The mission of the **Wild Salmon Center** is to identify, understand and protect the best wild salmon ecosystems of the Pacific Rim. They devise and implement practical strategies, based on the best science, to protect forever these extraordinary places and their biodiversity.

To find out more about the Salmon visit www.wildsalmoncenter.org.

Bella

By Sharon Waters

Early mist. Bird chit chat cut through the cover of silence and Bella roused, pushed her front paws far out in front and yawned. She opened one eye and looked around. It was dawn and time for her bed but Bella felt uneasy and her several attempts at sleep had been fruitless.

All was still but for the fading dawn chorus and Bella once again curled up and tried to sleep. She must have dozed for a while because she found herself racing through unfamiliar territory, dodging angry black crows who were screeching furiously at her unwelcome intrusion. Dark clouds threatened rain. The silence was tangible – a storm was brewing. On and on ran Bella, never seeming to reach her destination. She could see where she had to go to but no matter how fast and for how long she ran she never managed to get there.

Bella was a beautiful young fox, a female with a thick vibrant coat the colour of cinnamon and spice. She must have cut a striking figure as she slid and sliced through dusky landscapes on her daily quest for food.

Mostly solitary Bella had recently come of age, mating for the first time in her young life. She had matured fast after this encounter moving from remnants of playful cub to responsible expectant mother although there was still a while to go before her cubs were born.

Bella's nose quivered as she tossed and turned in fitful sleep. It was unusual: she normally slept well but not today and now she was awake – wide awake: sitting bolt upright as if frozen in time. *Something wasn't right.* Every instinct in her young body told her to be on her guard. A weak sun struggled in vain to break through the clouds and fear washed over Bella like a cold damp shower.

It was late morning. Bella listened intently, not daring to breathe, but all she could hear was the flutter of bird wings high in the trees. *Why did she feel like this? Why did her world feel so troubled today?* On her feet now she paced up and down unable to appease her fretful state.

She had to move: go somewhere else. She'd head for her earth, the one she used for shelter when the days were short and cold. She'd feel safer there. Although it was mild Bella felt an icy chill cut through her body and she shivered. Twigs and debris crackled underfoot as Bella made her way to the earth but to her surprise the entrance was blocked; packed tightly with clods of earth and stones. And the pungent sickening stench of humans hung in the air like cobwebs. Bella winced and backed off. *How she hated and feared that smell.* She looked around frantically trying to make some sense of the situation; trying to locate the source of her unease.

And then she heard something.

It was a sound that filled her with terror. The unmistakeable heart rending sound of dogs: not one or two dogs but what sounded to Bella like hundreds. Dogs with frantic, feverish, high pitched yelps that forewarned danger. For the second time that morning Bella froze, unable to move, unable to think clearly. She had not heard that sound before but her every instinct told her that it was bad. A trickle of urine made its way down her leg. She wanted to crawl somewhere underground where she would be safe. But her earth had been blocked and there was nowhere else to go.

She needed to run, to get away. Bella pricked up her ears to gauge the direction of the terrible din. She knew it was getting closer. Now she was on the move. Apprehensive at first but swiftly breaking into a run. Faster and faster she travelled, her movements becoming increasingly frenzied, desperate, urgent. Weaving in and out. Instinctively trying to disperse her scent which the day was keeping strong and thick above the ground. On she ran. Fierce, frightful sounds following her, petrifying her. She ran faster than she had ever ran in her life, tearing through alien countryside. Danger lurked everywhere. Trees loomed like monsters waiting to pounce. The blood surged through her in tumultuous waves. She reached the brow of a hill and paused for breath. She glanced back. In the distance she saw movement – lots of it – and it was heading her way.

Digging her hands deep into the pocket of her coat Fern stood on the sidelines amongst the other spectators. Her bottom teeth clawed a tense upper lip and she inhaled deeply, staring straight ahead. A squirming gaggle of hounds zig-zagged the length of field, frantic for fox scent. They found it quickly and broke into euphoric song which resonated far across the field and up the hillside to where Bella had taken brief respite.

Fern had glimpsed the fox break from the covert minutes earlier. Its beautiful coat blazed like fire through the greyness of the day. And she had closed her eyes and willed it to run – far, far away – *to escape these barbaric bastards in red with their dogs and grotesque traditions.* Dark clouds hovered menacingly over the landscape and the hunters spread out, red coats splashed across the field like drops of blood.

One of the hunters close to Fern eyed her suspiciously. *She sensed his mistrust* and held his gaze. His quivering fat podgy face reminded her of a trifle. She thought how ridiculous he looked.

The haunting chilling sound of a horn told Fern the hounds were still onto the fox's scent. Her stomach churned and she bit her lip even harder.

Countless people had tried to convince her of the necessity of hunting, how the alternatives were far worse for the fox, *as if they cared,* but she was having none of it. *They'd never win her over with their futile arguments as to how the fox was vermin, destructive, needed to be controlled. Who were these people to play God and anyway didn't cats kill birds*! Fern knew for a fact that her dog would go after a chicken given half a chance. It was instinct.

No. Foxes were hunted for sport. It gave people like this the chance to have a jolly good day out and now Fern was witnessing the spectacle first hand from the comfort of her human existence. She hated the sound of that bloody horn, blowing shrill from the mouth of one of these fancy dressed predators. It reminded her of those children's parties where kids run around playing games with blow out paper whistles in their mouths... Only *these were no children and this game involved a life and hours of frenzied terror.* It sickened Fern to the pit of her stomach and she watched isolated in her sadness: detached from the other partygoers whose pleasure seemed to increase the closer the dogs came to winning their prize.

Bella ran on and on, keeping close to hedgerows in an effort to hide her presence but it was too late for that.

The enemy was everywhere; eyes watching from their little metal containers; men with spades and dogs; people on horseback. They were everywhere! And the terrible sound of shouting – hysterical shouting – grown men with glowing eyes – almost frothing at the mouth in frenzied anticipation.

Bella felt tired, her swollen body where new life grew ached and she longed to rest, but blinding panic forced her on. Shrieks and yells followed her, wrapping her in a cloak of fear. The clouds grew darker covering the landscape in a gloomy veil.

Time passed by. One hour melting dramatically into the next as the chase went on. The young fox had used every instinct she possessed in order to try and outwit her pursuers. But now her strength was spent, her breathing laboured and rasping. She could run no more. Her tongue hung heavily from the side of her mouth, her legs were unsteady. She was having trouble standing now. The excitement behind her had grown to fever pitch and the dogs screams were deafening.

She looked desperately for somewhere to hide.

Anywhere.

But there was nowhere.

Bella crouched low, frantically trying to protect the babies deep inside her heaving body; frantically trying to protect them from this evil scene.

But she couldn't.

The party was almost over.

The games had all been played.

It was time to blow out the candle and cut the cake.

Bella turned to face the baying pack. A lone warrior pitted against the masses. Quickly surrounded by snarling, snapping mouths she fought to keep her balance but was soon upturned and set upon by the angry, brutal mob. Bella cried out in pain as teeth cased in powerful jaws sunk mercilessly, deeply, into her flesh: She became the victim of a frenzied tug of war as hounds ferociously clamoured to win a piece of her. Bella didn't stand a chance. This game was too one sided and her terrified piercing screams were gradually replaced by a series of low, pitiful whimpers as her life and spirit ebbed away. Cruelly taken on a blood soaked embankment to the jubilant sound of laughter and cheers.

Bella would have made a wonderful mother – proud, protective, and strong. But she never got her chance to shine in this world. Her unborn cubs never got their chance to rough and tumble and play hunt amongst the lush green fields and woodland haunts of their unknown mother.

Only one person grieved for the passing of Bella. Someone who had watched silently from a distance. Fern remembered the beautiful, proud outline she had seen on the brow of the hill. She remembered her feeling of helplessness at this poor animal's plight. She remembered the revulsion she had felt at the outcome. And she remembered making Bella a silent promise that she would always fight her cause.

As she left the party Fern took one last look back. All that remained was the blood stained canvas of a finished painting. One where a beautiful fox now lay broken and torn, her spirit destroyed in the name of sport, her once vibrant coat muddied and butchered. Silent tears mourned the passing of Bella – shed in secret and glistening with sorrow.

But as Fern walked, a glimmer of hope flickered in the air like a delicate nightlight. The hope that came in the form of a new breed of artists who, like Fern, was determined to paint a different kind of picture for this world. A picture that would show humanity, warm hearts, compassion and respect for all who share this planet. A picture that would show animals like Bella able to live freely without terror or harm. A picture that would show a beautiful vixen playing happily with her cubs on a hillside. It surely was something worth fighting for.

One day Bella! Fern silently vowed. *One day!*

Sharon Waters

Sharon Waters lives with her family in the East Midlands. She enjoys writing and is passionate about animal welfare and environmental issues. This is Sharon's first submission and she is thrilled to be included in this anthology.

Sharon has a lifelong respect and admiration for the red fox whom she refers to as 'a wonderful, enigmatic creature that has been persecuted beyond belief yet has still managed to survive in the face of adversity.'

Her story, *Bella* is dedicated to Ciannon, Sebastian and the countless Bellas everywhere.

~~~~~~~~~

Fox Facts

Species: Red fox (*Vulpes vulpes*).

Location: The red fox is native to much of North America and Eurasia, as well as northern Africa. In the 19th Century, it was introduced into Australia.

Habitat: The red fox inhabits almost every single habitat in the Northern Hemisphere, rural and urban alike.

Behaviour: Red foxes are solitary hunters and feed on rodents, rabbits, birds, and other small game. Although often seen alone, foxes tend to live in groups, often family groups. They are known for their ability to adapt well to many different environments and conditions.

Conservation status: Abundant across many areas, the IUCN Red List classes the red fox as 'Least Concern'.

Threats: Red foxes have been traditionally hunted for sport, and are sometimes killed as pests or carriers of rabies.

Action: N/A

To find out how to get involved in fox protection, check out **The Fox Project**.

The Fox Project is a wildlife hospital specialising in foxes, admitting and treating around 650 fox casualties per year including 250 fox cubs – the majority of which are returned to the wild under controlled conditions. They are also the UK's leading fox information bureau, incorporating a humane fox deterrence consultancy, designed to assist people in solving human/vulpine territorial issues without resort to capital punishment.

www.foxproject.org.uk

For Pepito

By Gail Richards

It was damp and dark inside and if someone appeared in the doorway there was nowhere to escape to. Anyway the chain on his neck didn't let him go far. But he preferred being outside and sometimes when a group of humans appeared at the fence he could keep very still beside the shed and they didn't even see him. He only ever saw humans now and the memory of his own kind had faded.

There's no going back now, thought Emma as she slipped the designer watch into her pocket.

She had seen the watch the day before when the middle-aged woman from room four left it on the table after breakfast. Emma ran after her with it. It had "Dior" on a face surrounded with diamonds. The woman thanked Emma with a wry smile and slipped the timepiece onto her bony wrist. "Five thousand pounds for a watch too uncomfortable to wear," she confided.

It was the same every morning with the couple in room four. Early breakfast, full English for him, cereal and toast for her. Emma took the loaded plates in and it was the work of a moment while making space on the table for the watch to disappear. Her hands trembled as she took the order from the people in room nine.

Ben, the young gardener, strolled into the dining room. Everyone turned to look as he hurried into the kitchen behind Emma.

"All going to plan?" he asked as the doors swung shut behind them.

"Yes," Emma answered. "Here, let me put this in your pocket. I'll be the first one they search for it."

She got out more eggs, mushrooms and tomatoes ready for the next order, her heart drumming. We're doing it for Pepito, she reminded herself, putting bread into the toaster.

Emma had taken on an extra task for herself after each shift. That day she did it during a lull in the serving, not knowing what might have happened by the end of the morning.

The bedraggled little monkey was crouched in his usual place by the shed in the garden. His brown fur had come out in patches on his body, giving him a threadbare look, but there was a dark cap of fuller fur on the top of his head.

"Here you go, Pepito," she whispered, putting down a handful of fruit and nuts for him to find.

It was impossible to escape his sadness but this was a special place for Emma, the place she had met Ben.

It had been her first day at the hotel. Having survived the confusing breakfast shift and before going home she decided to take some time to explore the hotel, anxious to get her bearings. "Is there a ladies' room down here?" a guest had asked and she felt foolish not knowing. Working as a general assistant in a bed and breakfast establishment in Brighton hadn't really prepared her for the move to a luxury hotel along the coast. The size and the choices offered were daunting and the wealthy guests' requests unexpected.

Trying to memorise the layout of the ground floor she'd wandered through the door into the gardens. It was a chilly morning so there was no one braving the patio, but the formal gardens were cheerful and well-kept. At the end of the path between the flower beds was a gate leading to an enclosed area, and she'd noticed more fencing further on.

It was as Emma approached that she saw a young man carefully measuring a distance from the dilapidated shed and digging small holes, then burying pieces of fruit in them. She didn't notice the monkey in the shadows until the man, who she was to learn was Ben, stepped aside and it crept out, digging up the food and bringing the delicacies to its dainty mouth.

"Don't move," Ben called softly to her and after a while he edged around to Emma's side. They watched the graceful creature for a moment.

"It's a capuchin," Ben told her quietly at that first meeting. "They're supposed to forage for food but with such a short chain round his neck that's the best challenge I can give him."

The monkey found all the food and slipped quickly back into the darkness, watching them.

"Is it legal to keep a monkey like this?" asked Emma.

Anger flashed in Ben's eyes. "They're getting away with it," he said. "No one listens to me. They know people high up in the council. I'm only an assistant gardener."

They stepped away to give the little monkey more space and talked, about themselves and the hotel. Emma saw the admiration in Ben's eyes but her glance was

205

drawn to Pepito. "Some monkeys have the understanding of a three-year-old child," she said.

Ben told Emma later that was the moment he fell in love with her and began to imagine the two of them with their own children.

While Emma was serving the late breakfasters, a white van drew into the car park to the side of the hotel. It had writing on one of its doors that she couldn't quite read and what looked like a drawing of a monkey. She wondered if her imagination was working overtime.

The elderly woman at the window table saw her looking as Emma put down the fresh pot of tea. The woman reminded Emma of her grandmother, except Gran always opened her mouth to speak without thinking first and this woman remained politely silent.

"Are you courting?" her gran always asked Emma. She never had been, only the odd outing to the cinema, or bowling in a group. Courting Ben was different.

"When's your afternoon off?" he'd asked the third or fourth time they met beside Pepito's space.

Emma blushed. This lovely young man was going to ask her out. "Wednesday," she'd said. "Wednesday I finish at midday and don't have to come back."

"Great," Ben said with a smile.

In a split second she'd had a million and one ideas. She wanted Ben to ask her to go for a walk so they could talk and find out more about one another. Then perhaps something to eat and the cinema. She could seek his steadying hand over a piece of rough ground and they would then be ready for Ben to put his arm around her when the film started.

"I'm meeting someone it would be good for you to talk to as well. I'll arrange it for Wednesday, shall I?"

"Ri-ight," she replied.

"Your input would be really useful," he'd said. "I'm at a loss."

Emma felt the same.

"This guy knows the law, can advise us where we stand," Ben said.

Emma liked the 'us' and 'we' but must have still looked doubtful because Ben added, "You don't have to if you don't want to. You've only just arrived. I'm in a hurry because I've watched this little scrap pine for nearly a year. He should be leaping through trees with others of his kind."

"Of course. I agree. I'll come."

He'd reached for her arm, touched it briefly. "Maybe we could go to the cinema or something afterwards?"

"I'd love to."

Ben turned back to Pepito and the smile he gave Emma was wan. "I can't bear it, Emma," he had said softly that morning all those weeks ago. "I can't bear it."

As she gave Pepito his treats, still shocked at herself that she had so easily stolen a valuable watch, Ben again crept up beside her. "I'm going to miss meeting you here," he said.

"You shouldn't still be here now," Emma told him. "Do what you have to do and get into hiding. I'll make them understand," she added with more confidence than she felt, "that it's for Pepito".

"I wanted to say goodbye so that whatever happens…" He left the thought unfinished but took Emma in his arms. They both knew that everything would be different by the end of the day.

They'd forgotten to ask what the penalties were for theft and criminal damage. What the world viewed as criminal Ben and Emma, cocooned in moral certainty, saw differently, even as they waited for the police to be called. They should have realised they were embarking on a risky enterprise. That Wednesday afternoon the first time they had gone out together, they met a man who wouldn't tell them his real name. They were to call him Martin. He was a cousin of someone Ben's brother had met once. He shared their concern but didn't want to lose his job. He had children and a wife with MS. You couldn't blame him, Ben and Emma agreed.

Martin insisted on total secrecy. They were to be in the café first with a copy of *Time* magazine on the table and he would find them.

Ben and Emma spent an hour in the library first, side by side at the computers. When the library administrator timed them both out at the same moment they looked up, surprised that the sixty minutes had passed so quickly.

"Do you think we know enough to ask this man the right questions, Ben?" Emma said.

"Perhaps, but I'm not convinced he'll answer. He won't even tell us his real name."

He was an ordinary looking man, dressed in a suit but no tie. He spotted the magazine on the table and sat down opposite Ben and Emma saying, "Sorry about the subterfuge". Emma's spirits lifted as the man smiled and his whole demeanour changed. "I can't afford to lose my job," he went on, "or get involved in anything outside of the law."

"You're a lawyer?" Ben asked.

"I work in the council legal department."

"And you know about the monkey that's being kept up at the hotel?"

"I didn't until my cousin mentioned it. Then I started to do a little digging."

"And have they got a licence to keep the animal?"

"I'm afraid so. To the owner of the hotel, Phillip Nicholls. All in order."

"And if they're not looking after it properly can the licence be revoked?"

"No."

"No?"

"I know it's not right. But the only way to get the owners prosecuted would be if the monkey constitutes a danger."

Ben and Emma looked at one another. Poor disheartened Pepito a danger? Not likely.

"And by having the barrier to stop guests going near they're complying with the law," Martin added.

After the man left they ordered more tea and got out their pages of notes from the computer research.

"Any wild animal can bite," Emma read.

"That's not the way our little friend is reacting, though," Ben said. "He's bored and frustrated but he just does that crouching and rocking that breaks your heart."

"We don't know how he'd react if someone approached him more aggressively."

"Emma, what are you saying?"

"I bet I could get him to bite *me*."

"NO!" Ben shrugged further down into his jacket as he realised everyone in the café was looking at him.

"I know, I know, bad idea," Emma said. "I'm just going through the options."

"He wouldn't want to hurt you, but it's too risky."

"It's worse than that – they might decide to have him put down."

Ben and Emma sat in silence, contemplating the thin line between rescuing the little capuchin and getting him sentenced to death.

"This is serious, isn't it?" Emma said.

"When you said you were going through options, do you have any more?"

"What happens if we cut his chain and report them for letting him be loose?" she asked.

"Probably he'd just cower where he was, but if he wandered..." Ben fell silent again.

"Yeah. It's a dangerous world out there and he knows nothing of it."

"Cut down the fence so guests can get closer?"

"Suppose a child approaches him?"

"Cut down the fence at a time when no one's allowed into the grounds."

"That doesn't happen. Anyway, they'd just build a new fence."

There was a silence while Emma realised that what she had thought of as options were probably just pipe dreams. Then she saw that Ben was looking intent. "I can see the cogs whirring in your brain," Emma said, looking at him. "You've got a plan, haven't you?"

"There are a lot of ducks to line up."

"We can do it for Pepito."

"It could backfire."

"What's the worst that could happen?"

"I don't know, we'd have to sort out the details. I could end up in prison maybe."

But getting arrested relied on some police presence and they were still conspicuously absent that morning.

She left Ben with the stolen watch in his pocket and the saw in his hand.

"Wouldn't the chainsaw be quicker?" she asked.

"It would frighten Pepito," Ben said. "I'll be as quick as I can. But I might be in prison the next time you see

210

me," he added. Then his face became serious. "Don't forget I love you."

"I love you too."

"Once all this is over, let's get married."

"Okay. It's a life sentence you're after, is it?" and she turned away to get back to work. It was only afterwards that she wondered at her jokey response and hoped she would have a chance to make sure Ben knew she meant yes.

Continuing with her work she longed for something to happen, even if it was for the police to come and arrest her. "Seal off the hotel," she and Ben had imagined the police saying. "The culprit must be inside. Don't let anyone leave." Then everyone would be safe and people would be throwing up their hands in horror at the idea of the intelligent primate chained to the pedestal in the gardens.

The ducks, as Ben put it, were lined up but no one had given out the parts to the other players. Finally she heard voices at the reception desk and the couple from room four were shown into the owners' office. Emma hesitated in the corridor, wondering whether to go out to Ben or wait for the police or the local press to arrive.

Before she could decide the office door opened again and Mrs Nicholls herself came out. "Ah, Emma," she said, as if she had been expecting to see her. "Could you come in here, please?"

Emma felt like a child caught with her hand in the biscuit tin. Twin thoughts were battling for supremacy in her mind as her legs shakily carried her over the threshold of the office: the childish 'if I tell them, they'll see we're right and let Pepito go' and the no more adult 'oh hell, why did we ever start this?'

She could hear Ben's voice at the reception desk. "Aren't the police here yet?" he was asking. The receptionists seemed baffled and he went on, "Just make sure no one goes into the garden. Nobody should approach the capuchin out there."

"The what?" one of the receptionists asked.

"The little monkey. He's on a chain but will bite if you go near."

The office door closed behind Emma.

She took some deep breaths, trying to stay calm. Mrs Nicholls moved around to stand behind her desk. The couple from room four were standing too and turned towards her. "Ah, Emma, dear," the woman said. Emma was immediately at a disadvantage because she didn't know the woman's name. Guests didn't have name labels like staff. But there was no hostility. "I couldn't find you in the kitchen. Did you pick up my silly watch again?"

The question confused Emma. She had expected animosity, accusation. The young woman from the local animal rights group had, Emma thought, been more frightening, with her close cropped hair and intense eyes and tattoos. She wanted secrecy as well, like Martin, because she had acted illegally more than once, but Ben laughed afterwards that if there had been a *Time* magazine on the café table she would probably have torn it up. They never did find out what things she had done but her nickname Snatch gave them an idea. Ben and Emma were afraid at the mention of the law that she was going to spit on the café floor.

They begged her not to do anything rash, though Ben admitted later he had been tempted by the idea of someone plucking Pepito to safety. She talked herself out of it in the end, thinking about the logistics of transporting a monkey.

Emma had a notion her experience was with half-dead beagles but there was no denying the young woman's depth of compassion for non-human sentient beings. At least she knew who they could ask for help with a more mainstream type of rescue and agreed to make some phone calls. Emma didn't think anyone would refuse to come if she summoned them.

"We didn't plan to keep it." Emma's voice was quiet and she felt like a child again.

Mrs Nicholls gripped the edge of her desk. "We?" she asked sharply. "So you did remove it? Who else is involved?"

"Just me and Ben."

"Benjamin Jackson, the gardener?" Mrs Nicholls asked and Emma nodded. "Which of you took the watch?"

"I did."

"And where is it now?"

"I put it in Ben's pocket."

"Did he know you were putting it in his pocket?"

Emma imagined herself as a reverse pickpocket, popping valuables into people's pockets without them realising. How wonderful to be able to do that, to imagine them getting home and finding gems and gold they didn't know were there. She stifled a nervous laugh.

"What did you both plan to do with the watch?"

"We just wanted to make sure children were kept out of the garden while we brought attention to the plight of the little monkey out there. We were going to give it back once Pepito was safe".

"A monkey?" asked the thin woman from room four.

"Yes," Mrs Nicholls put in. "It's an attraction for the hotel guests. Children especially like to watch it."

213

Children especially, Emma had observed, stayed for a maximum of a minute waiting for Pepito to do something entertaining and left disappointed. Most guests remained unaware of his presence. The two in the office exchanged a glance.

Emma recalled a snatch of conversation she had overheard while serving this couple. They seemed to have a little dog they were concerned about. Was Topsy being looked after well enough while they were away? In particular was Topsy being made to go on long walks she would find too much for her?

Emma allowed herself to feel hopeful. This woman was sentimental about small animals. She might be on their side.

"It's alone and chained up," Emma added, in case the woman needed to be convinced.

There was a knock at the office door and Mr Nicholls put his head round it. "Sorry," he apologised to the couple from room four. "All hell's broken loose out here this morning," he went on, turning to his wife. "There's someone from the local paper and a group of people who say they're here to pick the monkey up. Do you know anything about any of this?"

While everyone was floundering in confusion the thin woman, accustomed to having her wishes met, took control.

"Show me the monkey," she demanded, looking at Emma.

Emma turned to Mrs Nicholls and shrugged, then followed the couple. As she pointed the way to the exit into the garden it was clear they weren't the only ones headed towards Pepito. There was also a tall young man in jeans and a t-shirt and a young woman with a notebook in her hand and a huge bag over her shoulder, hurrying behind in chunky-heeled boots.

Ben was standing where the fence had been – he'd cut it down completely, leaving Pepito in the open.

The little creature didn't remember that day seven years before when at the age of only eight months he had been torn from his mother's arms. That was the last he had seen of his social group. Probably they had been killed, although Pepito could have no concept of that. He had learned to be wary of humans, though, and although depressed and lethargic he didn't know what to do with the panic that was starting to rise up inside him. He was too frightened to move, even the rhythmic swaying from side to side that he did a lot of the time without thinking.

"Don't come any closer!" Ben called quietly to the approaching group.

"He's terrified," Emma whispered, and the woman from room four looked at her.

"Where is he?" she said.

"Look, in the shadow of the shed," Emma pointed out. "The chain around his neck allows him to go from there and up to the pedestal where they feed him."

"Not inside the shed?"

"Yes, he can get in. See, there's no door. It's damp in there."

The man from room four cleared his throat apologetically. "A capuchin, you say? Didn't I read that they're one of the only animals apart from man who use tools?"

"You may indeed have read that, sir." The tall young man in jeans spoke up. He turned quickly to Ben. "I'm Greg, from the rescue centre. Snatch phoned us," he explained, and then turned back to the others. "They have the largest brain-to-body ratio of all the primates except humans and have invented the nutcracker and insect

215

repellent. In the wild you find other species of monkey tagging along with them as they travel because they're so quick-witted and good at dodging predators."

All eyes were on Pepito. Emma noticed Mr and Mrs Nicholls, the hotel owners, on the fringes of the little group. She wondered if they knew what class of creature they'd been keeping in a five metre square space.

"If you take him away will you re-home him back in the wild?" asked Mrs Room Four.

"And you are?" asked the reporter, writing rapidly in her notebook.

Emma thought she wasn't going to answer. She was looking the journalist up and down.

"Felicity Hillgarth," she finally said, her eyes quickly returning to Greg.

"That might not be possible..."

Felicity Hillgarth turned to the Nicholls, with her self-assured smile. "I suggest we go inside to talk," she said sweetly. "Might somebody rustle up some coffee?"

"Shall I...?" began Emma, but Mrs Hillgarth interrupted her.

"No, Emma, dear, you and I still need to talk."

Ben put his hand into his pocket and reached across to pass Mrs Hillgarth her watch. She gave him a small knowing smile as she took it. "Mission accomplished?" she asked.

"I hope so," Ben said. As the others trailed back to the hotel he mouthed to Emma, "The police?"

Emma shook her head. "Not called."

"What happens now?"

Emma had no idea. "We keep our fingers crossed," she said.

Ben remained with Pepito and in the end it was Mrs Nicholls who brought in coffee and biscuits for everyone but her husband heard all the conversation. Emma watched as he shifted uncomfortably in his seat and didn't look anyone in the eye.

"In the wild, capuchin monkeys live in groups of fifteen and more," Greg told them, handing around leaflets. "The hardest part for us at the rescue centre when we're dealing with animals like this from the pet trade is socialising them with others of their kind. They're usually taken from their family groups while they're still dependent infants so they don't learn about the hierarchies or body language and don't know how to behave." Greg turned to Felicity Hillgarth. "If they're reintroduced to the wild they have to be monitored and there simply aren't the resources to do that properly in the long term. The best we can do for your monkey – Pepito, did you say? – at least for now is try to give him an interesting, busy, stress-free life with others of his kind. Keep them well-fed and healthy and let them express as many natural behaviours as possible."

There was a long silence. It wasn't release back into the wild which was what Pepito deserved, but she believed this man if he thought that was dangerous. She would accept the next best thing. *Please please please*, she thought, *have room for Pepito*.

"We watch them really carefully," Greg went on. "But they're resilient. They always find their level in the group."

Emma had an odd feeling that this man was trying to 'sell' the idea of the sanctuary to them, as though they were wedded to the release and wouldn't accept anything else for Pepito. Once you tore a wild animal from its environment to be a pet or something to be used or ogled,

217

she thought, there was never going to be a perfect solution. But at least he could be somewhere where they understood the baggage the little creature was carrying. And who knew what they might make possible in the future for Pepito?

In the silence Mr Hillgarth cleared his throat, his habitual apologetic prelude to speech. When he spoke, though, he turned out to be the decisive one of the group. "Well, Mr and Mrs Nicholls," he said firmly. "I think that seems much better than the situation as at present, don't you?"

The hotel owners looked at one another rather sheepishly. They couldn't dig their heels in and maintain their dignity at the same time. And it was true the primate wasn't quite the attraction they had initially expected. They remained silent and nodded without enthusiasm. The creature had cost them a fortune but at the same time they couldn't afford to lose these customers or gain a bad reputation.

"So," Emma began, her eyes on Greg, "have you got space for him?" She hated her lack of self-control but her voice broke and the tears came. She would not see Pepito daily as she had, and if she did see him again he would be swinging through trees with others of his kind.

"We're ready to take him now," Greg told her.

Unable to control herself after the tension of the weeks and the sleepless nights and the anxiety, Emma folded her arms on the table, put her head on her arms and sobbed.

Felicity Hillgarth patted her shoulder. She had been browsing through the leaflets Greg had brought with interest. "Julian, dear," she said to her husband. "If you don't object, I'm going to sell the wretched watch and send young Pepito off with a dowry." She turned to Greg. "Would that be in order?"

Emma looked up and caught Greg's eye. "Five thousand quid," she mouthed.

"If that's what you would like to do," he answered. "We rely on donations, but we couldn't guarantee to use it for one resident only."

"No, no, no," Felicity said, waving a leaflet. "Vitamins and enrichment activities for all."

He looked so alone and anxious as he was loaded safely into the van with the monkey drawing on the side. The reporter took a last photo and hobbled off with her notebook and a bundle of leaflets.

"Well done, Mr and Mrs Nicholls," said Felicity, steering the owners back inside. "A good decision. All's well that ends well."

"Not so much a happy ending as a new beginning for young Pepito," said Greg, opening the driver's door. "You've done a good job here." He got into the van and wound down the window. "I'll get someone to write and let you know how he's settling in. They'll send you some photos. You'll see, he'll be a different animal."

At first he was afraid to move very far but he soon learned there was no restricting chain any more. The fence was lofty but his first enclosure seemed huge. From high up in the trees he could watch the other creatures in the enclosure next door and a memory came from deep within him. One of them was talking to him and he seemed to understand the communication. He was feeling stronger every day and his fur was growing back now he wasn't pulling it out. He was sleeping better too after a day exploring and finding his own food and the intriguing objects left in his enclosure. Soon he would gradually start to be introduced to the other monkeys to be integrated into the social group and the memory of the hotel garden would fade.

So if Ben and Emma Jackson had gone to visit they would have had difficulty recognising him and he would have paid them no attention at all. That was what they had done. For Pepito.

Gail Richards
Gail Richards is a writer of short stories and with her now grown-up son a long-term adopter of a capuchin monkey rescued from the pet trade. The courage and resilience of these animals is admirable. The story is dedicated to her adoptee and to all other primates not in their own environment in the wild, with a fervent hope that trade in these animals will be ended.

~~~~~~~~~

Capuchin Monkey Facts

Species: Capuchin Monkey (*Cebus spp.*)

Location: Capuchin Monkeys are found in Latin America as far south as northern Argentina.

Habitat: Rainforest dwellers, living off the ground. They are diurnal and arboreal. The Capuchins' intelligence allows them to adapt easily to new environments and changes to their habitat.

Behaviour: Wide ranging and living in large groups of about 10-35 individuals, they are very social. Capuchins can jump up to 3m (10ft) and move with ease through the trees. They spend most of their time up in the trees, sleep on branches at night, and only go to the ground to get drinking water. Capuchins are omnivores, eating fruits, seeds and nuts, but also insects, spiders and birds' eggs. Females can have young every couple of years and the infant stays with mother until they are old enough to get around on their own at six months. They are usually weaned at one year.

Conservation Status: IUCN classes most species of Capuchin monkey as 'Least Concern', but some are 'Critically Endangered'.

Threats: Being poached from the wild for use in the pet trade, bushmeat trade and for street entertainment.

Action: Born Free Foundation supports **Wild Futures** (formerly the Monkey Sanctuary) who campaign to stop the trade in primates worldwide.

Wild Futures is a UK-registered charity founded upon almost five decades of experience as a leader in the field of primate welfare and conservation, environmental education, and sustainable practice.

Wild Futures is committed to protecting primates and habitats worldwide. To find out more visit www.wildfutures.org.

Sniff the Air

By Dave Dolle

My young cub does not have my imagination. I shared my dream with him before he left. He scrunched his snout and said, "That's what comes of sitting in trees." He did not even reflect on my words. The young one only trusts what he can see, what he can smell, what he can taste. But there is more, how little life would be if there wasn't more.

Last year I was telling my cub the best place to rub your back was when you are sitting in the crux of a tree. As I age I enjoy climbing the tall pines the best, their branches are sturdy and the aroma fills my nostrils. I can let myself be lulled into a contented recollection of my life. A stand of pines, which I had ascended every spring, is now gone. When I awoke this year and took my usual first walk, to take in the air, there where only stumps. Granted stumps are fine for rubbing your rump but they don't give you a sense of lift. I enjoy a sense of lift.

I nosed the remnants, taking in the smell of spilled sap, the liquid had hardened on the ground, in spots clumped chips were scattered. I have learned there is no use dwelling on minor tragedies, if I did I would spend all my time weeping beside a stream. Life is filled with these little sadnesses, it is best to move on and find a new stand, which I did. They were different but with repeated climbing I became comfortable.

Sitting in a tree lets my bones rest. The sun strikes my fur and sinks down into my marrow. Sometimes I see myself walking off the end of a branch then; somehow, I would be floating off through the air. I wonder if the feeling is like when I've waded across a deep river letting the water take my weight. I close my eyes and the world becomes timeless. The universe holding me in the cup of its paw. When a cool breeze on a summer evening comes along I have to halt myself from trying out my dream. I know I would drop like a cub-bird before she has found her wings.

Old Big Paw was a climber when I was young. He had a light touch. Big as our people go but he could sit in a small tree and not bend the trunk. Old Big Paw said he could do it because he could sense how the tree took weight and he would spread himself out so the tree only carried his heavy parts where it would support. I am not Old Big Paw so I cannot do that, I keep on trying though and once in awhile I think I achieve it. A tree which should not hold me does and I feel light. There are few real pleasures, scratching my back and sucking fish bones are what are left to me. No more cubs, they are enjoyable at first, teaching them, keeping trouble away but a day comes when they look north and walk away to be on there own. I have tried to impart many lessons to my cub. My advice goes unheeded.

Being a male, my cub has his own ideas. Still, they are his own. At the bottom of a tree is where he likes to rub his back and rump. He is content to never leave the ground. Foolishness. I hope he grows out of it before it's too late. There will come a day when he won't be able to climb a tree and then will regret the times he didn't.

When I was younger my Mother would gently nuzzle me up to the branches. I would grip the bark tightly until she came and perched beside me. Together we would sit sniff the air and enjoy the setting sun. She taught me how to let one paw dangle while I rubbed my back. This allows me to stretch my arms and claws, almost feeling weightless, and let the ecstasy of the scratch run through me. When you've done it enough times you can balance and let two paws dangle. Granted the position takes skill but with practice anything is possible.

Our cousins to the north don't climb trees, they're too heavy and clumsy, all muscle and roar. I tried to install in my cub the benefits of being lighter, being nimble, better to get through the bramble and undergrowth. Better to be able to go high in the trees away from danger, away from the hardness below.

Of course he doesn't listen, he'd rather lope and swagger like our fatted butted northern cousins. Many of the young have started to imitate their rolling walk. They don't like the refinement of our bodies. How can a bear not love what he is? Very puzzling.

My cub asked me once why our cousins are larger than us. I told him the truth. Everything is bigger in the north. The deer are bigger, the mountains are bigger, the snow piles higher and colder, the winter lasts longer, and the trees stretch to the stars.

The cub wanted to go north so he could grow bigger. I told him life did not work that way. He would just be a small bear amongst his large cousins. They would not take kindly to him, they do not take kindly to anyone. Better to stay put. Be what you are. Enjoy where you are.

The young ones like to move off, which is fine, everyone should have a territory of their own. But they go too far. They want to be away.

I blame the sweet-stink smelling creatures, the ones with little fur who vocalize constantly. They crowd everywhere. The young ones get curious then follow their nose to where the sweet-stinkers feed. Then there is much hullabaloo and confusion.

I sometimes watch this from above. The actions would be humorous if I hadn't seen young ones hurt because of these encounters. The sweet-stinkers are as persistent as flies and as viscous as badgers.

The young ones are copying the sweet-stinkers bad behaviour. They stick their noses into places they don't belong, have no compulsion about treading through someone else's territory, and eat other's food. Shameful. They don't enjoy a good tree. Like my cub they all want to swagger around. Trying to impress who?

A bear is not brought to the world to push her will onto others. A bear serves her part of the land. She is born a guardian of her patch. We are the presence of the unseen spirit. We walk and take in all. The taste of food, the smell of the green, the sound of the stream. A good scratch on a tree. We experience the sensation of life for the unseen spirit. We sing a song of joy for the stars of the night sky.

If we become lost in ourselves, we are not conduits anymore.

Just beasts that run hither and thither like the sweet-stinkers, with no purpose. How can we change so much in one generation? Lose our sense of who we are. Dream of a way that is not our own.

Two springs ago I noticed an absence from the west, an absence which hurt my heart. The wind from there would bring memories, memories close to my heart.

The west wind is the best wind. It has always brought a whiff from my past. I know this wind can travel far. There are smells carried on its back which I scent when they flow through my patch of earth and they bring me peace. But those smells won't come again.

It is a strong, gentle wind, much appreciated on summer evenings, while I am nestled in the leaves watching the sun and the forest turn to night. The west wind is the wind which takes the most leaves before the winter sleep. I know this wind mixes and tangles bringing the distance to my nose.

The west wind brings change.

There was a place Old Big Paw had taken me, a rare place, it lay in the west. He had come to me one day and in his gruff way indicated I should follow. We then walked many days and sometimes through the nights before we stopped. I watched as Old Big Paw sat back on his haunches, eyeing me, not saying a word. In front of him was a stand of pines, old, much older than Old Big Paw.

The ground was covered deep in ancient needles and branches. These ones, these Tall Pines, had stood proud for a very long time. Pines, like our people, need a distance between each other. Each one was paces apart, their branches barely touching. Yet the covering was thick enough to block the summer sun. This was a place of coolness during the hot days and warmth through the winter. No footprints or tracks spoiled the grove, no creatures scat piled under the boughs.

A notion passed through me. I could curl up and sleep here during my own winter time. Maybe make the place my patch where I could go home to. In some way Old Big Paw must have sensed my intention. He let out a low growl which I knew meant, "Stay away," unless invited. This was a gift Old Big Paw wouldn't repeat. I must treasure every moment of it.

I nosed carefully around the Tall Pines, making sure I was respectful. Hoping one of them would allow me to be among its branches. Most of that day I let my nostrils lead me from tree to tree, finally, before late dusk I sensed one who would let me scale to the top of its person. It was an elder, maybe not scared of a young one like me. I nodded my head in thanks and let my limbs carry me upwards.

I took a spot near the top. This was the night when the unseen spirit first entered me. It came from the ground, through the ancient one, shooting through my fur like a waterfall of power and then flew into the night. I stayed awake until the dawn came. Old Big Paw made stretching sounds and began his slow walk out of the grove. I knew it was time to go. With reluctance I left my perch and followed Old Big Paw back to where we started.

After every winter sleep I could catch the scent of the Tall Pines grove, but the scent is gone. Like much I have seen near me they have changed. New smells are in the air, but I keep my dream.

At night before I sleep, my ear is on the ground and the thump of a heart beat comes through the earth. A rhythm which becomes part of me, gently vibrating through my marrow and grease then out through the end of my claws to echo through the dark. I dream the thumps echo around the world, one after another, and finding their way back they enter me. I allow them to go back in the ground. This is how I play my part.

The heart beat will tell me when to awake, whether after a certain number beats or a change in pace, I don't now. What is true is I awake before the light comes through the leaves and before it can settle on the waters of the lake. I pick my tree. After years of practice I know the shape and grooves of bark even if I can't see it. My climb is swift, as swift as someone many sleeps younger. If I have luck a white mist will have formed in the night, usually in a pocket where a valley has dipped in the forest. The valley will try to hold onto the mist and I will watch the valley slowly lose its grip. The mist will shrink and leave like a cloud rolling across the sky.

I am in my tree. The breeze shapes the mist, pushes the branches shaking the leaves, touches the grass, moving the top of the water. Scent from wet earth rises mixing with green smells, washes with creature sweat and is released to the sky. The trees crack themselves awake. Awake, the small creatures pad through the underbrush and the water laps as if the morning is drinking it.

I remain motionless, letting all around me become awake. May I live long, as long as Old Big Paw did, to be a part of all this. To be in a tree until I am no more. How many winter sleeps do I have left? Where will I go afterwards? I hope a good tall tree grows there, so I can climb to see, sniff the air – and have a good scratch.

Dave Dolle

David Dolle was born in Hokah, Mn and now resides across the mighty Mississippi in La Crosse, WI. He was not a gifted child but later in life, after many hardships and a number of adventures, he decided writing was the only thing a talentless backwoods American could do.

~~~~~~~~~~

Wild Bear Facts

Species: There are eight living species of bear of the family *Ursidae.*

Location: Bears are widespread, existing in the continents of North America, South America, Europe, and Asia.

Habitat: Bears are mostly forest species, apart from the polar bear. However, some species may inhabit or seasonally use other areas such as alpine scrub or tundra.

Behaviour: Solitary animals, bears are diurnal, active for the most part during the day. Bears are opportunistic feeders and consume both plants and meat.

Conservation status: Six of the eight species of bears are 'Threatened'.

Threats: Habitats have become fragmented and human-bear conflict has led to persecution. In addition, hunting and the use of bear parts and secretions for traditional medicine provide a real threat to the species.

Action: Born Free Foundation supports Turkish NGO, **KuzeyDoga**, which is undertaking research into the brown bear populations of the Sarikamis Forest National Park in North East Turkey, where they are threatened by hunting, persecution and habitat fragmentation.

For more information go to
www.bornfree.org.uk/campaigns/bears/adoptions.

Snowena

By Emma Lee

She misses. I bite my tongue so she won't hear my curse except as a faint whisper on the snow-heavy wind. She's accepted the hide I film from, but she's not eaten since yesterday morning. And I didn't realise how much I was willing her on to a successful hunt this time.

She licks her paw, disdainfully, as if to distance herself from her failure, as a domestic cat might. I watch her. Gorgeous snowy-grey thick fur with clear black markings that blend in with the mountainside, the fur-padded, clumsy-looking paws somehow graceful when she runs, the long, long tail, balance-keeper as she hunts over ragged rocks.

I'll have to return to camp soon, but while she's still here I can film. It took six months to find her. I don't want to lose her now.

She has a cave further up. It's tempting to kill a mountain goat and leave it for her but that would do more harm than good. She needs to hunt. Each failure is practice. Each failure a chance to try again. Each success buys a few more days of precarious life up here in the Hindu Kush. Evolution made her a specialist, otherwise the mountains would have become over-run with goats devastating the little vegetation that grows and turning this rocky outcrop into an inhospitable wilderness.

Amazingly people choose to live here too. Goat herders mostly who stick with the only life they've known for generations instead of seeking an easier, but unfamiliar life in the city. I guess we're all creatures of habit.

I couldn't do it. Those shacks made from timber, mud and thatch are precariously balanced on the mountainsides and always look as if they are about to collapse. At least I know my tent's temporary. How those guys actually live here... I watch them too. The women are up first, sweeping out, watering and feeding the domestic animals and getting water for the day. Breakfast is made and eaten, then the herders, wrapped in layers and hats, move their goats out onto the pastures, moving up and down the mountain with the seasons. They've seen a lot too. This area's been fought over by the Taliban and Northern Alliance and has been used as routes to distribute opium. No wonder the villagers always look fearful, as if death might tap them on the shoulder at any moment.

There was a kafuffle this morning. One of the domestic goats had been attacked and coats of others clawed at by some wild animal. The villagers blame the snow leopard they know we're trying to film. I don't think it's her though, but don't have the language to tell them or explain. But they need to know what is terrorising their animals so will name the snow leopard because they know she's there.

"Mum! It's starting."

"Give me five minutes, Rihanna."

I slump, that means mum's not going to join me. Still, at least she let me watch this one. I had to miss the wildlife documentary last week because it was on too late and the DVD recorder broke down again. I want to know as much as I can because I want to work with animals one day, maybe be a vet. I see the snow leopard before the man talking does. It's female. Her fur is gorgeous. I feel cold as the snow falls, but she must be toasty warm. I know she eats markhor goats that live on the mountains. Can't remember what the mountains are called though, Hima-something.

She's funny the way she chases off magpies. Don't like magpies much. Some of them can be pretty, but they squawk and are noisy. And they steal things. But she chases off the magpies because they alert other animals to where she is.

The talking man doesn't give her a name. I think I will. But not yet, I can't think of a good enough name. Rihanna would be nice but that's my name. My friend's name is Ciara but that's Italian and the snow leopard's not Italian. I don't know any names for where she's from.

It's funny the way she finds her prey but then rolls on her back and wiggles before stalking them. It's like she's trying to rub snow on her fur, but her fur already looks like snow so that doesn't make sense. Maybe it's to do with smell. Yeah, I think that's it. By rubbing herself in the snow, she takes on the smell of the snow and mountain so the goats smell mountain and snow instead of leopard. She hunts in the afternoon. Maybe it's still dark in the mornings and too dark at night to hunt. Must be really dark at night on the mountains. It gets dark enough in our garden at night, but the neighbour's lights come on if the fox visits and make it bright. There're no lights up on a mountain. I think she's like me and likes to lie-in in the mornings.

I'm going to adopt you for my birthday, I tell her. Well, not you, but a snow leopard like you. There are so few of you left, it's important. I'm going to get a certificate and maybe a toy snow leopard too. Another one, as mum would say, in her complaining voice. But I like my cuddly toys.

I know, I'm going to call her Snowena.

Day four of actual filming, if you ignore the six months spent tracking. The villagers haven't lost anymore of their goats but the snow leopard's managed to successfully hunt another markhor. She'll have plenty soon as the markhor begin to rut and the males fight on the mountainside, often sending losers plunging to the valleys below. They'll be too busy fighting and mating to check for the presence of a hunter, which is a good thing because most of her hunts end in failure. She'll never kill more than she needs to eat, unless she has a cub to feed, but she's part of the eco-balance that enables the strongest goats to survive as the weaker ones are culled.

It does seem ironic to be thinking of eco-balance when I'm filming an endangered species and the only way of getting here was to fly and then drive. I guess camping goes a little way to offset that. I'm not heating a home and making ten minute drives to the supermarket. But flying... my carbon footprint can't be small.

I do watch the villagers and think their lives are so simple and lack the electronic gadgetry that complicates mine. Some of it I can justify – can't film without decent cameras, need a mobile because I'm never near a landline, need to use fuel-hungry four wheel drives to get here because of the terrain. A nice little electric car wouldn't have the weight or traction and there's nowhere to re-fuel anyway. And for what? Is my filming making any contribution at all?

She's getting ready for another hunt. She's spotted a small female goat. She's stalking, stalking. Now she's rolled on her back and rubbed her fur into the rocks. She's on her feet again, padding forwards. She'll get as close as she can before she makes a move. Leopards are ambush hunters not sprinters. Easy does it and off she goes…

Got it! Oh, good girl! That's a relief. She won't need to hunt tomorrow.

But I couldn't do what the villagers do. I couldn't spend my days watching over goats, eating much the same each night and getting up and doing it all again tomorrow. I know I watch animals, but I'm filming them.

But what else would I do? Can't imagine not being able to travel. Can't imagine not being able to see such a gorgeous animal in her natural habit simply being a snow leopard. Sheltering, hunting and dozing in the weak afternoon sun. Her only concerns are the next meal and following the markhor up and down the mountain as they move to where grazing's best.

Will start packing up soon. She'll eat and retire to her cave to sleep. So won't achieve much more today. The journalist who's been liaising with the villagers wants me to show some of the film. Not sure what that will achieve, but I'll go along with it.

The villagers have gathered round a make-shift, dry stone wall where I've balanced a laptop. I've found a short section that shows the snow leopard hunting. As the journalist asked, I stop the film at the first sighting of the snow leopard. There's a kind of collective gasp. I can understand that. She's a beautiful cat, this one. I feel amazed that these villagers live in fear of her, yet have never actually seen her. Not as close and as special as this anyway. The journalist wants to keep the film on pause, but I start it again. Don't want them just to think this is about a picture of a cat. The next scene shows a successful hunt. There's another collective gasp and I'm not sure if that's down to the wonders of technology or that they, like me, were rooting for her success.

One of the elders gabbles something I can't fully hear and definitely can't understand. I fiddle with the laptop and wait for the translation. The journalist says something in reply. I show the picture of the snow leopard again. Let them take her beauty away with them.

As the villagers drift away back to their huts, the journalist tells me the herdsman had told him the snow leopard was his friend now. When they saw the snow leopard hunting markhor, they understood the leopard only hunts wild prey and not their domestic animals. So they don't blame the snow leopard for the attacks on their animals.

I take a deep breath. Maybe I'm doing something worthwhile after all.

The teacher calls my name. I stand up. I wanted to do my show and tell about Snowena. But I didn't have a picture of a snow leopard and every time I tried to draw her, it didn't work and I couldn't get it right. I walk up to the teacher's desk and put my panther on it.

"This is Ebony. She's a panther. She lives in the forests in Asia. She's a big cat, like other leopards, lions and cheetahs. Panthers will eat deer, mice and rats and any other meat they can find. They store any meat they don't want to eat up in trees where other hunters can't get at it. They are very good climbers.

"Panthers look like they're completely black but have normal leopard spots on black fur so you can't see the markings very well. A panther is a black leopard.

"Panthers can have babies with normal leopard colours and sometimes their parents are normal coloured leopards too. Some leopards become panthers because of something called mel, mel, m, melanism."

"Thank you Rihanna. But I think you'll find a panther is a panther, not a leopard."

235

I hurry back to my seat, running but trying to make it look like I'm walking. I know I've gone bright red. I don't want to cry but I know I will. Panthers are black leopards no matter what Mrs Jones says. It's not fair.

Ciara's next, which is OK as I don't have to listen as I know what she's going to say. I have to listen to the others because sometimes Mrs Jones asks questions to make sure we're listening. I hug Ebony. It's not fair.

I wish I had a laptop that connects to the internet. Then I could do my show and tell by showing that programme. She'd have to believe me then. But I wouldn't do my show and tell about Ebony. I'd do it about Snowena, show everyone how beautiful she is.

Emma Lee

Emma Lee's stories and poems are widely published. Her poetry collection, *Yellow Torchlight and the Blues* is available from Original Plus (UK) and novel *Bitter Fame* via http://www.bitterfame.webs.com.

She blogs at http://emmalee1.wordpress.com.

~~~~~~~~~~

Snow Leopard Facts

Species: Snow Leopard (*Panthera uncia*)

Location: Mountains of Central Asia

Habitat: The snow leopard likes steep and rocky places high up. They have even been known to live around Mount Everest. Snow leopards live higher in the summer but come down to lower altitudes in the winter, following their prey.

Behaviour: Solitary and uniquely adapted to life in mountains, they have long tails for balance and are excellent leapers with very strong legs to help them jump as far as 15m (50ft). They hunt the bharal (a form of sheep) and the ibex. This can lead to conflict with local livestock farmers. Cubs stay with their mothers for the first 18-22 months. The snow leopard is usually most active at dawn and dusk, and tends to move around a lot, staying in the same area for only a few days at a time.

Conservation Status: The IUCN Red List classifies the Snow Leopard as 'Endangered' which means that it 'faces a very high risk of extinction in the wild in the near future'.

Threats: Persecution by farmers, poaching for pelts and body parts for Chinese medicine, loss of habitat.

Action: N/A

To find out more about Snow Leopards and how to help any of the big cats visit www.bornfree.org.uk/campaigns/big-cats/big-cat-rescue.

Peace Crane

By Hilary Taylor

I will always remember those burning eyes. Never have I known such a sense of calm, of peace, as that which passed from the bird to me. It was a miracle, and I will always be grateful.

It is almost dark when I find it. Colours have shifted from the clear, sharp contrasts of a perfect spring day – blue and gold and green, through a rich copper glow, then a thin wash of pale lemon, to greyscale. The air is cool and though the day has been still, a wind is stirring now. I walk quickly, fists in pockets, chin down, kicking at stones on the path, replaying the angry words that forced me from the house. When they start on each other I have to get out or I will be consumed by it. Accusations, denials, threats and curses fly like barbed arrows across the tiny kitchen, or between the rooms, from the hall up to the bedroom, from the bathroom to the living room and back, until it seems as if the whole cottage is criss-crossed with hate, like a giant insect wrapped in the threads of a poisonous spider, ready to be devoured. I've stayed out all night more than once this spring. I shelter in the old bird hide this side of the Broad. The last time was three nights ago, and I grabbed my old sleeping bag as I stumbled out of my room and down the

238

stairs, trying not to listen. In the morning I left the sleeping bag in the hide, stuffed under one of the benches and got back to the cottage early, before they missed me. When my mother came downstairs her eyes were puffy and red, her lips slack and hopeless. My father came into the kitchen, eyes dull, mouth a thin line, and the silence was thick and hard between them, like a wall.

I'm on my way to the hide now. It's not used any more. The path kept flooding, so they built a new one further round the shore. The power lines hum as I pass below them and a few steps further on I notice a creature – I can't say what kind – lying in the grass at the edge of the path. My pace slows and my hands come out of my pockets. Roadkill, I think at first, but this track is hardly used by vehicles. As I come nearer there is a small movement, so small I wonder if I imagined it. The creature is still again, and then another tremor flutters across the pale shape. Is it alive? Or maybe it was the rising wind riffling the feathers, for now that I am almost upon it, I see that it is a bird, a large grey bird, with a long neck and black and white markings on its head. One huge wing is stretched awkwardly behind the bulk of the body, and I can see immediately that it is broken. The enormous flight feathers are darker than the rest of the plumage, and only one of them is damaged, torn half way along its shaft. Is it a heron? There is a heronry further round the track, where tall trees line the shore on the edge of Horling Broad. Squatting beside the huge bird, I wait for it to move again. The burnt-orange eyes stare at me. There is no mistaking the life in them. The head is black, with a broad white stripe either side, and a patch of red on the top. I don't think herons have red on their heads, and I know they have long black feathers at the back of the neck, which this bird hasn't got.

I may not know what the bird is, but I know what has happened to it. It has flown into the power lines. It happens all the time. It's been on the news. Last summer there was a swan found the other side of Horling with a broken wing and a broken leg. They managed to fish it out of the Broad with a net, and nurse it back to health. Mostly the large birds die if they hit the lines. Even if they aren't killed outright, a broken leg or wing will usually prove fatal before long.

The bird moves again. This time it is more than a tremor. It lifts its head, lunges towards me in a feeble attempt to protect itself. The bill is long and sharp, making futile stabs at the air. Then its body shifts and its legs and one wing begin to scramble frantically as it tries to lift its huge bulk and stand on its long legs. The other wing hangs low, useless, trailing on the ground. It fails, sinks down into the grass, lowers its head and neck and is still. Then it makes another attempt, legs scrabbling in the grass, trying to balance with its good wing. I crouch helplessly beside it. I am desperate to do something, but I don't know if I can. Eventually it flops down again, exhausted, lays its long neck and head on the ground, and stops moving. But still it stares at me, eyes like glowing coals in the dusk.

I return its stare, and it makes no more threats to me. After a time, I reach out my hand and gently touch the smooth feathers at the base of its neck. My hand rests there and we remain motionless, the two of us, as the darkness deepens and the wind drops and silence enfolds us. A profound peace seeps into my bones and from somewhere the thought comes into my head that I could stay like this for a thousand years. Time seems not to matter, and I don't know how long we remain like that together, but eventually I become aware that I am talking to the bird, and I have the strange feeling that my words are a response. The bird was the first to speak, I know it, although I can't say I actually heard any words.

"Don't worry," I murmur. "I know you can't get up by yourself. Your wing is broken. But I can help you. I'll look after you. Broken wings can mend, and I know a place where you'll be safe."

I move my hand from its neck, along its back, stroking the feathers gently. "I won't hurt you. You can trust me. I'll come back. Now please don't try and move. Rest there, and I promise I'll come back for you."

Again it is as if the creature speaks to me. This time, I am aware of just three words. I can't hear them, exactly, not in the normal way, but as a half moon rises, the wind stirs again, and it is as if the bird is whispering through the night breeze. "Thousand," it says, and then, "Coming home." What does it mean? I don't know, but the words are a comfort somehow. For a few moments more, I let my hand rest there on the soft smooth feathers, and a calm certainty fills me that all will be well.

Now I must move, and quickly. I leave the bird and run on down the track in the dark, turn off along the path that leads to the shore and the old hide. I could try to carry the bird in my arms, but I am worried about making its injuries worse. I splash through the flooded section and across the bridge, round the bend and I'm there. I push open the door and feel under the bench for my sleeping bag. Not there. I can't see anything. There's a pale moonlight outside but it's quite dark in here. I feel around the floor, under the benches at the other end, and eventually I find it, definitely not where I left it. Someone must have been here, but I can't worry about that now. Scrunching the sleeping bag into a bundle, I run back. What if the bird is gone? What if it has managed to get to its fee Even if it can't fly, it could wander off the track into

241

longer grasses and reeds where I'll never find it. And then it will be sure to die. My throat constricts and it's hard to breathe. I can't let that happen. The peace that filled me when I touched those feathers, and when those fire-red eyes looked into mine, suddenly seems on the point of evaporating. It will be lost if I lose the bird. And suddenly I realise how much I need to keep it alive, to make it well and let it go free. I don't know how, I don't understand it, but I am sure it spoke to me. I force my legs to keep moving, and with the rhythm of my steps the words come back. "Thousand. Coming home. Thousand. Coming home." What can it mean?

It is there, pale grey in the moonlight, as I left it.

I fall to my knees beside it, my breath coming in shallow gasps. Its eyes are closed and there's no movement.

"No, please, don't be dead. Please. I came back." My throat is dry and my voice shakes. "I told you I'd come back. Please." I lean in towards the bird, and with the tips of my fingers touch the feathers on the top of its head. The eyes open slowly, deep red, even in the moonlight, and relief floods through me. The bird is alive. "Now, let's see if we can get this round you. Support that wing." I spread the sleeping bag beside the bird, reach over to the other side of its body, and try to nudge it gently towards me, on to the bag. My idea is to use it as a kind of net or one-man stretcher, so that the whole bird will be supported as I carry it, and I won't cause any further injury. All the time I am talking to it, reassuring, telling it what I'm doing, talking rubbish probably, but it's working because the bird is calm and still, and is easily persuaded on to the bag, until eventually I can pick it up and carry it comfortably. The funny thing is that while I'm talking to the bird – "You'll be all right. I'm going to look after you. We'll soon have you comfortable…" – I can hear the bird talking to me. It's like a voice in my head, or whispers carried on the wind. "Thousand… coming home. Thousand… coming home." And every time I look into those burnished eyes, calm flows through me. It is as though it is the bird that is doing the reassuring, the bird that is comforting me, and letting me know that all will be well. And I can't help thinking of my mother and my father, of the cottage and the anger that fills it, and how I long more than anything for peace.

By the time I get the bird to the hide, push open the door, and lay it in the corner on its sleeping bag bed, I can hardly bear to leave it. But I must. I need to fetch water. I have no idea how long it was lying there by the path, stunned by the crash, unable to move. But I know it will need water if it is to survive. There is fresh water nearby of course. The shore is only metres away, but what can I use as a container? I could go home to fetch something. It wouldn't take long. I could even carry the bird to the shore and let him drink there. Then my foot kicks against something on the floor in the darkness, and I hear it clatter across the boards. I feel around with my hands until I find it – a plastic cup. When I get it outside in the moonlight, I see that it is the lid of a flask. How did that get here? It's not mine, and I thought I was the only one that still used this old hide. Then I remember that someone had moved my sleeping bag too. I take the cup down to the water's edge and fill it. I bring it back and persuade the bird to drink. It does so, but makes no further attempt to get to its feet, so I think it will be safe to leave it for the rest of the night. I cannot worry about the mystery intruder. It has to be safer here than outside, where I might never find it again. As for the broken wing, I'll have a better look at that in the daylight, and see if I can work out the best thing to do. As I turn to close the door behind me, the moonlight catches the fiery eyes. I shiver as something passes between us again – it is like a moment of knowing, a realisation of some truth that is infinitely bigger than my little life, but that cannot be put into words.

I am woken by the rain, and even before I reach the hide, I can see that someone has been here. There are footprints in the wet earth outside, and the door is ajar. My heart thumps as I rush forward with my bag of grain. Please let the bird still be there. Please don't say someone has let the bird go. I step into the hide. There is an old man in a dirty wax jacket and a knitted hat kneeling beside the bird, wrapping something round the injured wing. The bird is quiet, still, allowing him to do as he likes.

"What...?" I say. "What are you...?" My breath is coming in gasps.

He doesn't stop working on the bandage. "I've put a splint on the break, and now I have to immobilise the wing by taping it to his body. It should heal perfectly. He'll fly again eventually. And he'll be able to look after himself till then. This is a good place. Plenty of food. Quite safe." He looks up at me. He has a scrappy grey beard, and his face is wrinkled. "I take it you brought him here," he says.

"Yes. Last night. I found him. I think he crashed into the power lines."

"I reckon you're right there, lad. He's lucky you found him. You'd think he'd learn, wouldn't you?" He finishes bandaging, and tapes the end securely against the bird's body. Then he settles the bird back on the sleeping bag, and sits himself on the bench.

"What do you mean, learn?" I sprinkle grain where the bird can reach it, and it pecks at it hungrily.

"He's done it before. Broke this same wing."

"How do you know? Who are you?"

He leans towards me, hand outstretched. "Ben Clark. Local birdman. Pleased to meet you."

I shake his hand. His skin is rough and cracked, but warm. "Adam Lucas. I live in the End Cottage. Up the track."

He nods.

"Birdman?"

"I've been watching birds at Horling for sixty odd years. This one's an old mate of mine."

"Old? How old? And how do you know it's the same one?"

He laughs, looks down at the quiet bird, and then back at me. "You just know your friends, don't you? This was the first one to come home. Nineteen seventy-nine. Fifteenth of September. I was right here in this hide – brand new it was then, and I watched them fly in. Couldn't believe it at first. Amazing. Two of them. This one and a female. They didn't breed that year though, nor the next. It took a while."

"What is it?" I ask. "I thought it might be a heron at first, but it's not, is it?"

"No, you're right there, lad. It's a crane. Common crane. Gone for hundreds of years they were, from these parts. Used to be common before that. Rich folks in the middle ages liked to eat them, they did. Greedy. Hunted them out, they did. But at last they came home."

"A crane!" I say. "Nineteen seventy-nine? And it's the same one? They live that long?"

He chuckles again, and I sense something from the bird too. It's that knowing again, that feeling of rightness, harmony, perspective. Ben looks at me, not smiling now. His eyes narrow. "Some say they live a thousand years," he says, his voice low, and when I look into the crane's eyes it seems almost possible.

"A thousand years," I breathe, and I remember the words whispered on the wind.

"And if we're lucky, we'll see the rest today. I'll show you."

"The rest?"

"Yes. The rest of them. They'll be here to feed I reckon. Usually are. Unless they're across at Bockley Marshes. Listen out. I'll open these." He stands up, closes the door and then opens the viewing shutters. We wait. I don't know how long it is, but after a time, loud, low trumpeting calls echo round the Broad, a thrilling other-worldly sound. The old crane lifts his head, ruffles his feathers, and attempts to stand. We look out and there they are. Seven, eight, nine of them, necks outstretched, wings spread wide, and long legs trailing behind. They circle in and land, and a few moments later there are more. Seventeen of them altogether, out there at the edge of the water only a few metres away. The rain has stopped and the surface of the water shimmers in the thin sunlight.

We watch for a long time, and then one of them stretches out its wings, and I think it is going to take off, but it jumps up into the air, wings flapping, legs dangling, and then lands. It repeats the performance, then bows its head, picking something from the ground.

"What's it doing?" I whisper.

"Just watch," Ben says. "You'll see."

The crane jumps up again, throwing the stick it just picked up, and then stabbing at it with its bill. Another bird joins in, mirroring the display, and then another, until almost the whole group is dancing together, jumping, flapping, bowing, throwing sticks, in the most spectacular piece of bird theatre ever seen.

246

"But what is it? What are they doing?"

"It's the Crane Dance," Ben whispers. "Isn't it fantastic? You'll never see anything like it." He fishes something out of his pocket, a crumpled piece of paper, an old scribbled note or shopping list by the look of it. He flattens it and smoothes it on the ledge in front of him. Then he begins to fold it, first one way, then turns it and makes another fold, pressing the creases carefully.

Behind me, I hear a movement, and when I look round, the crane is standing quietly by the door, looking at us with his burnt orange eyes. His good wing wobbles, flutters a little as he uses it to balance, while his broken one is taped to his body.

"He'll be all right," Ben says, still folding and creasing and turning his paper. "He'll be back when it's healed and I'll take off the bandage. You can open the door. But tell him first."

"Tell him what?"

"Your dearest wish. Didn't you know that cranes can give you what you wish for? They're good luck, cranes."

I move from the window to the door, and I look into the crane's eyes, put my hand once more on the smooth feathers of his back, and without words, I tell him my dearest wish. Then I open the door and, picking up his feet, he walks gracefully, sedately, quietly, out of the hide, round the corner, and is gone.

Ben hands me the folded paper. It is a miniature bird, a tiny crane. "This is for you," he says.

I take it. I cannot speak.

Ben looks at me. "It is said that if you fold a thousand of these, the cranes will grant your wish."

"A thousand? But I don't know how to... I can't..." My dream is slipping away. I want the bird back. I am on the point of running after it.

Ben chuckles again. "It's all right," he says quietly. "This is my one thousandth."

I stare at the paper crane resting in the palm of my hand like a silent promise. A thousand. He's made a thousand of these.

"And did I tell you," he continues, "that the crane is a symbol of peace?"

I bring the paper crane to the window. Holding it in my fingers, I look out at the dancing cranes. Our injured bird walks towards them. I watch him join the group. Then I turn and slip out of the hide. I walk down the path, and turn on to the track towards the cottage.

"I'm coming home," I whisper to my paper crane. "Coming home."

Hilary Taylor

Hilary Taylor grew up in Suffolk and Hampshire, and spent her student years in Edinburgh before returning to Suffolk. She has five grown up children and teaches in a Primary School. In her spare time she writes stories and is working on a Young Adult novel. Her story *Sightseeing* is published in *Going Places*, the Bridge House travel anthology. She is good at making flapjack, would like to grow vegetables without weeding, and has recently discovered how to make mosaics.

~~~~~~~~~~~~

Crane Facts

Species: Common Crane (*Grus grus*)

Location: A long-distance migratory bird, the vast majority breed in northern Europe and Asia, nest in Russia and Scandinavia, and winter in Africa (south to Morocco and Ethiopia), southern Europe, and southern Asia (south to northern Pakistan and eastern China).

Habitat: The common crane's breeding sites are wetlands. Non-breeding wintering and migration habitats of the species include flood land, swampy meadows, shallow sheltered bays, rice paddies, pastures and savannah-like areas.

Behaviour: The common crane is fully migratory, although isolated breeding populations east and south of the Black Sea may be resident, or only undertake local movements.

Conservation status: The IUCN Red List classes the common crane as 'Least Concern'.

Threats: In both its breeding and non-breeding ranges the common crane is threatened by habitat loss, fragmentation and degradation through dam construction, urbanisation and agricultural expansion.

Action: N/A

The Great Crane Project is a partnership between the Wildfowl & Wetlands Trust (WWT), the RSPB and Pensthorpe Conservation Trust, with major funding from Viridor Credits Environmental Company. Their aim is to restore healthy populations of wild cranes throughout the UK, so that people can once again experience these beautiful birds.

A Final Word

We hope you've enjoyed this special collection and that it will inspire you to look at other short story anthologies published by Bridge House.

If there is a single take home message from all that you've read here it's that animals deserve to be born free and to live free. This is the philosophy of Born Free and the premise of their Zoo Check Programme. There are many alternatives to seeing animals in zoos and we strongly urge you to find out about these. If you're unsure about any organisation even if its claims sound good please check them out by contacting Born Free.

To find out more about Zoo Check visit
www.bornfree.org.uk/campaigns/zoo-check.

As part of the Zoo Check programme we also urge you to be a careful traveller – don't support animal attractions or have your photos taken with animals used as props. Think very carefully about how the animals are being used to *enhance* your holiday experience and if you really need it. Consider how these animal are treated. For example, due to a change in public attitudes, there are no longer any dolphinaria in the UK. To find out more check out the Zoo Check web pages and report any incident of animal exploitation.

If you can't see an animal in the wild, then it's best not to see it all.

Please check out the many organisations listed after each story and the general list that follows. These are all organisations that promote seeing animals in their natural environment.

Thank you for supporting this project and remember to look out for next year's charity book, a collection of uplifting children's stories to raise funds for **Children's Hospices UK**. Children's Hospices UK is the national charity that gives voice and support to all children's hospices in the UK. Their vision is for every child and young person not expected to reach adulthood to have access to the highest standards of care and support for every step of their journey.

Other Useful Links and Organisations

Global Federation of Sanctuaries

The Global Federation of Animal Sanctuaries (GFAS) was formed in 2007 by nationally and globally recognized leaders in the animal protection field for the sole purpose of strengthening and supporting the work of animal sanctuaries in the United States and abroad.

GFAS does not operate animal sanctuaries, but rather helps sanctuaries help animals by establishing clear, specific standards for the humane care of various species in captive facilities and provide the best care possible for rescued animal

GFAS, through s. their Captive Wild Animal Protection Campaign, also serves to provide education on the causes and conditions of displaced animals and what can be done to stop exploitation and cruelty.

Web site: http://sanctuaryfederation.org

Royal Society for the Protection of Birds

The RSPB is driven by a passionate belief that we all have a responsibility to protect birds and the environment. Bird populations reflect the health of the planet on which our future depends. The need for an effective bird conservation organisation has never been greater.

Web site: www.rspb.org.uk

Wildlife Extra

Wildlife Extra aims to promote wildlife-watching as a means to conservation. Wildlife watching is becoming a key factor that enables protection of the wildlife and wilderness of the world by making it an economic force for local communities, thus it becomes in everyone's interest to preserve the environment.

Web site: www.wildlifeextra.com

Wildlife Trusts

There are 47 individual Wildlife Trusts covering the whole of the UK, the Isle of Man and Alderney. They are the largest UK voluntary organisation dedicated to protecting wildlife and wild places everywhere – at land and sea.

All 47 Wildlife Trusts are members of the **Royal Society of Wildlife Trusts** (Registered charity number 207238).

Web site: www.wildlifetrusts.org.

Index of Authors

Other Anthologies by Bridge House

100 Stories for Haiti

100 Stories for Haiti is a unique collection of stories bound together by paper and glue and massive amounts of hope. This is no ordinary book. One morning a writer woke up and decided, "I must do something." Hundreds of talented authors worldwide sent him their stories and the result is an anthology that anyone can enjoy.

Proceeds go to helping the victims of the Haiti earthquake. So open this book and pick a page. There's nowhere to start and nowhere to finish. If you find one story, one page, one line entertaining: buy it.

"A good read for a great cause. It's a cracking read – very different styles and very different takes on the theme of 'hope'. No story is over 1,000 words long so it's excellent to dip in and out of." (*Amazon*)

Order from www.bridgehousepublishing.co.uk

Paperback: ISBN 978-1-907335-03-7
eBook: ISBN 978-1-907335-05-1

Bridge House

Twelve Days

Twelve Days is a collection of darker, longer stories which will
give you something to think about. Elegantly crafted by some
of Bridge House's finest writers, these thought-provoking tales
will occupy you during some of the darkest days after Yuletide
festivities. These stories can of course be read at any time of
the year but the collection is named after the twelve days of
Christmas and provide one a day for this season.

Order from www.bridgehousepublishing.co.uk

ISBN 978-1-907335-02-0

Bridge House

In the Shadow of the Red Queen

The Red Queen's shadow falls upon us in all sorts of circumstances. She may help us to play tricks on each other while she plays tricks on us. She has a streak of cruelty and can make us cry. Yet she also has a sense of humour and being the wily female that she is, she excels at making us fall in love.

A story for everyday of your holiday – and the day before you go and the day after you come back.

"This is a delightful and entertaining collection of stories, ranging from the heart-warming to the humorous, from action-packed to downright bizarre. There is one for every mood and an abundance of great characters. I think Bridge House is doing an excellent job of bringing together this group of talented writers for us to enjoy. A must for anybody's holiday luggage." (*Amazon*)

Order from www.bridgehousepublishing.co.uk

ISBN 978-0-955791-06-2

Bridge House

Do you have a short story in you?

Then why not have a go at one of our competitions or try
your hand at a story for one of our anthologies? Check
out:

> http://bridgehousepublishing.co.uk/competition.aspx

Submissions

Bridge House publishes books which are a little bit
different, such as *Making Changes, In the Shadow of the
Red Queen* and *Alternative Renditions.*

We are particularly keen to promote new writers and
believe that our approach is friendly and supportive to
encourage those who may not have been published
previously. We are also interested in published writers and
welcome submissions from all authors who believe they
have a story that would tie into one of our themed
anthologies.

Full details about submissions process, and how to submit
your work to us for consideration, can be found on our
website

> http://bridgehousepublishing.co.uk/newsubmissions.aspx

Lightning Source UK Ltd.
Milton Keynes UK
10 June 2010

155381UK00001BB/7/P